MIDLIFE TREMORS

DRUID HEIR BOOK 2

N. Z. NASSER

THE PLAYERS

Alisha Verma - Druid Heir
Marina Ambrose - Alisha's best friend
Echo - Alisha's leopard sidekick
Ezra Neuhoff - Alisha's half-werewolf, half-wizard mentor
*Fei Yen, Faeza, Marek, Tomás, Santiago, Farzad, Nagma, Ethan,
Hassan* - Alisha's night class students
Flinar - a dark elf
Mirabel - Wildwoods student
Joshi Verma - Alisha's father
Sahil Verma - Alisha's brother
Gaia - Goddess of the Earth
Robert Jameson - Detective, Shadow Squad
Phinnaeous Shine - Shapeshifter, Prime Sorcerer
Orpheus Might - Vampire, Minister for History and the Today
Rayna Willowsun - Druid, Minister for Education,
Headmistress of Wildwoods School of the Wondrous
Lavinia Drach - Witch, Minister for Defence
Gunnolf Zev - Werewolf, Minister for Justice
Helio Woodwink - Fairy, Bestiary Minister
Cillian O'Meara - Leprechaun, Minister for Finance
Margola Silver - Selkie, Minister for Information

Erelim - Angel, Minister for Diplomacy
Mr Costello - executor of Rosalie's will
Calypso Archer - the Custodian
Nightfall - a horse in the Celestial Library
Tielbu - a dragon
The royal gamekeeper

1

I stood in front of the desk in the community centre and lifted my fists in a fighting stance. Two rows of faces smiled back at me, eager to learn. Kickboxing was their favourite part of this night class, after all. After the sun god killed a student in my class, it seemed only fitting to take my students' training up a notch.

Only three weeks ago, my friends and I had defeated the murderous sun god after he'd killed my mum and a host of other scientists, including Nita. We had run towards danger and won. After a lifetime of living in the slow lane, I had avenged Mum's death and stacked up new experiences at a tantalising rate. A whole new world had opened to me, and I had magical talents and a toned butt to show for it. Plus, a hot new romance with Ezra, my werewolf-wizard mentor.

Not bad for a forty-year-old divorcée.

But a woman needed money, and I liked my job, so I'd spent the evening teaching holiday vocabulary, followed by a bout of kickboxing drills.

"Keep those feet moving," I said. "Fists up. Turn those wrists. Punch, punch. No, Tomás and Santiago, play punching each other is not what I called for."

"Forgive me, miss," said Tomás, turning all the charm of his Portuguese heritage on me.

I smiled. "Four deep squats next. Let's get those thighs and glutes working."

"I don't know what a glute is, Miss Verma, but if I do the squat, can I eat more cake?" said sixty-five-year-old Nagma, who didn't let her traditional dress hold her back from achieving as deep a squat as any of the younger students in the class.

I grinned. "They are muscles in your bottom. And more squats definitely mean more cake. Next one, lunge back and kick up. Repeat." I did the move myself, modelling the breath work, trying not to think about the empty seat where Nita had once sat. "Well done, Hassan. Try the kick a little higher, Marek. Remember, class, if you can't do the move for whatever reason, then adapt it. Take it down a level. Don't stretch your body all at once. With each practice, you'll get better."

I turned to the two Chinese women in my class, Fei Yen and Faeza, and my heart skipped a beat.

There they were again, showing unbelievable flexibility for two women of advanced age. They had to have a decade or two on me. Not that I could tell by their wrinkle-free skin. But here they were in traditional Chinese dress, lifting each other to execute the most perfect high kicks as if age wasn't a barrier at all. As if they had an innate strength and fluidity of movement that scoffed in the face of mere ageing.

I kept my voice upbeat even as I plotted how to get to the bottom of their secret. "Excellent work, Fei Yen and Faeza. You've improved. Did you have martial arts training in China?"

"No, Miss Verma," said Fei Yen.

"Definitely not," said Faeza, as they reverted to performing the moves like decrepit old women.

As if I'd not seen. As if they hadn't given me a dozen other reasons to believe they were from the Otherworld.

Well, tonight, I would get to the bottom of it.

It wasn't like I wanted to go home to the dragon nightmares that plagued me no matter how much lavender-scented mist I sprayed on my pillows—reptilian skin. Amber eyes. Fierce wings slashing through the pink sky. Lofty monuments smashed into rubble. The dreams left my heart pounding.

So, I would do what any grown woman with worries did. Distract myself. And my two sneaky students had given me just the way to do it.

I DUCKED behind buildings on the rain-slicked London street after locking up the community centre. Around me, high-rises loomed with glowing television screens visible through windows. Londoners sprawled on their sofas, stuffing fistfuls of crisps into their mouths, and a restless baby's cry rang out into the night. Up ahead, two of my students meandered under the streetlamps and heavy clouds, oblivious to my presence. I'd grown convinced there was more to my students Fei Yen and Faeza than met the eye. Come hell or high water, I was going to get to the bottom of it tonight.

Their clothes made them easy to track, despite the dark night. Tonight's night class had celebrated cultures from around the world. Fei Yen and Faeza had come in traditional Chinese dress. Their silk qipaos were ankle length, with high necks and simple knotted buttons with loop fasteners. The dresses stood out against the black starless night: Fei Yen in red with intricate phoenix embroidery and Faeza in blue, with dragon and floral embroidery.

I felt plain in comparison, but then I had channelled my chic French side rather than Indian extravagance for the lesson. That meant faded jeans, a camisole with a silk scarf tied around my neck, a jaunty beret and a black blazer to hide the sword Gaia had given me.

I darted after Fei Yen and Faeza, pleased that my flat shoes muffled the sound of my progress and that I'd tied my unruly hair in a ponytail.

Approximately fifteen metres separated us. At first, nothing out of the ordinary happened.

But as we left the main road and all other pedestrians slipped away into the night, Fei Yen and Faeza transformed. A shiver ran up my spine. Gone was the slow heaviness brought on by age. They bounded along the pavement arm in arm, like gossiping teens. I strained my ears, but they weren't speaking English, although they were the strongest students in my night class. Wisps of Chinese floated my way.

My phone trilled in my blazer pocket. I took my eyes off my targets and hissed into it. "Not now, Marina. I'm on a mission."

My best friend's laughter bubbled down the line. "One success, and you think you're Jane Bond."

"I'll call you later." I flattened myself against a tree trunk.

"I'm just wrapping up at the surgery," said Marina. "Fancy coming over for a quick gin?"

A movement flashed in the corner of my eye. A street bin arced through the air and bounced onto the road, spilling its contents across the asphalt.

"Alisha? Your heartbeat just spiked." Her empath skills grew with each passing day.

"I have to go," I ended the call and spun around.

There was no sight of Fei Yen and Faeza.

The street bin lay on its side in the dim light of a dilapidated bus stop shelter. No drunken louts or wayward schoolchildren out long past bedtime filled the South London streets. So who had shunted the bin across the road?

I stepped closer.

A dozen fat rats scurried around the bin, pulling, pinching and kicking a bony, dull-grey body trapped by the bin. Judging by the pallor of the man's skin, he was seriously ill, and the rats were trying to finish him off.

My skin crawled. It wasn't the first swarm of rats I had seen in London, but the thought of the poor man being cannibalised churned my stomach. London rats were absolute stinkers, opportunists and always ravenous.

I sprang into action. "Hey!" I shouted, running towards them. "Leave him alone."

A rat the size of my forearm turned beady eyes on me. "Stay out of this, druid."

My jaw hit the floor.

The loathsome thing reminded me of the Banksy artwork, where a medallion-wearing rat held up a Welcome to Hell sign.

I composed myself before I swallowed any flies or the rodents got the better of me. "I said, step away from him."

I'd met talking rats before. Some had formed part of the team that had helped me defeat the sun god. I'd seen them at the witch Lavinia's gym too. As Minister for Defence, she had trained her coven's familiars to be formidable spies. They were the ears of her operation, cleaned her gym, and by all accounts, could cook up a storm.

I had no idea they were bullies too.

"Make us stop if you dare." His toothy rat grin sent shivers up my spine. "Come on, lads. Let's teach the druid not to mess with witches' work."

The rats gave the man a last flurry of kicks. Then they lined up in a semi-circle formation on their hind legs, showing their muddied bellies and yellowed claws. I counted seven in all, with some right hefty beasts amongst them. No doubt they could do some damage in those numbers.

And I didn't fancy a battle on the streets of London with no backup and the chance of falling foul of the Magical

Constitution. Severe punishments awaited those who compromised the secrecy of the Otherworld. No doubt, the rats had Lavinia to vouch for them, but I had no one. And I was on a short leash with the Sorcerer's Senate after breaking the first law: never meddle in the affairs of the gods.

The man groaned and freed himself from the bin trapping his body. He shook off greasy wrappers from the nearby kebab shop, retching as he heaved himself up. He was short for a man and wore a Roman tunic and knickerbockers as if he didn't give two hoots about fashion. No wonder the rats had taken a dislike to him. Bullies always picked on those who stood out.

He turned, and the light from the bus shelter illuminated his face at last.

I gasped.

This wasn't a human. He had knobbly legs and arms attached to a small, muscular body. One of his arms hung limp. His large, milky eyes were suspended within a dull grey, triangular head with wisps of grey hair. A deep cut above his eyebrow marred his smooth face. He had a small nose and full lips, but it was his ears that stood out. They sat high up on his skull, shaped like the sails of a ship, angular and billowing, and twitched with emotion.

"What, you've never seen a dark elf before?" the chief of the stinky rats said.

My leopard companion Echo had warned me about elves once before. They were employed by the Sorcerer's Senate to clean up magical residue but were also mischief makers. They were more likely to graffiti buildings and tamper with street signs than to sweep the roads.

I addressed the elf. "Are you okay?"

Milky eyes searched my face. "Go on your way, druid, or they will harm you. Elves are used to being the lowest in the pecking order."

The rat sighed. "For good reason. You're new around

here, so you probably don't know he's not worth your trouble. His kind was responsible for the Battle of the Celestial Library. The scoundrels almost toppled the Otherworld and outed us all. So we give them a kicking every few weeks or so, just to show them who's boss. Witches' orders."

I frowned. "Listen up. This gentleman doesn't seem to deserve a kicking for something his kind did. Do I give you a kicking just because one of your lot once left its droppings in my kitchen?"

"I'll have you know that Otherworld rats are far superior to humdrum rats. We're house-trained, for one."

I pretended to be awed. I hadn't been best friends with a vet all my life without learning a few tricks of the trade. It was far better to persuade an animal to do my bidding than to get into a fight I might not win. "How clever of you. You're far too clever to make the mistake of picking on this elf when I've asked you not to."

"We do, druid," the rat said.

"I think you'll find that Lavinia and I are friends."

"I'm afraid that is old news. Our mistress is displeased with you. She suspects you might be more foe than friend."

I winced. "Charming."

If Lavinia had found out we had cheated her of Ezra's blood, then a storm was brewing.

"So you see, druid, we have no reason to spare you." His front teeth gleamed in the moonlight like two knives. "Attack!"

They sprang in my direction, bouncing off surfaces, somersaulting through the air. The stench of wet fur and putrid breath made me gag. These rats weren't like the coven's familiars. They were coarser in appearance and nature. They were Lavinia's fixers rather than her favourites. Any second now, they would land at my feet, chew my ankles and drag me to my death like the poor elf.

"Wait!" I held up my hands, and my palms tingled with power.

They froze in the midst of their advance as if they were far more accustomed to taking orders than using their own initiative. The lead rat glared at me, all bulging black eyes and twitching whiskers, a few inches from my calf. "You wish to share your last words, druid?"

"No, actually. I wanted you to double-check you're not making a mistake. I am dating Lavinia's nephew, you know. You wouldn't want to come to blows with his new lady love, would you?" I gave him my most charming smile.

Okay, love was pushing the nature of my relationship with Ezra. What we had was a friendship with more than a hint of frisson, plus one sexy-as-hell date in bonne Paris, but framing it as love might save a whole heap of trouble.

"Just leave the elf alone," I said, "and we can all go home safe and sound."

Behind him, the elf, to his credit, awaited his fate. His knobbly body curved over as if we had already been defeated, but there was a fragile courage in the set of his lips. If it had been me, I would have scarpered while no one was looking.

The rat's eyes turned cold. "We take orders from the coven, not you. And you ruined a simple evening's pleasure."

I shrugged. Backing down wasn't an option. I couldn't stand bullies. "Don't say I didn't warn you."

The rats came at me en masse, their gnawing teeth and claws threatening mortal damage.

I bit my lip to swallow the scream that built in my throat. My fear was instinctive, but I had a chance of coming out on top if I held my nerve like Ezra had trained me to do.

The tingling in my hands signalled I was ready. My beret flew off as I kicked and punched, my routines from kickboxing classes triggering my muscle memory, interspersing the moves with gusts of winds that sent the rats flying. The elf helped, too, making projectiles of the rubbish, infuriating but not slowing down the rats.

But they were too many.

With each rat I cast away, another returned. I wanted to subdue them. To kill them would earn Lavinia's wrath, and I had already risked making her my enemy.

I breathed hard and fast, cursing as a rat crawled up my trouser leg and sank its teeth into my calf. If it were a case of the rats or me, I'd have to kill them, but it went completely against my vegetarian, peace-loving nature. I shook my leg, and the rat spun through the air and thudded against the side of the bus shelter.

The chief rat led a charge up a lamppost. "Grab her ponytail."

Rage swept through me.

I pulled out the sword Gaia had given me. I'd mostly carried it around like an ornament, but this was as good a time to practice using it as any. A weapon blessed by Death promised to be devastating. At the very least, it would scare them off.

A woman could hope.

I gripped Transcender in both hands. Its ivory hilt felt cool to the touch, a huge relief, given how I was slick with sweat. I swung round, slashing the obsidian blade through the air.

The rats scattered.

Voices surged in my head, and I dropped the sword like I had been burned.

Seven pairs of black beady eyes turned in my direction, and my last thought before the rats rushed at me was how the poor elf would be next.

2

The elf gave a blood-curdling scream that signalled our end, there on a dimly-lit, rain-soaked London street fouled by rubbish. No doubt the noise would alert nearby humdrums in their homes. Even in death, the Sorcerer's Senate would insult me for outing the magical community in the most ignominious circumstances. The chief rat would take Transcender to be his own, and armed with my sword, he'd rule over London.

My headstone would read: *Here lies a druid, outsmarted by rats.*

What an end.

They knocked me off my feet by targeting the backs of my knees. I fell and let loose another two gusts of wind before the seven rats colluded to bind my hands with a vine. Then they dragged me into an alley, uttering a spell to make light of their load.

I spat the words. "You won't get away with this."

I meant it. That's the thing about endings: they depend on the life you lived and the love you gave. My friends and family would avenge me. I was sure of it.

The chief rat preened over his swarm's work, his pot belly

puffing up with pride as he approached, twitching in anticipation of his bite. "The time for talk is over."

I cursed. Being told to shut up reminded me of my ex-husband. I closed my eyes, not wanting his wretched face to be my last.

Where was a teleporting werewolf-wizard when you needed one?

I hadn't even managed to bed him yet. What a waste.

Suddenly, a woman's cry of distress met my ears. I opened one eye.

There, at the end of the alley, stood two vivid red foxes with fur more silken than I had seen on any London fox. They were medium-sized and well-fed, with intelligent, inquisitive eyes.

I couldn't believe my luck. Hopefully, we had stumbled into their territory. I was pretty certain rodents were a dietary staple for foxes. That meant I had a chance to turn the tables.

The rats, too, recognised the stakes had changed. Their whiskers twitched, and their beady eyes bulged.

The foxes glanced at one another, their bushy, white-tipped tails swishing, before baring their teeth and running into the fray. The leaner one was quicker. It arrived first, snarling and snapping at the rats, picking one up by the tail and hurling it with ease. The second one was more of a brawler. It reared up on its hind legs, seeking to crush the slower rats, its mouth gaping open, the vocalisations ear-splitting with intensity.

I wanted in on the action. With my hands tied, I used my non-existent stomach muscles to manoeuvre into a sitting position and my teeth to tear off the vine. Fuelled by anger, the tingling in my hands reached a crescendo—better late than never— and I released a whirlwind that sent the rats scurrying up buildings and into the sewers.

The trembling elf cowered a few metres away, and the foxes' posture relaxed. Their tails no longer swung wildly, and their closed mouths hid their teeth. So they probably didn't want to eat me.

"Thank you." I gave them a wide berth before inching out of the alley, where two piles of clothing caught my eye.

A scream built in my throat as I took a closer look. Two pairs of lacy knickers, an A-cup and a B-cup bra from Marks and Spencer, two pairs of ballet pumps, a red silk dress with phoenix embroidery and a blue one with dragon embroidery.

Fei Yen's voice behind me made me jump. "So now you know our secret as well as our bra sizes."

I whipped round, my heart hammering. "Holy moly."

There stood my two students, half-smiling in the moonlight, in all their naked glory. They had dishevelled hair and muck under their nails. A deep gash marred Faeza's thigh, blood red against her olive-toned skin.

I stared open-mouthed. "I *knew* you were different."

Faeza covered her bits. "Do you mind passing us our clothes?"

"It's the least you can do after stalking us," said Fei Yen. "Then we can talk."

Heat rushed to my face as I handed them the two piles. "Er, sorry about that. I'll be right over there with the elf."

I spotted him across the road at the dilapidated bus stop. I retrieved the bin rolling in the street, set it aside and joined the elf on the bench at the bus shelter, his eyes moving skittishly across my face as if he still didn't know whether I could be trusted, despite all the trouble I had gone to in order to protect him and the bruises and stinging cuts I had to show for it.

Not to mention the rabies injection I probably needed.

I laid a gentle hand on his knobbly grey arm. "I'm Alisha."

"Thank you for seeing me, Alisha," he said, his voice brittle from shock. "Not everyone does. Most other peculiars would have gone along their way. Elves are not beloved."

I frowned. "I'm sorry to hear that."

Dirt and blood smeared his face. "Why did you help me?"

"All creatures should have self-determination, and the rats were trying to control you. It wasn't right." I paused, searching the street. My heart dropped like a stone in a well. "Oh no."

"What is it?" said the elf.

"They took it. They took my sword."

The elf lifted his hand of four fingers and reached into the darkness. When he drew his hand back, it held Transcender as if he had plucked it from a pocket of night. He handed it to me with a slight bow of his triangular head. He picked something else out of the void. "And here's your beret."

I gasped, put the beret on my head and accepted the sword, stashing it in my blazer before any harm came to it. "How did you do that? Why couldn't you hide yourself from the rats with a trick like that?"

"Elven magic isn't what it used to be. Everything changed after the Battle of the Celestial Library. We aren't welcome at Wildwoods School of the Wondrous. We aren't allowed to gather for long. We are harassed and harried. Our magic is depleted and untrained, and while I can create pockets, it takes time. The rats raging at you bought me time to hide the sword. It is much easier to hide a small object than a large one."

I kissed his cheek. "Thank you."

His ashen skin creased into folds as he smiled. Then he eased himself off the bench and turned into the night. "I must go, Alisha, and you should too, lest the rats return. The streets of the city are not safe at night. Thank the foxes for me."

"Wait," I said. "I don't know your name."

"I am Flinar," said the elf.

"Will we meet again?" I asked.

"Perhaps one day." Flinar cast a worried look over my shoulder. "But I don't like crowds." He limped away in his torn tunic and ridiculous knickerbockers, and I quelled my instinct to mother him.

"Charming." Fei Yen dressed once more in her red phoenix qipao. She plonked herself down next to me in the bus shelter, exhausted. "He could have stayed to say hello. It's not every day you meet a dark elf."

Faeza joined us more slowly, her face pale in the moonlight. They must have been in their fifties. Despite their slim dancers' bodies, the fracas with the rats had taken its toll. Her wound bled through the blue silk of her qipao.

The odd car sped past, but the drivers paid us no attention. We were just three women waiting for the bus.

"You really should find a safer place for your sword," said Fei Yen. "It's been flapping about inside your jacket for weeks. You're lucky Neighbourhood Watch haven't noticed it, let alone the police."

I frowned. "Surely I wasn't that obvious?"

"You jerked in fright every time it poked you," said Fei Yen. "It's been rather hair-raising watching you. It's a wonder you're still whole."

"How's your leg, Faeza?" I asked.

She sighed. "I'll survive. At least until we work out why our night class teacher was following us. Were we mistaken to save you, Alisha? I'm not sure it was your best professional decision to stalk us, and I'd hate to have to give up your class. We enjoy it so much."

Fei Yen nodded. "It is a wonderful group of people, and the kickboxing moves help keep us fit."

"Ha! I knew you weren't attending primarily for the language side," I said.

"Why would we need a class to practice English?" said Fei Yen. "We even dream in English."

"We have lived in London for over seventy years," said Faeza, "But it is in our nature to be able to speak all languages common to the area we inhabit, as well as the language of animals."

"Bloody hell."

They looked so toned in the nude for women of their age. Between them and Lavinia, it was enough to give me a complex.

"I had it all wrong, didn't I?" I asked.

If they were over seventy, their boobs were doing marvellously well. They were positively springy, the lucky cows—or rather foxes.

Faeza's eyes narrowed. "So tell us, Alisha, why on earth were you following us?"

They were right, of course. I had violated my duty of care. Technically, it would have been more sensible to ask Detective Jameson to investigate. That was what the Shadow Squad was for. Except, I wasn't the most patient woman.

I stood up to look them both in the eye and give myself more room in case they attacked. I had seen them in action. These two definitely had teeth.

A bus pulled in, crushing remnants of rubbish.

I waved the driver on and then focussed on my students. "I agree. You deserve an explanation. You see, I clocked the clues that there was more to you than you told me. Demanding answers was a big no-no in front of humdrums and would have led to me falling foul of the Magical Constitution, so I decided to follow you home. I'm sorry. I really am. In my defence, I did try waggling my eyebrows at you during night class, but it didn't provoke the confession I hoped."

"We just thought you had developed a nervous tic," said Fei Yen.

Faeza swatted her and gave me a sympathetic look. "It's been a hard year for you."

"You know, the Magical Constitution isn't worth the parchment it's written on," said Fei Yen. "Neither is belonging to the Otherworld. We don't need to register as peculiars to feel valued, and we certainly don't need to follow their rules. Foxes are natural outsiders. Our cunning tells us to live on the outskirts and not to risk our skin."

Faeza nodded. "Except we consider you a friend, and when we saw that bin arc through the air and the scuttling, devilish witches' rats, we knew you were outnumbered. We couldn't look away, even though our instincts told us to avoid confrontation."

"Thank you for risking your skins for me," I said. "Faeza, you need to stop that bleeding."

"I'll be fine. You think we haven't been in scrapes before? Finish explaining." Her look brooked no nonsense.

I took a deep breath. "Okay. You saw transformation and great pain in the cards the night the sun god killed Nita. As if you knew of my druidry and what the night held in store."

Fei Yen smiled. "This is true. How else do you think we fund all the Chinese take-aways Faeza likes to order? Card reading is the largest source of revenue at our shop."

They ran a tea and occult shop called Shanghai Moon around the corner from my flat, and the card reading table was always full. I had always thought it to be hocus pocus, but Marina was a real convert.

I nodded. "Then there was how you weren't fazed by Ezra appearing in wolf form in the classroom."

"Of course not. A wolf is part of the Canidae family. Like foxes," said Fei Yen.

I spluttered. "Are you telling me that Ezra has candida? Isn't that a fungal infection?"

Fei Yen laughed. "No, silly. Canidae is the Latin name for the biological family tree from which foxes, wolves and dogs branch."

A wave of relief flooded me. "Phew."

Faeza gave a watery smile. "Are you two up to hanky-panky then?"

I blushed. "Let's get back to the subject at hand. Neither of you fell for Detective Jameson's explanation that Nita had been killed in a rogue attack. As if you knew the killer was a god all along. So those were my reasons. There's nothing else to it. Except maybe your spooky thing of finishing each other's thoughts. If that doesn't scream Otherworld, I don't know what does."

"That's not spooky. That's love." Fei Yen turned to Faeza with concern. "Are you sure you are okay, my darling?"

Her wispy voice wasn't her own. "I was just thinking that Alisha should have a baldric to keep her sword safe."

Then she slumped and slid off the bench, transforming into her true self as she did.

I gasped. There was no cracking of bones, just a shifting of skin, a shrinking, a reframing, that all happened in a blink of an eye. Like Faeza was both woman and vixen, and both identities were as fluid as water.

Quick as a flash, Fei Yen caught the limp vixen in her arms. Her eyes were closed. Her clothes pooled at our feet.

Fei Yen looked at me aghast, her eyes filling with tears. "How could I be so stupid? She always takes the brunt of it when we have to fight. I didn't think it was that bad."

I gripped her shoulder. "There's no time for emotions right now, Fei Yen. We must get her some help."

"We can't take her to the hospital. We'll have to take her back to Shanghai Moon."

"No, I have a better idea," I said. "Do you trust me?"

Fei Yen nodded. "I do."

"Then we have no time to lose."

3

———————

I thanked my lucky stars for friends like Marina, who raced across moonlit London in her van to pick up a wounded fox. Twenty minutes later, Fei Yen scooped up Faeza and followed Marina into her surgery. I trailed behind with the discarded clothes.

My job had been done. This was Marina's domain, and I could rest easy knowing Faeza was in safe hands.

The smell of disinfectant filled my nose. I hovered in the treatment room as my best friend worked on her patient with a whirr of rainbow hair and deft fingers. Within minutes, she hooked up Fei Yen to fluids and cleaned and bandaged the wound. Finally, she placed gentle hands on the vixen's head and closed her eyes, synchronising her breathing with the animal.

Within seconds, the vixen stirred. Her bushy, red tail sparked to life, and then she rolled over, startled at the strange, sterile environment.

My best friend, the empath, the animal whisperer.

"It's okay, sweet thing," said Marina.

"I'm here," said Fei Yen. "It's okay. You can shift here. You are safe."

Only when she heard Fei Yen's voice did the vixen's stress ease. She sighed and curled up in a ball, and her silken red fur became a woman's skin. Her vixen's ears became human ones, and her snout receded to become a petite nose.

Marina trembled as Fei Yen embraced Faeza and covered her in a blanket.

I rushed to Marina's side. Her fingernails had been chewed down to the quick. "Are you okay? You're quivering like a leaf."

I didn't need her to tell me the truth. I knew her well enough to recognise the signs of anxiety—the signs that heralded another fight with her mum or an exam at school she was worried about. I didn't need a therapist to fill me in. Marina's quivering showed she hadn't managed to control her empath powers yet. Just like my dragon dreams were a sign of my fears that I'd never measure up to my long-dead grandmother, the legendary animator Rajika Verma.

Marina's blue eyes clouded over. "Just ignore me. The important thing is that Fei Yen is going to be okay. We got her here just in time. That wound might not have looked terrifying, but rats can be terrible carriers of disease. She'll need a course of antibiotics."

I grimaced. "Yeah, I might too. I'm covered in bites from the bloody things."

Marina looked at me in horror. "What on earth happened tonight?"

"We'll need a huge gin while I fill you in. And maybe a lasagne from Tito's," I said. Marina just happened to have one of London's best Italian restaurants next door. "But first, can you tell me why you're trembling? I'm worried."

"I'm finding it hard to switch off the empath thing after helping patients. Like their residual pain and fear seep into me."

I squeezed her. "We're a right trio, aren't we? Less than a month to our magical trial, and there's you with no off switch.

There's me with unreliable wind druidry, a flat zero on animation powers and a deadly sword that, in my hands, might as well be a toothpick. And Sahil, who has failed to find any powers at all."

The door to the treatment room swung open, and in padded a familiar creature. His thick, golden coat of rosettes gleamed in the fluorescent light. His scarred face, with its emerald eyes, provoked gasps from my students.

"No one said being a peculiar was easy," purred Echo, leaving us with no doubt about his superior hearing. "You went out looking all chic, Alisha, and now you look like you've been dragged through a bush backwards."

I wasn't surprised to see him here. Since her entry into the Otherworld, Marina had been receiving more and more peculiars as patients. Echo acted as a consultant for her. It wasn't like the Royal College of Veterinary Surgeons would have been any help. Marina's approach to Otherworld patients was a combination of veterinary knowledge, winging it, and Echo filling in the gaps.

God help us all.

"Hello, Echo." I scratched his ear. "I thought you were hunting tonight."

He inclined his magnificent head. "I was, but I rushed over when Marina paged me about an Otherworld fox."

I raised an eyebrow. "She paged you?"

Echo honked with laughter. "Of course not. I have neither opposable thumbs nor a pager belt. But since I'm now employed here, I like to use professional lingo."

Fei Yen and Faeza gawped.

I turned to them. "Ladies, I'd like you to meet my magical leopard, Echo, who started life as my Bengal cat."

"The pleasure is all mine." Echo grinned as Faeza's blanket dropped, and she scrambled to cover up again. "You need not worry. I prefer to eat animals who aren't scavengers. Deer are my current favourite. Herd animals are an easy kill.

You can always pick one off. Sometimes I even sing the Bee Gees's *Stayin' Alive* at them. The chorus, not the mumbling bit. You know, to give them a bit of a boost before I go in for the kill."

He paused and yawned, showing pristine rows of jagged teeth. I had brushed those teeth when he'd been a Bengal cat.

"But truth be told," he continued, "I am turning over a new leaf. I promised not to eat the animals in this surgery, and so far, I have upheld the bargain. Although outside of this surgery, you could be fair game, dependent on how terrible my hunger pangs are. And I always leave enough of the carcass to allow for burial. I'm not a Neanderthal."

"I'm injured. He'll eat me first." Faeza clutched Fei Yen. "Save yourself."

"Don't mind him," I said. "He talks a good game, but he doesn't actually kill that often. One kill can sustain him many months, and I keep the freezer well stocked with salmon and steak."

"She's very generous," said Echo. "And since you are her students and, therefore, indirectly pay for my sustenance, I shall give you a free pass from a mauling."

"How kind," said Marina. "We'll hold you to that. Now, will you please zip it and let these poor women tell us what exactly they are since we missed all the fun on the streets of London."

Echo turned steely emerald eyes on her. "Marina Ambrose, you do not need—"

Marina straightened her spine, all hint of trembling gone, and imbued her voice with quiet authority. "My surgery, my rules." She smiled at the foxes. "Tell me who you are."

Faeza stood supported by Fei Yen, but they spoke as one. "We are *hu hsien* from China."

"We didn't hide that from you, Alisha," said Fei Yen. "*Hu hsien* are foxes who can shapeshift into maidens of renowned grace and beauty with a fox's tail. They heal quickly, can speak many languages and become an ephemeral spirit. A man who falls in love with a *hu hsien* is in great danger, for the *hu hsien* can devour the souls of such men and leave them as mindless zombies."

"But that was a long time ago," said Faeza. "When we left China, we evolved past *hu hsien*. We can no longer become spirits and no longer have tails in our human form."

Fei Yen laughed. "Thank the gods."

Faeza smiled. "It took me a long time to walk as a maiden without my tail for balance."

"It did," said Fei Yen. "But we have adapted well these past decades. "London was the perfect place to blend in once we left China. Do you know how many foxes are in this city?"

"I do," said Marina. "Approximately ten thousand."

"But why did you leave China?" I frowned. All this time as their teacher, and I had no idea why they had left their home.

Marina smiled at me. "Because they are in love with each other. And some men would rather crush beautiful women than let them love freely. I didn't need to be an empath to know that."

Faeza nodded. "So we were forced to kill. Over and over again."

"One day, we just couldn't do it anymore. So we saw the pictures of China Town in London and decided to come here," said Fei Yen. "Except it was too expensive to live there."

Faeza kissed Fei Yen's cheek. "So we opened Shanghai Moon in Balham."

"The rest is history," said Fei Yen. "Thank you for recognising our love, Marina. And for helping my love to heal. We don't know how to thank you."

"Some longjing green tea and oolong would be just perfect." Marina poked me in the side. "My best friend promised to get me some but kept forgetting."

"What in the heavens? You have the same surname. I thought you were sisters," I said.

"Oh my goodness, Alisha. You're terrible at love," said Marina. "They're married, doofus."

Fei Yen and Faeza held up their rings.

"Since 2014," they said as one.

I furrowed my brow. "What I don't understand is why you choose to live amongst the foxes and humans of this city yet reject closer contact with the Otherworld."

"Because, while we trust you, we don't trust the Sorcerer's Senate. As long as the senate is in charge, we will continue to live in the shadows, where it is safe," said Fei Yen.

Faeza nodded. "We are your friends, Alisha, and as your friends, please think wisely about whether you want to take the Wildwoods magical trial."

"You are surprised that we can hear as well as the leopard," said Fei Yen with a twinkle in her eye. "Your rainbow-haired friend is not surprised. Even as we stand here now, I can hear the burrowing of rodents underground."

"And I can hear a wall clock ticking in the surgery reception area right now," said Faeza. "Your footsteps behind us were like the stomping of an elephant."

I made a mental note to get tips from Echo.

"Mark our words, Alisha," said Fei Yen. "Once you are a registered peculiar, the senate will have a claim to you. And what the senate wants, the senate gets."

4

———————

Wildwoods School of the Wondrous had become a second home to me since the revelation that I was a druid. Sometimes it seemed as though I spent more time there than at my own flat. Up in the cluster of treehouses surrounding the great oak, I felt safe to explore my druidry. Little wonder generations of peculiars had gravitated here to learn and push the boundaries of their magical side. How sad that Fei Yen and Faeza didn't trust the Sorcerer's Senate enough to take advantage of all Wildwoods had to offer: the community of peculiars, the library with its cherry-wood shelves and carpet of desiccated leaves, the arena that adapted to the training needs of students and the guiding hand of headmistress Rayna Willowsun, the Minister for Education.

When the Prime Sorcerer had wanted to banish me from the Otherworld before my magical trial due to my disobedience, it was Rayna who had vouched for me.

Like a grown woman's priority should be obedience. My top values were loyalty, authenticity and hope. Obedience came at the bottom of the list. I had spent my whole life unlearning that crap.

What mattered was being true to myself.

Still, acquiring new knowledge and skills took effort, and part of me would have been relieved if Phinneous Shine had kicked me out and I'd returned to sitting on my sofa dipping fistfuls of Doritos into guacamole. It had been so long since I'd really rested. Since my head had been empty of questions. There was much to be loved about the contentment of not striving for answers.

And this morning, in a cabin suspended like a bauble from a sycamore tree, I was faced with a teacher who demanded nothing more than my best.

"I must tell you, Alisha, these history lessons with the three of you really are the bane of my life," said Orpheus, the scariest and only mind-reading vampire I had ever met.

"Well, Minister, if you could just tell me how you would like me to behave, I will do my best," I said. "It must be a relief not to have to teach me, Marina and Sahil all at once."

Orpheus sighed. "Yes, it's just wonderful to prolong the pain threefold."

I chewed my lip. "Perhaps you can outsource this particular responsibility."

The fact that he could read every thought made me twitch with anxiety. Ezra had tried to teach me how to shield my thoughts, but as a new druid, my skills lagged aeons behind a hundred-year-old vampire.

Orpheus gave me a steely look. For a miserable vampire, he was pretty smoking hot—something about those dark eyes against skin as white as the cliffs of Dover.

"What?" he said. "And miss all this fun? No, druid. As Minister for History and the Today, this duty is mine alone. And for all that is unholy, can you please stop thinking about the werewolf?"

I couldn't keep Ezra out of my thoughts since he whisked me to Paris on our first date. He teleported us to the top of the Eiffel Tower and showed me the Louvre, Montmartre and

Notre Dame. I should have jumped his bones there and then before his pack summoned him.

Let's face it, he'd earned it.

Orpheus turned beetroot red. He'd obviously read every carnal thought.

It served him right. If I couldn't keep him out of my mind, maybe I could gross him out enough that he chose to stay out.

I wrenched my attention away from Ezra's come-to-bed eyes and low-slung jeans. "You know, from an English teacher's perspective, placing 'the' before 'today' in your title is grammatically odd. Would you consider changing it?"

His eyebrows shot up into his hairline. "You want me to change a title that has been passed down through the centuries and denotes the importance of the present over dusty history books? Hmm. Let me give it some thought." He scratched his beard so theatrically that I regretted showing any initiative. "No. I don't think I will. Do you know your problem, Alisha Verma?"

I sighed. "I'm sure you'll enlighten me."

"You have no hope of passing the magical trial."

I had to give it to him. Marina and I had come to the same conclusion. She could just about manage to keep her focus when the emotions of others became too overwhelming, but I was as unpredictable as Russian roulette. What's more, there had been such a buzz amongst Wildwoods students about our impending trial that my stress levels had skyrocketed. By all accounts, the trial took place in front of an audience, like some sort of gladiatorial show.

There was every chance we would be humiliated.

Since Fei Yen and Faeza had raised doubts about the Otherworld, my terrifying dragon nightmares had morphed into scenes of humiliation: my trouser seam splitting to reveal my control pants in the middle of the trial; Ezra lustily grabbing my hips and pulling me closer, only to change his mind when he saw me naked and just last night; my sword deciding I wasn't worthy and stabbing me in the eye.

"Alisha, if those winds don't die down, this cabin will become a projectile."

I slammed my tingling palms against my thighs. "That isn't me."

Only a desk separated us. He reached for me with long fingers, his dark eyes unfathomable, and laid his hand on my shoulder. "There, there. Calm yourself, druid."

The clouds in my mind cleared. It wasn't that my worries lifted, more that they no longer seemed insurmountable. Outside, the winds quietened. "How did you do that?"

"I can do more than read minds, move fast and bite necks, you know." He wasn't joking. "I also have the ability to wipe minds. Sometimes an emotion, sometimes a singular event, sometimes completely."

A shiver ran down my spine.

"These traits are passed down in a minor way to the vampires I have sired. You see, I have experience teaching new peculiars to master themselves and others." He peered down his Roman nose at me, making me feel small in comparison. It would have been sexy if he hadn't been such an arsehole. "I want you to take your studies seriously, Alisha. Can you do that? Passing the trial isn't just about raw talent or luck. You have proven you have that. There has never been an initiate who has a goddess on her side. I thought you were an imbecile when we first met, but you faced up to a god. You have proven yourself not to be the fool I took you for. However, you still show foolishness in spades."

"Well, aren't you a delight?"

"Nothing wastes time more than being delightful just to save feelings. Or are you too fragile for the truth?" The sleeves of his gown flapped angrily as he wagged his finger at me, and I wanted to bite it off. "Then listen, druid. Being a peculiar is about grit and the choices you make on a daily basis. Take your grandmother. She changed the course of the world by standing firm when it most counted. All her learning, all her magic and experience, led to that moment when she fought against dark forces at the Battle of the Celestial Library." He bent to open a drawer of his desk and placed a thick history book in front of me. "Read aloud from the top of page 581."

On the front was the Wildwoods crest: an embossed W, crowned with posies of plants.

I flicked through featherlight pages edged with gold. "The Battle of the Celestial Library. On 9 March 1982, when Uranus entered retrograde motion, a fifty-strong group of dark elves led by Meriel Naehorn breached the defences of the Celestial Library in an attempted to seize the magical artefacts stored there. The Custodian Rajika Verma, a druid who had warned for many years of the nefarious intentions of Naehorn, together with her leopard Chanakya Gunbir Hredhaan of Maharashtra, fought valiantly to defend the library..."

I shivered with anticipation. I'd known Echo had fought at my grandmother's side—that was how he'd received his scar, after all—but reading it in a history book filled my heart with pride for my loved ones.

"Continue," said Orpheus.

"With the stolen magical items, the dark elves planned to shred the Magical Constitution and turn the egalitarian council and Otherworld into an elf dominion. When Meriel Naehorn's forces disabled the Celestial Library's defences, Rajika Verma and her leopard stood singlehandedly against them until Defence Minister Lavinia Drach's army heeded the distress call. The Custodian then retreated to guard the inner sanctum. The battle raged for thirty-six hours. While Rajika Verma ultimately lost her life, her actions prevented the dark elves from gaining possession of a single artefact."

I exhaled loudly. My grandmother had only ever been a

ghost to me, but I could sense her spirit now. I understood why she'd been held up as such an example.

A half-smile played on Orpheus' lips. "You are beginning to understand. Finish the paragraph, Alisha."

"Defence Minister Drach apprehended the dark elf leader Meriel Naehorn and her followers, who were subsequently stripped of their magic. On 11 March 1982, with the conjunction of the Moon and Mars at hand, after all-night deliberations with the Sorcerer's Senate, the Prime Sorcerer Phinnaeous Shine cast out the dark elves from the senate and expelled elven children from Wildwoods School of the Wondrous. Their return to the school would be permitted only on condition of a generous donation to the Wildwoods coffers." I gasped. "But that's not fair. How can all elves be blamed for the actions of a few?"

"The senate took decisive action. Thank the stars they did, or you would be living in a dark elf dominion right now."

"It was nearly forty years ago."

He frowned. "They murdered your grandmother."

"And would the senate's decree have been any different had she lived?"

"Bad behaviour has consequences. The attempted destruction of our society is a grave crime."

I thought of Flinar, my new elf friend, and the sadness in his eyes. "Are you so sure that the senate is above reproach?"

His conviction chilled me to the bone. "I am. And your grandmother would have been too."

Something told me Ezra wouldn't have been as quick to write off a whole section of the magical community. He'd put himself in harm's way to help me avenge Mum's death. A man who went to such lengths for a stranger had more compassion than the senate had when they had cast out the elves.

"You do realise that the werewolf was thinking with his carrot and veg rather than his brain when he helped you? You could have lost your life against the sun god. A true mentor would never have acted so recklessly." He paused and leaned forward, and I was struck again by how his handsome, chiselled face was wasted with his heartless personality. "The werewolf is not fit to be your mentor. It would be in your best interests to switch to me."

I gawped. "You want to be my mentor? Why? You don't even like me."

Orpheus shrugged. "An immortal vampire runs out of challenges. You are a challenge."

I pictured the vampire and the werewolf fighting over me like in *Twilight*. It wasn't my favourite fantasy, but I could get used to it.

His sculpted lips curved into a smile. "My intentions are anything but romantic, druid."

I laughed uncomfortably. "That's a relief. What *are* your intentions?"

"To take you to the next level. It's particularly disappointing you haven't managed to access your grandmother's powers yet. What is the werewolf's strategy? Surely he has one?"

I sighed. I had been a little disappointed at how often pack business took Ezra away from my training needs and my side. How was I ever supposed to gain my confidence if he kept disappearing? Not to mention the lack of opportunities to seduce him.

"The pleasures of the flesh are all well and good, Alisha, but sometimes you have to think with your mind."

"Rather than my lady parts?" I said helpfully.

He spluttered, and I gave myself a point for ruining his composure. But Orpheus wasn't the kind of man who'd let me get the upper hand for long. My adrenalin spiked as he moved in a sudden blur and came to sit on the desk. He towered over me, dark eyes holding mine, and I caught a whiff of dark chocolate and sweet cherry.

My hand slipped under my jacket to grasp Transcender's hilt.

"Whoa, you're a fast mover. Is that beard oil I can smell?" I blurted out to mask my nerves.

"Vampires have dry skin. So what if my goatee needs a helping hand?" he said in exasperation. "And don't think I haven't noticed your sword. Stop posturing. You wouldn't have a chance to get in a strike if I wanted to kill you."

I gulped. I had a feeling that duty of care meant far less at Wildwoods than it did in humdrum society.

"I'll only make this offer once, Alisha. You are too enamoured with the werewolf to take proper instruction. The results of your magical trial depend on your decision. What do you say, druid?"

My mind whirled. I had already made enough enemies in the Otherworld to fill a granny annexe. I didn't need another one.

The cabin rocked as if we were caught in a storm.

A note of warning. "Alisha—"

I gave him a blank look. "I promise that isn't me."

Then we fell.

5

Orpheus and I clung together. I cried out as we hit the rafters before plummeting in a mass of flesh, books and classroom furniture. Screams filled our ears. Any second now, we'd hit the ground and be smashed to a pulp in our wooden casket. Not that Orpheus should have minded. I was pretty sure he couldn't be killed by falling, and vampires liked caskets.

Still, he seemed hellbent on getting us out of this one. He gripped me tightly against his chest as we fell, his eyes narrowed in concentration.

Little did he know, I didn't need to wait for a knight to rescue me.

My palms tingled as I formed a cushion of wind around us.

"What are you doing?" he grunted, his feet floundering in the air, the current giving him oscillating fish lips.

I panted with exertion. Sustaining the wind took all my focus. "Saving us with a cushion of wind, so we don't break our necks."

"Let me do my job, you cretin." He pinned my hands to my sides. When the cushion of air dissipated, he propelled off the falling debris and launched us into the woods.

My scream stuck in my throat as we ripped through the air. We tumbled to safety by a grove of trees, rolling over and over before coming to a stop in a tangle of legs and arms and hair and dirt.

A couple of hundred yards away, the cabin broke into a hundred pieces.

I groaned in the vampire's arms. My body would be bruised black and blue by our fall. What's more, the jutting edges of my sword hilt had imprinted themselves onto my skin during our tumble.

Orpheus shoved me aside without ceremony, stood up and dusted himself off. His eyes flashed in surprise as the ground shook with tremors. "What is going on? Has there been a mishap in the arena? Whatever it is, someone is going to pay for that lesson interruption. My history classroom has been all but destroyed. What are you still doing sprawled on the floor, druid?"

The tremors subsided at last, and I sat up.

My heartbeat jumped as a familiar face loomed into sight behind Orpheus.

Ezra's eyes, full of concern, drank in the sight of me before he tore them away to speak to Orpheus. "I take it you haven't seen the news, Minister."

Orpheus snorted. "Humdrum news has been taken over by a clan of Murdochs and is little more than fiction. Better to trust my own eyes."

He disappeared in a flash towards the arena.

Ezra crouched by my side. "Thank the stars you're okay. I came as soon as I realised what was going on."

"My knight in denim jeans." I stared up at him, dazed by the fall. He hadn't had a shave in days, and his rumpled clothes indicated he'd slept in them, but butterflies still darted in my stomach.

He pulled me to my feet and kissed the top of my head.

I melted into him, then pulled away to check how much damage Wildwoods had sustained. My jaw slackened. "Oh my goodness, we have to see if anyone is hurt."

I ran full pelt towards the school.

"Stay here. It might not be safe." Ezra cursed and followed, hot on my heels.

My lungs burned as I ran. Only when we stood in the middle of the site did we stop, aghast.

Two cabins that had fanned out from the great oak had fallen in addition to ours, leaving huge craters and debris on the ground. Torn books, discarded school bags and shattered glass crunched underfoot. Some rope bridges had been twisted or torn, and many others had become dislodged altogether. Felled beech trees had crushed apparatus in the training arena. The cable car track had been mangled.

"The luck of the leprechauns was on our side today," said Ezra. "If this had happened in the evening, Wildwoods would have been full to the rafters."

Orpheus's vampire speed had propelled him ahead of us. By the time we arrived in the thick of it, he loomed over the clusters of distraught pupils, taking names. Rayna Willowsun tended to three pupils on stretchers with capable hands, uncorking clinking healing potions from her belt, her expression solemn.

"There were fewer than fifty people on site, but the children need calming. Rayna is already tending to the injured, but their injuries are mild, especially in the hands of a druid with healing powers," said Orpheus to us. "You can help calm the children. What are you waiting for?"

Ezra and I rounded up the children away from the rubble.

"This way, children," I said, putting on my brightest voice. "It was just a little mishap. Your parents will be here soon, and you'll get a day at home. It's just like a snow day. And everyone knows how fun snow days are."

They gazed at me in awe.

The Wildwoods rumour mill had gone into overdrive after my intervention during the Kraglek ceremony. Once word had got around about my antics with the sun god, I'd been turned into a heroine overnight.

Not that I was complaining.

I spotted a familiar face amongst the assortment of shapeshifters, druids, vampires and witches. Mirabel, the gutsy fairy who'd refused to back down from a pack of werewolves and had faced Kraglek, sobbed a few feet away.

I wrapped my arms around her slight shoulders and pushed her auburn ringlets out of her tear-stained face. "It's going to be okay, Mirabel, I promise."

"But that's just it, Alisha. It's not going to be okay. Everyone is saying it's the dark elves." Mirabel gulped back her tears.

I frowned. This didn't look like an enemy attack. I spotted neither assailants nor weapons. How could the dark elves have pulled something like this off unseen, with all the magic and defences that dwelt in this place?

Ezra knelt next to us to tie Mirabel's trailing shoelace. "That's highly unlikely, Mirabel. People say all sorts of things when they are scared. That doesn't make them true."

I nodded. "You're safe now, Mirabel. Just hang in there until your parents arrive. A duvet day always makes me feel better. Tomorrow this will all seem like a bad dream."

She brightened. "Do you think I can get out of doing my history homework?"

"I'll have a word with Orpheus," I said.

"You're the best." She floated back to her friends.

I turned to Ezra with a frown. "Dark elves? Sounds a bit farfetched to me."

His grey eyes smouldered. "I agree. I haven't caught their scent, and my nose never lies. If it were the elves, Lavinia would have called in her army already. Orpheus may scoff, but the BBC is reporting an earthquake measuring magnitude 6 on the Richter scale. A chunk of Westminster Bridge even fell into the Thames."

"Bloody hell. An earthquake in London is impossible. There aren't any major fault lines here."

He rubbed the back of his neck as if he'd been working long nights and needed a little kneading of his muscles to set him to rights. "I thought you knew by now, Alisha? Nothing is impossible."

Orpheus came up behind us. "You don't belief that codswallop, do you, Mr Neuhoff? An earthquake of this magnitude in London? It beggars belief. The dark elves are a far likelier explanation. Your aunt has been warning of an impending attack for quite some time."

Ezra raised a dismissive eyebrow. "My aunt has been a sworn enemy of the dark elves since the Battle of the Celestial Library. Unless she provides actual proof, I hope you'll take her declarations with a pinch of salt."

"The yew tree rune has been compromised. Would an earthquake disable the school's defences?" said Orpheus coldly.

My mind flashed to my loved ones. I needed to know they were safe. "So Ezra can teleport in and out of Wildwoods?"

Orpheus looked down at me. "Indeed. And the dark elves can use their black hole magic to wreak havoc. Now do you see the stakes?"

My heart hammered in my throat. I clutched Ezra's arm and got a whole load of bicep. "Ezra, will you check on my family for me? I can't breathe if they might be in danger."

He locked eyes with mine. "I won't be a second."

Then, he disappeared.

Orpheus's jaw hardened. "What a loyal sheepdog you have there. It's plain to see who is in charge. No wonder he is failing as your mentor."

I chewed my cheek to still my sharp tongue. Now was the time to pull together.

Just because Ezra had agreed to check on my family, it didn't make him a sheepdog. It made him someone who had recognised my anxiety and done the human thing. I bet Orpheus was a caveman—the type of man who expected women to launder his Y-fronts and be happy about it.

He stalked off as the rest of the cavalry arrived: the Prime Sorcerer, flanked by Defence Minister Lavinia and her two sisters, the Bestiary Minister Helio Woodwink and his assistant, the Justice Minister, the alpha Gunnolf and two burly werewolves. A vice tightened around my heart as they huddled together like a war committee on a battlefield.

Inside my jacket, Transcender pulsed against my skin like it was trying to tell me something.

Like it knew that danger approached.

My anxiety grew like a tidal wave. When Ezra reappeared with Echo at his side, I breathed a sigh of relief.

"Joshi, Sahil and Marina are all well and accounted for. The leopard insisted on coming, but he doesn't travel well." Ezra wiped the drool from his trouser legs.

A dizzy Echo padded over to nuzzle my leg with the gait of a drunken sailor. "I am relieved to know the dark elves have not torn you apart, Alisha Verma. Although you are no longer completely incapable of protecting yourself, I would be breaking my ancestral oath if I had allowed the wolf to return alone."

I scratched him behind his ear. "How is Dad?"

"Glued to the humdrum news with your idiotic brother," said Echo. "Marina is soothing her animals at the surgery."

Ezra ushered us forward, his warm hand on the small of my back, lingering there. "Come, you two. The Prime Sorcerer calls."

Phinnaeous Shine had reigned over the Otherworld as Prime Sorcerer longer than any other peculiar. As Echo had explained, a wizard with skinwalking powers was singularly suited to the brief of Prime Sorcerer. He could infiltrate top levels of government as easily as a woman slipping on a new dress. His transformations were not limited to his own gender. He could walk in anyone's shoes, and his skinwalking extended to voice and mannerisms, although his target's memories were, of course, alien to him. Still, with a little research, he could emulate just about anybody on earth and wear his new skin for as long as it took for the sun to rise and fall.

However, his skinwalking didn't impress me that day; his sheer resourcefulness and strength did.

"Children, stay out of the way." His black skin shone with perspiration as he bellowed.

Phinnaeous Shine stood, legs in a wide stance, his gown billowing behind him as he raised his arms left and right, like a conductor of an orchestra. The debris around him rose: the splintered cabins, torn rope bridges, the derailed cable cars and broken crockery. He hoisted them into the air, and they knitted back together in front of our eyes in such a spectacle of power that even the most troubled students cheered.

Helio sprinted away to check on the bestiary and round up any errant creatures. Up amongst the tree canopies, silver-haired Lavinia flew on her dull brown umbrella with its shimmering brass handle alongside her sisters Chandra and Isadora on their umbrellas. They looped through the sky, lassoing Wildwoods back together, their lips synchronised in their spells. Gunnolf, Ezra and the two burly werewolves heaved the fallen beech trees out of the arena while druid Rayna used her knowledge of plants to repair the yew tree that served as Wildwoods's primary defence.

Lucky old me and Echo had been assigned to Orpheus to patrol the ground for dark elves.

"I will rip out the throats of any elf I see." Echo's emerald eyes gleamed.

"It would be better to check with me first, Chanakya Gunbir Hredhaan of Maharashtra. There are still some elves who are pupils here, whose parents managed to raise the tuition fees," said Orpheus. "Although I have my suspicions that the money comes from dark dealings."

"Your instincts are as finely tuned as Ravi Shankar's guitar," Echo purred.

"I'm more of a Jimi Hendrix fan myself," said Orpheus. "It is an honour to have a warrior from the Battle of the Celestial Library here on the day the dark elves have returned."

"Steady on." I pushed through thick foliage. "We've not found a shred of proof."

Echo growled. "They are a tricky race, Alisha. Do you think it was just anyone who killed the great Rajika Verma? It was these treacherous elves that conspired to kill your grandmother. They do not deserve your compassion."

I sighed, grateful Echo hadn't been at my side the night I had met Flinar. He might have sided with the rats.

How quick these two were to judge. While geography had never been my strong point, I agreed that earthquakes in London were a ridiculous thought. But I would not cast blame on an entire group of magical individuals without more evidence, and for that, we needed Detective Jameson. That was after we had finished patrolling the Wildwoods boundary for non-existent boogeymen.

"Tell me, leopard, have you yet written a memoir of your life? You are talented in that respect, I seem to remember, and as the Minister for History and the Today, I would like to remind you how valuable eyewitness accounts are."

Echo lifted his chest with pride. "You heard where Ursula K. Le Guin got her ideas from?"

Orpheus nodded. "I did. But writing fiction is entirely different to non-fiction. I would be happy to read samples once you have a manuscript for your memoirs."

"I would be indebted, Minister. First, we have dark elves

to hunt." Echo prowled close to the ground like he had caught a scent. He pounced on a bush, flushing out a red squirrel who scampered up a nearby sycamore.

I rolled my eyes.

A deep gong sounded, rippling like a wave across Wildwoods.

"Come, the Prime Sorcerer summons us," said Orpheus.

We hurried to the now spotlessly clean arena, where Phinnaeous Shine clapped for the attention of those gathered. Lavinia stood at his side, dressed as usual in bubble gum pink, her shoulders pushed back and her posture as straight as a military general.

By now, the numbers had swollen. We gathered in a throng of not only pupils, teachers and ministers but parents who had hurried to the school to check on their offspring and individuals from the magical community who had felt the pull of Wildwoods in their hour of need.

The Prime Sorcerer raised his voice above the sound of the breeze and the rustling leaves, and the crowd fell silent.

"Wildwoods is many things. It is a school. It is a safe haven. It is the seat of the Sorcerer's Senate. It is our most treasured resource. And yet, today, our treasure has been plundered by forces who, as yet, hide in the shadows. And we will be ready when they show their sorry faces. The dark elves will be punished."

The women laid protective arms around their children. The men in the crowd cheered and stamped the ground.

A shiver ran down my spine as Echo, too, threw back his head and roared his approval.

The most experienced faces, the ones lined with age, who had seen battles before, stayed quiet.

This is ridiculous, I thought, though I didn't say it out loud. Who was I to speak up against Phinnaeous Shine?

Orpheus, next to me, leaned down to murmur in my ear. "You see, you're learning to trust others with more wisdom."

I pledged to find a way to keep him out of my head.

An enigmatic smile danced around Orpheus's lips. "I haven't yet earned your trust, Alisha. But I will. I'm right about the dark elves and being the superior mentor."

"That remains to be seen, Orpheus," I said.

The Prime Sorcerer led the way back into the reconstructed building with the air of a triumphant king at his homecoming.

Dread bubbled up inside me.

Phinnaeous Shine stood out even amongst the deeply impressive and jaw-dropping peculiars I had met on my Otherworld journey. But what were resourcefulness and strength if they made you rush headlong into mistakes? The senate had a duty to act responsibly, but instead of pausing to gather evidence, it had doubled down on a decades-old grudge. Had Fei Yen and Faeza been right to warn me about where I placed my trust?

6

Twilight had fallen by the time we reached my family home overlooking Tooting Bec Common. At this hour, the streets would usually have been filled with the sound of spluttering engines, drivetime radio and hooting as stony-faced drivers sat in traffic jams.

Not today. A quiet fear gripped the city.

Families sat glued to their television sets, where regular broadcasting had been interrupted by footage of the tremors and their aftermath.

It wasn't only Westminster Bridge that had been damaged. A deep crack had desecrated memorial stones in Westminster Abbey, and the foundations of the London Eye had become unstable. The city's emergency services had been working themselves ragged all day. News agencies reported hospitals full of patients suffering minor injuries and countless insurance claims from civilian homes and businesses.

Echo padded alongside Ezra and me, his tail swishing in disappointment. "I was rather hoping to terrorise hapless dogs having their walkies on the way to Joshi's house, but the streets are empty. Trust the elves to ruin everything."

"Not you too, Echo." Ezra stopped short on Dad's driveway. "You can't believe all that guff from the senate."

"I can, and I do," said Echo. "I fear there are troubling times ahead. This has elvish fingerprints all over it."

Ezra shook his head. "All I see are pieces of a puzzle and a lot of folks eager to jump the gun."

"Well, if I had opposable thumbs, I would point a whole armoury of guns at them," Echo growled. "Since I am lacking in that department, my claws and teeth will have to do."

I clenched my jaw in frustration. "And what if you are wrong?"

Echo yawned as if he didn't care either way. "It doesn't matter. I feel nothing but disdain for the dark elves since the night we lost your grandmother. If the dark elves receive boots up their backsides because of this morning, it reminds them to stay in their place. Look what happened to your fox students when they intervened in elvish troubles. Nothing good comes of siding with them."

I massaged my temples, tired of explaining the obvious. "But it was the coven's rats who hurt Fei Yen and Faeza, not Flinar."

"More like the rats knew the dark elves were up to something. Flinar could very well be a dark elf general."

My tone was sharp. "He was nothing of the sort. You didn't see him, or you would think the same."

"I have been a peculiar for centuries longer than you, Alisha. What you see with your newly unveiled eyes is not always accurate. Now, if you'll excuse me, I can hear the gentle flapping of koi in Joshi's pond that require my attention." He bounded up and over the side gate, and within seconds, splashing indicated he was toying with Dad's koi.

Ezra and I headed across the block-paved driveway to Dad's front door.

"You didn't have to come, you know." I rang the doorbell. "As far as we know, this morning was a geological anomaly."

Ezra leaned against the pillar of Dad's porch with his thumbs hooked in his jeans pockets. "Can't a guy miss his girl?"

My heart leapt a beat. "Is that what we are to each other?"

The lines around his grey eyes deepened as he smiled. "What do you want us to be?"

"I want us to have enough time to find that out."

"I wish I could whisk you away again, but my gut says things are hotting up. You have the trial to concentrate on. And then there's this ridiculous thing with the elves. I've never seen the senate so gung-ho. I would have stayed away today, but I needed to know you were safe."

"It's sweet, but it seems like all the men around me are rushing in to protect me—even Echo. Take right now. I'm perfectly capable of breaking bad news to Dad myself."

Ezra's grey eyes glimmered with amusement. "I know by now that you're an independent woman, Alisha. Just because I rush in to stand by your side doesn't mean I don't respect you. I just thought it was fairer that Joshi heard Rayna's decision from me. If your dad's unhappy with me usurping him as Sahil's mentor, I'd rather take the brunt of it. Besides, it's about time your brother and I bonded if I'm going to mentor him too."

I gave a throaty laugh. "So that's why you're here? For Sahil? I thought it was for me."

Ezra pulled me closer, and the scent of sweat from the morning's exertions and the tang of soap travelled up my nose. "If I'm honest, Orpheus sniffing around you made me a little possessive."

I grinned. "Vampires don't sniff. That's more of a werewolf thing. And you didn't look too bothered when you and the pack were playing at being lumberjacks in the arena."

His eyes dropped to my lips.

My heartbeat raced, but there was no way I'd let Dad catch us smooching. Mum would have given me a cheeky wink and offered to take me corset shopping. Her French heritage meant romance and sex were no big deal. Indian dads were more uptight. Even when their daughters were forty. Mine would rather have eaten his own toenail than see me locking lips with Ezra.

I pulled away and murmured in Ezra's ear. "Much as I love your hands on me, I don't want to make Dad's day any harder than it is already. No need for him to see his daughter in a compromising situation."

His eyes twinkled. "My apologies. I had no idea you were so...proper."

I fidgeted to hide my flushed cheeks. I thought my divorce had turned off my need for romance, but it turned out the right man could switch it right back on. "Oh, no, Mr. Neuhoff. I'm not proper. Just a daughter sensitive to her father's needs."

The air smouldered between us.

"In that case, a rain check," he said.

The door opened, and my brother Sahil emerged with a look of surprise. "Hey, Alisha, good thing you're here. Dad's been wound up like a spring since the quake." He nodded warily at Ezra. "Thanks for checking on us before, Ezra. Glad the tremors didn't flatten you."

"So you felt them here too?" I said.

"A shudder. Nothing more. Like a train had passed by. Weird, though, isn't it? It's not like we're in Tokyo or San Francisco. It was worse for some of my tenants. I was just about to nip down to Peckham to look at a crack. You can babysit Dad while I'm gone."

I grimaced. "That bad, is it?"

"Uh-huh. And you know what we're like. We exist in the same space like passing ships because we have no idea what to say to each other. Anyway, top timing." He grabbed his keys and stepped out over the threshold.

"Actually, Sahil, I wanted to have a word. Alisha's going

to tell your dad, but between the two of us, Rayna wants me to take over mentoring you for the trial in a few weeks."

A look of horror crossed Sahil's face. "You know, about that, I reckon I'm not a peculiar. I have no magical talents. Me taking the trial is a waste of time."

Ezra put a hand on his shoulder. "Once the trial date is set, it must be taken, or you forfeit your chance. Let me see what I can coax out of you. What have you got to lose?"

Sahil heard the challenge and squared up to Ezra, all bristly, thin-lipped five-foot-nine of him. Ezra cleared him by a few inches and exuded calm. Which meant nothing because if there was one thing ingrained in me from the days my brother would pin me down when my parents weren't looking, it was that he was a live wire and knew how to play dirty.

I cringed, staying out of it only because Ezra held up a hand to say he could handle it.

"I could lose my pride," said Sahil.

Ezra raised an eyebrow. "Perhaps. But I can't see how it's any different if you chicken out."

Sahil often brought the child out in me. I was tempted to do a chicken dance there and then, but Echo came bounding around the side of the house, stinking of pond life and trailing water with him.

Sahil visibly shrank as the leopard approached. "You."

"Yes, who else?" said Echo. "Were you expecting The Lion King?"

Sahil wrinkled his nose. "You smell like a marsh."

His fur was bedraggled, and algae clung to his ear. "You speak the truth. I, too, cannot stand my own smell. Unfortunately, there is such an infestation of algae in the pond that I can't locate the koi. Assuming they still live and haven't succumbed to the poor water quality."

I sighed. "Dad has no idea how to maintain the pond

without Mum. You promised you were going to call an expert in."

Sahil's eyes flashed. "How much more do you all want to ask of me? See to Dad, will you? With me, Echo. You need a hose down."

Echo's tail swished, and he bared his teeth. "I am a majestic leopard from India. Not a toddler from kindergarten."

"How about I help with the cleanup?" Ezra ushered the grumbling leopard back around the side of the house. "And we can talk over your options about the trial? Between your sister, Marina and me, I'm sure we can get you up to scratch. That is if you want to be a part of this world."

Sahil followed, keeping his distance from Echo's swinging rump. "Marina has agreed to help me? Why didn't you say?"

Ezra caught my eye. "Yes, I thought I had mentioned that already."

I shut the front door and walked past the shrine with Mum's garlanded photograph. In the kitchen, I found Dad looking worse for wear with mad professor hair and his shirt buttoned up wonky. An old school television stood on the counter—Mum would have hated that—blaring out news of the tremors. I turned down the volume.

Dad swung around, his face brightening at the sight of me. "Alisha, thank the gods you are here. I can't seem to find my comb." He closed the spice drawer. "I could have sworn it was in there."

I turned my full attention to him and picked up his comb from next to the kettle. "Your comb is right here. Sit down; let me help."

He sank into a chair while I fixed his buttons and tugged a comb through his errant hair.

"Why are you dressed in a shirt?"

"Oh, I don't know. When Rosalie was here, it was easy to take pride in myself. She was such a beautiful woman. I didn't want to let her down. But now, I walk about all day in my pyjamas."

"Well, that doesn't sound so bad."

He slumped. "It is if the pyjamas have three-day-old chilli stains on them. So today I thought I'd wear a shirt. And the first thing that happens is the city experiences an earthquake. If that isn't a sign, I don't know what is."

I put the comb down. "Don't be ridiculous. That was nothing to do with you."

"Well, of course not. It's all over the BBC. It just *feels* that way." His brow furrowed. "Unless there's something else. What's going on, Alisha?"

"Oh, nothing much," I lied, wanting to shield him from more worry. "Phinnaeous Shine was very impressive. The building took some knocks, but everything is now as it was."

"He pursued my mother romantically once, long before I came along." He squinted at me. "Hang on a minute. I know that face. I have known it your whole life. You're hiding something. Like when you missed the potty and covered the poo on the carpet with a doll's blanket."

"Dad!" I thanked the heavens Ezra hadn't heard. Through the window, I could see him and Sahil grappling with Echo and the garden hose. I gave a heavy sigh. "The senate think the dark elves are behind the tremors."

Dad let out a wail and covered his face with his hands. I'd never heard him make that sound before, not even when Mum had died. It was as if a dam had burst within him, and he didn't know how to stop.

I held him tightly, bent down so he'd hear me and be comforted by my presence. "Dad, what's wrong?"

He lifted his stricken face, his breath coming in gulps. "The dark elves are here again, just as my children have stepped into the Otherworld. They killed my mother. How can life be so cruel?"

His wails recommenced, rising in pitch until they became hysteria.

Ezra, Sahil and Echo gathered at the kitchen window to peer at us, the garden hose forgotten.

Do something, mouthed Sahil.

It felt wrong, but I slapped Dad's face.

He sighed and then collapsed into my arms. "I'm sorry. I needed that. Sometimes it's hard being the adult."

I gestured at our onlookers to give us some privacy and pulled back to make eye contact with Dad. "I know it is. For what it's worth, there's no evidence the dark elves are behind this. I'm sure there's a simple explanation."

"This is why. This is why I never wanted the two of you involved."

"Dad, I have something to tell you. Rayna has decided you are too distracted to train Sahil properly for his trial."

He let go of me, and his ageing hands, which had once painted so joyously, curled around his middle. "She wants him to drop out? Maybe that's for the best. Maybe you should step back too."

I shook my head. "No, she wants Ezra to train him too."

His chin trembled. "So be it. But the trial is two weeks away, and none of you is ready. You will fail, and it will be for the best. And then we won't have to think about the dark elves ever again. I will ask for the same fate."

I frowned. "Whatever do you mean?"

"Alisha, if you fail, this will seem like a dream to you. You won't even remember the Otherworld exists."

"I don't believe you. Surely we'd just learn for the trial again and retake it?"

Dad fidgeted. "There are no do-overs for the magical trial. Once you enter Wildwoods grounds, the decision is out of your hands. If you don't take the trial or if you fail it, you lose your memories of the Otherworld. The senate's vote is binding. Anything magic has touched—your mother's death, our talents, Echo. After a visit from the magical clean-up crew, it would be as if those memories warp into something humdrum. Not entirely different, but with the magic sucked out of them. You would wake in the morning and believe that your Bengal cat had simply gone missing."

My heart pounded. How cruel to find our true potential, only to have it snatched away should we fail. "You're just saying that because you don't want us to succeed."

"No, my darling. I'm saying it because it's the truth, however painful."

"Your painting would revert to humdrum level."

"Like most of my married life. I wasn't unhappy. There is much more to being above than being a peculiar."

My stomach clenched. "Dad, it might not be the elves."

"It will always be something."

7

———————

I bristled with anger. Not at Dad so much as at Ezra. Why had he left me in the dark about the trial and all that was at stake? It was his job to fill me in. Orpheus flashed into my mind. At least he told it how it was. At least he didn't try to protect my feelings.

Ezra had a lot of explaining to do.

And then there was Dad. How was I supposed to concentrate on getting through the trial with him in such a state? If the dark elves were out of the picture, he could rest easy that the immediate threat had diminished. Then maybe he would get behind us. Maybe his fear would seep away, and he would find joy in his life again. He had always been the more cautious parent. That was nothing new. But right now, he was in danger of crawling into his shell and never coming out—more mollusc than man.

Dad stood up shakily. "I'm sorry, Alisha. I know you didn't want to hear that. Please stay for dinner. Shall I set up the dining room?"

Mum had made all the hosting decisions.

"Sure, Dad. The dining room will be just fine. I'll come

through in a minute, okay? I have to make a call." I dialled Detective Robert Jameson, Marina's current fling.

Robert was my contact at the Shadow Squad, a small team of humdrums working off the books from the Metropolitan Police, whose remit was supernatural. He picked up on the third ring, sounding harried. "Alisha, it's not a good time."

"Robert, I need a favour."

"The city is in freefall. Can it wait?"

"Dude, I'm your only druid friend. And you're dating my best friend."

He sighed. "Be quick."

"The senate seems to think this morning's tremors were the work of the dark elves. Are they on the money?"

"I'm not a hundred per cent. Not yet. My sort of grunt work takes time. I've been out all morning, checking in with my Otherworld contacts, taking in the damage with my own eyes. If you want a definitive answer, you're not going to get one today."

"I just need your best guess, Robert."

"Okay, well then, I'd say the senate is talking bollocks. The dark elves no longer have the resources to pull off something like that. Their networks were shredded back in the eighties, and we've heard no whispers of plans. Nada. Tell the senate it's barking up the wrong tree. The last thing we need is them stirring up tensions in the Otherworld while the city is reeling from a natural disaster."

I breathed a sigh of relief. An earthquake was bad but not half as bad as an old enemy rearing its head. "So you think it was an earthquake?"

"I think it could be. The scientists are saying London's not as geologically stable as was once thought. What makes it worse is our overloaded infrastructure. Nine million people, diminishing green space, more and more high-rises, jammed roads and densely populated areas, even in the richest parts.

It was pretty hairy this morning. Anything further up the Richter scale could cause loss of life."

"Yikes," I said. "Well, let's hope it was a one-off."

"I've got to go, Alisha. Give that rainbow-haired best friend of yours a kiss from me. I'll get over to her as soon as the clear-up's over today."

"Kiss her yourself. And Robert? Thanks." I hung up and turned around.

Ezra leaned against the door frame, his T-shirt drenched. He'd be right at home in a hot-stuff car wash or a Magic Mike show.

A shiver of pleasure ran through me. "How long have you been standing there?"

He crossed his arms with no self-awareness about how damn attractive he was. "Long enough to wonder why you're getting involved with this when you have the trial to focus on."

I cursed my traitorous body and adopted a cool tone. "Are you serious? After all you've been keeping from me?"

"What do you mean?" He stepped forward.

"When were you going to tell me that if I fail the trial, there are no second chances? That I'll be back in my humdrum life faster than I can blink?"

A shadow passed over his face. "Shit, you can't think that of me. I was protecting you. You've already had so much more pressure than a normal initiate. I didn't want to add to it by laying that on you. It was a tactic to keep your mind focused."

My restraint snapped. "Well, I'm not focused, Ezra. And do you know why that is?"

His voice was flat. "I'm sure you're going to tell me."

"I'm not focused because you've been prioritising pack business over me for weeks."

His eyes pleaded. "You have no idea about the rules of the

pack. About what a fine line I walk. You don't know everything yet, but I really want to share it with you."

"Well then, tell me."

"I really want to, but we need to get through the next few weeks. Get through the trial. Then we can get to know each other slowly, I promise."

I clenched my fists. "I barely even know what the trial entails. How on earth are we supposed to prepare when the requirements are so nebulous? It's two weeks away, and I still have no idea what to expect. Without you being present, our chances of success are nil. And yet you have the cheek to tell me I'm distracted?"

His jaw clenched. "No, Alisha, I'm trying to tell you that the senate is a law unto itself. Whatever you find out about the tremors, you're not going to change the senate's path. You're not even a fully-fledged peculiar yet. And you're not doing yourself any favours by not falling in line."

I arched an eyebrow. "Do wolves always fall in line?"

A vein throbbed in his neck. "That's not fair."

"Isn't it? Maybe I just don't like turning a blind eye to the things that are wrong in the world. Maybe I'm focused on more than myself. You know what I think? I think you've run out of ideas, and you're staying away because then it's on me when I fail the trial."

He sighed. "It's okay to be scared about the trial, hellfire. Most peculiars take it far earlier."

"You're saying teenagers are more capable of this than me?"

"Stop putting words in my mouth. I'm saying it's different taking it at a young age with the rest of your contemporaries, compared to at your age."

I seethed. Had Orpheus been right after all? "You actually went there. Age has nothing to do with how well I'll perform. Yes, age has drawbacks. Maybe I'm not as fit as I was. Maybe my boobs are less bouncy. But dammit, my experience and intuition more than make up for it. I know my flaws, I know my strengths, and I know who to trust. Except maybe I made a mistake with you."

His voice was a low note of warning. "That's ridiculous."

"Is it? How do I even know I can trust you? How do I know you're not some shady geezer who will never put me first?"

He shrugged. "Because actions speak louder than words. I'll always be there when it counts."

"Yeah, well, I won't hold my breath." I gave him a look that might have sent a lesser man running for the woods.

"Careful, you might say something you can't take back. Look, I'm soaking wet. You're right that you need more of me in the run-up to the trial. Let's meet at the Wildwoods arena tomorrow evening. Sahil and Marina can come too. And the leopard, if I ask nicely."

I chewed my lip. "I'm teaching night class."

"In the morning then, with Sahil and Marina. We'll go through the trial and get some practice in." He paused. "Look, I'm sorry. I've been neglecting you. It's a wolf thing. My duty to serve the pack clashed with my desire to be with you. It won't happen again."

"I want to believe you. I really do." I sucked in a shaky breath. "If we fail, all this falls away. I saw past the veil, Ezra. I learned new things about myself. I can't lose that. I can't lose Echo. And I don't want to lose you."

He pulled me into his arms. "You can do this."

I went to him reluctantly and laid my head against his hard chest. "I don't want to go backwards. I can't give it up."

"You have to promise to leave the matter of the dark elves to the senate. Phinnaeous, Gunnolf and Lavinia won't rest until justice has been served. You can't stop a rocket in motion."

I stiffened and mumbled into his chest. "I can't promise that, Ezra."

"I thought you might say that."

8

———————

Sleep was not my friend that night. I fell from great heights, grasped by a teleporting werewolf, a cold vampire and an amber-eyed reptile. They fought over me like meat. The pieces of me scattered in the wind for vultures to find, so there was nothing left for Dad to bury.

In the morning, I pulled on some workout clothes and piled on the concealer before heading out the door with Dad's picture of Tielbu in my pocket—I was apparently an animator, after all—and Echo at my side.

A half-hour later, the early morning sun glinted through the trees as Ezra, Marina, Sahil, Echo and I trudged towards the Wildwoods arena. Marina and I let the men and leopard walk ahead. They had somehow found common ground in Dad's garden. Ezra and Sahil had bonded over the struggle to wash Echo, and Echo was delighted his tormentors had ended up as wet as him.

"Oh love, you look like shit. That sounds like a rotten fight," said Marina. Her rainbow hair was tied into space buns, and she wore workout gear bought from Baba Yaga's Gym: a bubblegum-coloured sports bra and leggings get-up that would have looked at home on Lavinia's own clothing rail had she been as buxom. "Joshi's just scared, that's all. You're still his baby girl."

"The only thing I have in common with a baby girl is my need for naps."

"Last week, my biggest desire was to watch *Grace and Frankie* and stuff my face with ice cream. But I've had itchy feet since the tremors. The city is pulsing with worry. I can feel it. Robert said it was all hands on deck, and here I am, twiddling my thumbs. I should be doing something. You know, comforting those in need. Or at least comforting him. My newest push-up bra hasn't even had an outing yet. I'm gagging to give him an eyeful."

I grinned. "It'll be worth the wait, I'm sure. But there's no bloody way you're going out helping humdrums using your empath skills. What happens when people start asking questions about you? The Magical Constitution rules that out for a good reason."

"Just imagine, though, Alisha. I helped Elvira. I could help the sick ease their pain. Like a shot of morphine, you know? Only natural. There'd be no side effects."

I tucked my arm into hers. "Except on you. Your skills aren't ready for that yet. I know your instinct is to help, but I saw what toll your talents took on you when you comforted Faeza. Besides, at this rate, we'll be back to being our bog-standard selves before we can say abracadabra."

Marina gave a weighted sigh. "Quick, before we get started. Tell me how it's going with lover boy. I get you're angry at him and why, but are you still hot for him? You know, you've got eyebags from hell, but your dewy skin tells me another story."

"He hasn't paid me the slightest bit of attention in weeks."

"That's not what I heard. Echo told me he hasn't been able to keep his eyes or hands off you. He said you have Ezra by the short and curlies."

Echo bounded over, his hearing too acute for his own

good. "This much is true. He rushed to Wildwoods when the tremors occurred to be her knight in shining armour, and the vampire had saved her first. The wolf is as hot for Alisha as I am for a harem of newly groomed and fluffed Persian cats."

His glamour made him a beacon for household cats. He had grown to like frolicking with the local feline population. He revelled in the attention. Although I most certainly did not like coming home to sheets soiled by excessive rubbing and rolling that he got up to with his little friends.

I folded my arms. "For the millionth time, will my closest friends realise I don't need saving?"

Marina waggled her eyebrows. "There is a world of difference between being strong-armed by a man and being able to rely on him. I wouldn't be so quick to complain if I were you, my love. It might have gone tits up with Alex, but Ezra's cut from a different cloth. Speaking of which, looks like it's time to roll up our sleeves."

We scurried to catch up with Ezra, handsome in blue jeans and a vest.

Ezra led us to a stone table with cube seats at the edge of the arena. He had his work cut out with the three of us, and the clock was ticking. "What's with the glum faces? This could be the day you unlock your potential. Half of being a peculiar is about belief. That's what we're going to work on. Take a seat."

"What I want to know is why every other test I've taken in my life has a list of content I'm required to know." I chose a cube and crossed my arms.

Marina nodded. "Preach, sister."

"Because every trial is different," Echo purred. "It resembles neither a driving test nor a school exam. It's not even like a lawyer taking the bar or an athlete at the Olympics."

"Well, that's about as helpful as a chocolate teapot," I said.

"What made you think the trial should be easy?" Echo

prowled up and down. "It is because it is difficult that it is worthwhile. But we are here to make sure you are ready. I am here to be the cat to Ezra's dog. The head to his tail. The Diana to his Supremes."

Sahil grinned. "Was that supposed to be a pep talk?"

"I don't suppose you brought a sedative for the cat, Marina?"

She grinned. "Not this time, but I'll be sure to remember next time."

Echo sat and curled his tail around his body. "No need to be tetchy. I was just trying to lighten the atmosphere."

Ezra slid onto a seat around the stone table. "The magical trial isn't based on humdrum boundaries. The Otherworld has no boundaries. Therefore, the test is naturally more ambiguous. Magical trials test courage, quick thinking, creativity and loyalty. The purpose of the trial is for the senate to ascertain your chances of surviving or destabilising the Otherworld. Rayna will devise one she feels adequately tests the newest initiates. The rest is up to us."

Us. The word reverberated in my head, and I fell in love with him just a little bit.

Marina bit her lip. "Okay then, hotshot, how do the foxes survive without being sanctioned by the senate? Why do they get to keep their magic?"

Echo growled. "Because once you walk through the doors of Wildwoods into the bosom of the magical world, once you've taken the blood bond with the Magical Constitution and broken bread with the senate, only one of two paths are available to you. Why do you think I didn't want you following the wolf to Wildwoods? The foxes are cunning. They knew the reach of Wildwoods, and they knew to avoid it. You jumped in headfirst without even understanding the ground rules. And if you fail, the curtain falls. Just like that. This is the way it has always been. Do you understand now what is at stake?"

My pulse raced. "Is that true, Ezra?"

"It's always been true that there are rules for belonging to organisations and penalties for disappointing them. It's also true that being an outsider is not easy. You know that from your work at night class. I was doing my job the night I first brought you to Wildwoods. I'm trying to do it now."

"Well, this is awkward," said Sahil.

Ezra rubbed the back of his neck. His biceps flexed as he did, and I tried not to notice. "It's not the only thing that's awkward. Let's lay it all out on the table. Why do you want to live your life as a peculiar? You first, Sahil. You have the longest way to go here."

"This feels less like a training arena and more like a psychologist's office," Echo purred.

"No freaking way," said Sahil. "I'm a forty-two-year-old man. This is all blooming weird. I'm practically constipated with fear. Let the others go first."

I swallowed down my anger. "It's okay. I'll go first. I want to be a peculiar because, for the first time in my life, I understand who I am, and I don't feel trapped or that a part of me is missing. And when I summon the wind, I feel free."

Ezra nodded. "How about you, Marina?"

She looked down at her hands with her gothic-black nail varnish. "I want to help. My hands are magic. I can sense how people feel. It's the key to unlocking everything. I can't lose that."

"Now, your turn, Sahil. Go on. There is no shame in the arena," said Ezra. "We are all learning, but we can only learn if we are honest with ourselves."

"I'm here for Alisha."

Ezra shook his head. "No, that's not it. Shall we get a helping hand? Marina, will you do the honours?"

Marina took Sahil's hand. "He's lying."

Sahil snatched his hand back.

"Why are you here, Sahil?" said Ezra.

Sahil's brow furrowed. "If you have to know, I'm here because I don't want Alisha to have all the glory. She was always the golden girl. Always sunny. Always willing to help others. Then she goes and makes friends with a goddess and solves the mystery of Mum's death. She even got the better of the sun god. I know I should be grateful, but it makes me sick."

"You make it sound like I did that all alone. It was blind luck." I frowned. "What makes you sick?"

Sahil shrugged. "The thought that you get all the power. I want a piece of that pie."

Marina winced. "I guess being the only child isn't that bad. At least you're telling the truth now."

"This is the reason I will always prefer Verma women," said Echo. "The men are pansies or have no honour."

"Do you feel lighter now, Sahil?" said Ezra.

"A bit. Still constipated. But lighter."

"So, now we all know why we're here—finding our true selves. Helping others. Power. I've worked with worse." His grey eyes met mine. "The question is, do you want to work with me?"

I lifted my chin. "I don't see what choice we have."

His eyes dropped to my lips. "Then let's begin. We'll get you over the line. Anything else will have to wait."

Echo edged forward. "The trials always take place away from Wildwoods. This is for a good reason. Your magic will be tested in the real world, not here, where the school adapts to your every need. Out there, there are no safety nets."

"I can tell you that your trial will take place in the London Underground after the tube lines have closed."

I breathed a sigh of relief. I felt at home on the tube. I knew the London Underground as well as the lines on my palm. It didn't seem daunting to be tested down there. "Will there be an audience?"

Ezra nodded. "The Prime Sorcerer will send orbs to follow

you, which will show your progress to the senate and school community back at Wildwoods. A small staff from the infirmary will be present at the site of the trial in case any medical assistance is required."

"How long will it last?" asked Marina.

"As long as is required to determine the outcome," said Ezra.

"You will have to prove you can get by alone and as a team—and without breaking the Magical Constitution. Do you remember the laws?" said Echo.

Marina waved her hand in the air like the class swot. "Ask me!"

Echo inclined his head. "Go ahead, Marina Ambrose. Speak slowly and clearly. We will only go over this ground once."

Marina turned her blue eyes to the sky like she was taking an oath. "1. Never meddle in the affairs of the gods. 2. All peculiars and magical artefacts must register with the Sorcerer's Senate within three lunar cycles. 3. A sentient peculiar who uses magic to harm a humdrum will have their magic drained ad infinitum. 4. Peculiars must hide the existence of the Otherworld from humdrums and re-establish secrecy upon accidental arousal of suspicion. 5. It is forbidden to interfere with the compos mentis of another peculiar. 6. The delicate power balance between co-existing peculiar communities must be protected. 7. New users of magic must be supervised until they pass the trial. 8. Black magic and necromancy are forbidden."

Sahil's eyes bulged with incredulity. "That necromancy thing is wild."

"Can anyone tell me which law, in particular, is going to be the hardest to follow on the night of your trial?" said Ezra.

I gave a curt nod. "Number 4. The Founder's Law. Peculiars must hide the existence of the Otherworld from humdrums and re-establish secrecy upon accidental arousal of suspicion."

"Exactly. With the trial taking place out in the open, away from Wildwoods, this is the biggest pitfall. It is this law that leads to the biggest proportion of initiates failing. If our existence becomes common knowledge, the whole survival of the Otherworld is compromised. Secrecy is the one thing all magical races agree on. Which means when it comes to a vote, if you break that rule, each and every senate member will vote against you."

"Point taken. We'll guard our secrecy," said Marina.

"Then it's time for the next lesson. Teamwork." The copper flecks in Ezra's eyes glinted. He pointed to the triangular frame that pierced the clouds. "Sahil, I'd like you to climb that."

Sahil squinted at the dizzyingly high structure. "Then what?"

Marina and I exchanged glances. We knew what was coming next.

A glint in Ezra's eyes. "Then you jump."

"You're out of your mind. Why would I do that?"

Echo toothy grin showed his mirth. "Joshi's style as a mentor was to wrap you in cotton wool, and it brought nothing. Our way is much better. We fling you off a building to rule out flight, instant armour and reactive adaption."

Sahil jerked his head in fright. "Over my dead body."

"I told you he was a pansy," purred Echo.

"Don't worry, Sahil. The arena will catch you," I said. He might be a lousy brother, but he was *my* brother. "You can do it."

Ezra cleared his throat. "Actually, Alisha, this time, it will be your job to catch him. Let's stretch those wind powers of yours. See how you do under duress."

I gulped.

"And Marina, you're going up to see if you can use your

magic to soothe Sahil's fears. I have no doubt you can. Hell, you managed to assuage a dying woman's fears." He lit a roll-up cigarette and took a drag like this was a walk in the park and not life and death. "The test for you is to keep your own emotions in check. Being an effective peculiar is all about balance. As a werewolf, I balance my duty with my desires. My anger with my passion. You have to learn to balance negative emotions with positive ones. Focus on good memories to anchor you. A past success. A loved pet. A joyful experience. Think of it less as a gushing river and more as a canal lock. You are not at the mercy of the tides. You control the levels."

Marina pressed her palms to her cheeks. "I got it. A canal lock." She took a deep breath and stood up. "I'm ready."

"I'm bloody not." Sahil dragged his feet in the sand of the arena as we tugged him up.

Glee bubbled up inside me. I relished the chance of unleashing my power on Sahil. All the times he'd wrestled me to the ground as a child. I planned to bring him to the ground like a ricocheting rollercoaster. "You want power? This is your chance, big bro. I'll be waiting at the bottom. I won't let you fall."

He followed us with a pinched expression, fingernails digging into his palms. "If I don't make it, I don't want this getting out. You hear me?"

Marina put an arm around him, her forehead knotted in concentration. "It's going to be okay. I'm here, aren't I?"

He relaxed enough to climb up the structure alongside her, pausing every few minutes to look down, his eyes wide.

Ezra and Echo joined me in the arena. From the ground, I could make out Marina murmuring in Sahil's ear. Around us, the trees rustled, and the birds chirped. Every now and then, the cable car juddered to life, taking pupils to Wildwoods.

Just when I thought Sahil was going to chicken out, he jumped.

Falling like a brick, faster than my eyes could track. Screaming, high-pitched like a woman, as if he'd shed his coat of manliness.

Echo's roar filled the arena.

"Now, Alisha," said Ezra with urgency.

My palms tingled. I held them towards my brother, and the breeze became something I could mould and direct. I focussed, narrowing my gaze, so I saw only him, ready to cocoon him.

Just a bit closer.

Then poof.

His clothes tumbled through the air and landed strewn across the arena. His Calvin Klein boxers dropped inches from my feet.

The bottom dropped out of my stomach as though I was the one who was falling.

"The Verma boy has revealed his true self," said Echo.

My tall, handsome brother, with his designer stubble and Saville Row clothes, had transformed.

In his place was a feathery creature common in London.

A grey breast, pink clawed toes, orange beak and green-tinged head with fiery eyes.

Echo rolled around on the floor, cackling. "Karma is good. He wanted power, and the universe made him a pigeon."

Sahil swooped closer. When he came to a standstill at our feet, he stood more upright than a pigeon, as if he were half man, half bird, albeit only as big as a Wellington boot. His chest was more muscly than a pigeon's, his feathers ruffled, not smooth.

He looked as mad as hell, and when he opened his mouth, he had teeth. "I don't feel right. Will someone tell me what's going on?"

I recoiled in horror. "Er, Echo, I don't think he's a pigeon."

Marina ran towards us, heavily panting in her haste. "Where's Sahil? What did I miss?"

"He's right here, Marina," Ezra scratched his jaw. "That's progress for you. Always a surprise."

I stared at my brother. "But what is he?"

Ezra knelt in the sand to Sahil's level. "I'm not a hundred per cent sure, but I think he's a werepigeon."

Sahil made a mournful, throaty coo and passed out.

9

"It's not that bad, Sahil," I said. "Remember when you were little, and you wanted to fly?"

It had taken him a while to come around, but smelling salts from the infirmary had helped. Only that had also brought a stampede of pupils from Wildwoods into the arena to gawk at him. They pooled around us like Sahil was a circus curiosity and not a peculiar in need of some privacy at an unsettling time. It only took one to break into giggles, and the domino effect rippled through the rest, a belly-clutching hilarity at his weird muscly bird body, his pointy teeth, his cooing and strutting.

My brother usually loved attention, but their laughter struck a nerve. He stamped his pigeon toes. "Will you tell this lot to piss off?"

The Prime Sorcerer sighed and turned to the pupils gawking with a swish of his gown. "Ignore his bad language, children, and come along. Perhaps Mr Verma can come and speak to us about his transformation once he has got to grips with this new side of him."

"Not bloody likely." Sahil ran at the children with flapping wings.

"I must get Orpheus to take a look at your genealogy again. This is most unusual." Phinnaeous Shine gave me a stern look. "You know, I think back to Rajika Verma, and I wonder, where it all went wrong? She had such vitality and strength. To think, her descendants may be too lacking in focus to even pass the magical trial. Is it true you have been unable to animate the dragon yet? You do realise the resources that have been invested in you and your merry little crew?"

I gulped. The man made me feel five years old, not forty.

Gaia's voice chided me in my head. "You didn't think that wind was all you could do?"

Ezra's hackles rose. "You have my word she will pass the trial, Prime Sorcerer."

"I'll hold you to that, Mr Neuhoff. I seem to remember you spoke up for Ms Verma after her last disaster. I hope I wasn't wrong to give her a second chance. Talent is not everything. It's character that is the real game changer." He glared at me, nostrils flaring. "You have neither your grandmother's talents, druid, nor her beauty, but you can make something of yourself yet. Maybe try a little more sleep, a little less booze and a whole heap more moisturiser. Hers was honey-scented. Her yoga regimen gave her great flexibility and focus and kept the love handles at bay. Perhaps you should try taking a leaf out of her book." Phinnaeous Shine stormed off.

I stared after him. "I should give him a piece of my mind once I've planned a stinging retort."

Marina stared after him. "Mansplain much? What a wanker." She hugged me. "Don't worry; we'll get there."

"Ignore him, hellfire. He's got a lot on his plate. The senate has been war-gaming through the night. Gunnolf didn't get back to the farmhouse until the early hours."

"Right, I'm off, you two," said Marina. "Echo's taking me to work my magic on some creatures in the bestiary to practice some of Ezra's balancing techniques. Unless you want some help with him?" She grimaced at Sahil, who was pecking the sand of the arena like he wanted to tunnel out of Wildwoods. "I don't think he realises he has wings."

Sahil flapped in our direction. "I heard that. You can laugh all you like. You still have your body. I can't leave looking like a bloody werepigeon. If they catch me on Trafalgar Square, they'll take one look and think I have rabies."

"There is no rabies in the United Kingdom." Marina edged away.

"Fat lot of good you were," said Sahil. "This bloody well wouldn't have happened if I hadn't listened to you."

"Go, Marina," I said. "It's not her fault. And I think you are pretty powerful. Think about it. Not only can you fly, but pigeons have awesome camouflage. This city is so grey. Think of all the concrete and rain, not to mention the other pigeons. You blend right in."

"I don't want to blend in. I want to stand out. This isn't what I imagined. I'm a laughingstock." Sahil plopped down in the sand, rocking his green-grey head back and forth like a lunatic. Or a bird.

Ezra gave him a hard look and sat down in the sand next to him. "Sahil, I'm a *were*-something."

Sahil tilted his head and pinned one fiery eye on him. "A werewolf. That's a massive difference."

"Not how I see it. The *were*- prefix is a corruption of the Latin *vir*, which means man. It means virility and strength. Like me, you'll be strongest at the full moon. You will learn to shift between man and bird. You have teeth and claws that can do extensive damage. You can soar. That's more than I can do."

"Also, pigeons can produce loads of poo, so that's your secret weapon," I said. "You can destroy an entire area in seconds if you put your bowels to it."

"Not helping, Alisha," Sahil cooed.

"You don't even need your posh flat anymore. You can make as many nests as you want to."

"Jesus," said Sahil. His werepigeon voice was more nasally than his human one, possibly because all his components had to fit into a smaller form. Although a pigeon's brain was much smaller than a human one, so there might have been some shrinkage. I decided it was best not to bring that up.

I petted his head. "I'm proud of you."

He pecked my foot. "Too soon, Alisha. And stop pretending you're not enjoying this."

"Okay, Tweetie. Sorry, I meant sweetie."

"Now, can someone find my clothes and teach me how to shift into human form? Being this small is giving me an inferiority complex and making me feel quite murderous."

I backed away. "Ezra, teach the man what he wants. Or failing that, does Wildwoods have a therapist?"

Ezra grinned. "All part of being in the were-family. I've got a better idea. Ready to whip up a breeze, Alisha? Let's watch him soar."

The morning became afternoon, and with the arena being used by Lavinia to drill Wildwoods students in defence skills should the dark elves attack, Ezra and I retreated to the shade of a sycamore tree.

I lay on my back, looking up at a bank of cumulus clouds. "Thank goodness Sahil went home. What an exhausting morning. I can't believe that a few hours with you unlocked his magic. I'm just not sure how Dad will feel about it."

Ezra cocked an eyebrow. "So you're done doubting me then?"

"You put us first for a morning. You're just getting started."

A laugh rumbled through him. "You're sexy when you speak your mind."

"I am?" I said. Alex had hated me pressing a different point than him. It was always the start of an argument.

"I love a woman who can challenge me." He held up a hand. "But I wasn't the key to Sahil's breakthrough. It was a team effort. Sibling rivalry is a potent thing, and Marina's empath skills played a role too. Rayna knew what she was doing when she suggested group sessions for us. She's not Minister for Education and Wildwoods Headmistress for nothing."

I squirmed. "It's weird, though, isn't it? Him being a werepigeon?"

Ezra snorted. "I can't say I've met many. They don't fly around in a flock. We'll have to keep an eye on him. It's not like he has a pack. He's going to be lonely."

"I can pretty much guarantee he's in the pub right now, drinking away his sorrows."

"Yeah, well, right now, we have something else to worry about. Did you bring what I asked you to?"

I nodded. Out came Death's sword, Dad's drawing of Tielbu the dragon and a leaf from the park.

"That sword is a thing of beauty." He lifted Transcender and turned it over in his hands in awe.

"And yet when I hold it," I said, "I hear voices that overcome me. It happened when I tried to protect Flinar. I dropped it like a hot stone, and only then did the voices still. Maybe it's more of a burden than a benefit."

He shook his head. "I don't believe that for a second. Gaia is a friend to you. If she gave you this, it is with good reason. Maybe what you need is to relax and not overthink. It doesn't matter that your grandmother was Rajika Verma. It doesn't matter that she was a huge figure in the Otherworld. Right now, all that matters is that you are on your own path. As imperfect as you feel you are, your journey is not yet over. Your path is just beginning. So take a deep breath, lie back and close your eyes."

I sank back against the ground, feeling every twig in my back, aware of the rise and fall of his breath and mine. The soil was cool against my back, and my eyelids fluttered as the light changed above me, and the nebulous pink was shadowed by Ezra coming closer. I stiffened as he trailed the leaf over the bridge of my nose and down one cheek, across the curve of my chin and onto the other cheek.

"What are you doing?" I asked.

"Relaxing you."

"You didn't try this with Sahil."

"Different strokes for different folks."

"I'm starting to get that." I held onto his hand and opened my eyes. "I'm still angry at you."

"I'm trying to make it up to you." He lay down next to me and kissed me, soft and sweetly, as if in apology, before nibbling my bottom lip and deepening the kiss until I was hot and needed him more than I had ever needed my ex-husband.

In fact, it took me a minute to remember Alex's name.

Ezra pulled away and grinned. "So, are you relaxed?"

I was pretty sure I saw stars, and we weren't even in Paris this time.

"Pick up your dad's drawing."

"Huh?"

"Pick it up." He uncurled my hand from his shirt and pushed the drawing of Tielbu into my hand. "You have no need to be scared. You are on your own path. And it's just me and you here. No Joshi, no Sahil, no Gaia. Reach into the picture and find Tielbu there. Not an inanimate dragon but the real, breathing, fiery one you know from your stories. Who won't hurt you, who is bonded to you and is just waiting for you to awaken him."

I pressed my lips together and felt the calm of the leaf across my skin, the comfort of being in Ezra's arms and the quiet of the woods. I touched the page and trailed my fingers over the strokes of Dad's paintbrush. Tielbu was turquoise blue like he'd risen from the Pacific Ocean, not Dad's imagination. I filled my lungs with the smog-free Wildwoods air and imagined Tielbu's own lungs inflating, the beating of his colossal wings, the life in his amber eyes, the dry iridescent scales of his skin.

The page deepened, and I was no longer sure what was in my head and what was under my fingers. Heat travelled into my body from Tielbu's fiery breath, and his veins throbbed beneath my fingertips as if he and I were one.

I reached into the page.

"Well," said Lavinia's plummy voice. "About time you worked on that, Alisha."

I dropped the page as if I'd been scalded and opened my eyes.

Ezra was on his feet. "Now's not a good time, auntie. We were in the middle of something."

"I could see that," said Lavinia. "I thought I could offer some words of encouragement. Impress upon you just how important this is."

"How important what is?" I asked. Dejection washed over me. I'd been so close.

"My dear girl." Lavinia strode over to press her powdered cheek against mine before kissing her nephew.

I'd not seen her at close hand since our battle with the sun god. The spell to stop him had aged her. She'd been far too busy rebuilding Wildwoods after the tremors to find me, and I had avoided her like the plague after my run-in with the rats. After all, they'd said she had suspicions about whether I was friend or foe. Far better to leave sleeping dogs lie.

"You don't look yourself, Aunt Lavinia," said Ezra. "You should take it easy."

She waved a dismissive hand. "Hogwash, Ezra. I am Minister for Defence, after all, and we are under threat." She primped her helmet of silver curls and sighed. "Although, I suppose you could say the spell against the sun god took its toll. Not only did we lose poor Elvira, but my skin lost at least a decade's elasticity. It really is a shame. Especially since that vial of your blood didn't bring us closer to the secret of your teleporting." Her eyes narrowed as she searched our faces. "Some might say we were hoodwinked." Her voice brightened. "Still, we live and learn. And there is another battle on our plates right now. We're going to crush those brutish dark elves once and for all. How dare they trample sacred ground?"

"Auntie, about that. Aren't you barking up the wrong tree?" Ezra said.

She cackled. "I'm not a wolf, Ezra. I have known this was coming for a long time. The coven is ready. Wildwoods is ready." She swung round to me. "But there is something that would make it easier."

I darted a look at Ezra. "What do you need, Lavinia?"

"You know how much I'm a fan of efficient transport. Especially after the terrible disappointment of transferring the teleporting skills to the coven. Efficient transport has the capacity to lighten the load during wartime. You can't underestimate its impact. Particularly when the transport has military potential." She bent down to pick up the drawing of Tielbu.

I clenched my fists and bit down hard on my lip to stop myself from taking what was mine.

Lavinia's shrewd, hard eyes assessed me. "I want to trust you, but something just doesn't sit right. It's an easy fix, though. Raise the dragon, Alisha. We could do with a dragon in the fight against the elves. The war would be over before it had even begun. Just think how pleased the senate would be. How pleased I would be."

My skin grew clammy, but I held her gaze and turned the corners of my lips into a tight smile. "I'm afraid, Minister, that

I have failed at this task every time I've attempted it. But if I succeed, you'll be the first to know."

She pushed her shoulders back. "Well, that's all I ask. We must spend some time in the reading nook again at some point. Toodaloo, lovebirds."

She shimmied away.

My breath came in rasps, my gaze unfocused.

In an instant, Ezra was at my side, his hand on the small of my back. "Breathe, Alisha."

Lavinia turned around. "It just occurred to me. Why don't the two of you join us for dinner at the coven flat? All the movers and shakers will be there. In fact, you should all come. Bring your dad and the empath. Heavens, bring the werepigeon. Not the leopard, however. The rats wouldn't like it. It'll be such a giggle. Friday night, 8 p.m. Don't forget. And make sure you dress the part. The ladies like to put on some sequins and heels every now and then."

I waited for her to leave, then covered my face. "What are we going to do?"

Ezra tipped my chin up with a gentle hand. "We take this one step at a time. What Lavinia says and what the senate decrees are two entirely different things."

"Maybe I should leave Tielbu on the page. Maybe this is the reason I'm struggling to bring him to life. Like the universe is telling me not to put a weapon in the senate's hands."

He gave a firm shake of his head. "It's the wrong decision to give up a major win just because the consequences are difficult."

I chewed my lip. All my biggest turning points had required blind courage: my university degree, my freedom after the divorce, and my right to know this side of me.

"You were on the verge of a breakthrough, Alisha. The colour on the page began to oscillate just before my aunt arrived. I've never seen anything so spectacular. You can't give that up."

He was right. I had felt Tielbu taking shape beneath my fingers. My senses tingled with the knowledge. The thought of never meeting him made me despair, but I couldn't let him fall into Lavinia's hands.

I took a deep breath. "Putting Tielbu in a drawer doesn't mean I can't animate another creature. I can ask Dad for another drawing."

Ezra's face tightened. "That would be a mistake. I've been thinking for a while. You failed at your attempts to animate in your father's attic, right?"

"Don't remind me."

"That's just it. When Joshi gave you the picture of Tielbu in the infirmary, he inadvertently gave you your best chance of success. Your connection with Tielbu is why you were almost there. We only have ten days until the trial, Alisha. This is your best shot. Animate Tielbu, and it will unlock everything else."

"There has to be another way." I put space between us, thinking hard, staring through a clearing in the tree canopies towards the clouds. "I've got it. Maybe I can animate him where Lavinia won't know."

"That's brilliant." A slow smile spread across his face. "It couldn't be here. Or even in another city. Her rats and their network of snitches are too good. She always finds out eventually. No, it can't be here. There is only one place that is hidden from Lavinia."

"Where, Ezra? I would say the sewers. No CCTV and no self-respecting humdrum would hang out down there. Only that would be a natural habitat for the rats. How about the royal palaces? Security has to be pretty tight in there. Or maybe the end of the Northern Line? That's pretty much No Man's Land."

His grey eyes glinted. "The place we need keeps itself hidden within the seams of the world. Even Lavinia's moles can't find their way there. It'll buy you some space to bond with the dragon without my aunt staking a claim. You're going to animate Tielbu in the Celestial Library, and she will never find out."

10

The day of Mum's will reading arrived. So much had changed since her death. She had known the minutiae of my life from the moment of my birth: my tottering first steps, my favourite books, the women I admired, and the lay-back-and-think-of-England state of my marital sex life. It seemed cruel that she didn't get to be there for the next stage of our lives.

Dad, Sahil, Echo and I waited for the solicitor in my parent's mahogany dining room. I'd hoped to find Dad in a better state, perhaps painting, but there were no tell-tale stains on his person. No paint splotches to show that he was getting back to his happy place. Only a stale house in need of airing, dirty dishes piling in the sink and dirty laundry spilling out of the utility room.

"I'm not ready to hear Rosalie's final wishes." Dad sniffed. "She doesn't even know you're a werepigeon, Sahil. She'd be so proud."

Sahil looked up in surprise. "She would?"

Dad grimaced. "Maybe not, but she'd definitely find it amusing, and her scientific brain would be in love. It's rather impressive that Ezra managed to unlock your peculiar nature so quickly. We got nowhere together. It's enough to make a man feel useless."

"Yeah, well, I'm glad you didn't witness it," said Sahil, downcast. "It wasn't pretty. There were all these kids pointing at me, and my clothes went AWOL."

Ezra had managed to teach him to shift back into his human form, but there was still something feathery about him in the fall of his hair. It had always sat smoothly against his head, but now he had more of a ruffled look. It suited him and made him look less uptight.

"Take a page out of Eric Idle's songbook. 'Always Look on the Bright Side of Life'," said Echo.

Ruffling Sahil's feathers was no way to be supportive. I shot Echo a look of warning and turned to Dad. "Mum must have told you what's in the will?"

Dad shook his head. "I thought I knew, but the solicitor said Rosalie went to see him the week before she died."

"Well," I said. "We'll just have to face it together. Like we do everything else."

"I don't know. I feel quite alone in this pigeon saga," said Sahil.

"I can count the number of leopards in this city on one paw. You are certainly not alone amongst pigeons in London, Sahil Verma," purred Echo. "As Michael Jackson would say, 'You Are Not Alone'."

"Mock me all you want," said Sahil. "Mum is gone, and I am a werepigeon, and life couldn't be any worse."

"Echo, stop it," I said. "Otherwise, I'll cut back on your freezer goodies. The butcher's bill this week was astronomical."

The doorbell rang.

"Saved by the bell." Dad heaved himself up to get the door. "You kids and your fighting. Some things never change."

We listened as Dad greeted the solicitor and ushered him past Mum's shrine into the dining room.

"My condolences once again," said the solicitor as they entered the room. He was a bald man in his fifties with a tummy that bulged over his suit trousers.

"Thank you, Mr Costello. Please take a seat," said Dad. "This is Sahil, my son, and Alisha, my daughter."

"I'm sorry for your loss. What a beautiful Bengal cat." The solicitor bowed as deeply as a Japanese businessman.

"He bowed to me, did you see?" Echo purred.

"Bengals are so rare." Mr Costello sat down. "I had no idea how vocal they are."

"You don't know the half of it." I stared at his briefcase, a glossy red leather decorated with diamanté studs.

Mr Costello snapped it open and pulled out some papers. "Oh, the sparkles were my granddaughter's doing. In fact, she insists I wear sparkly underwear too. I'd do anything for her. Being in my line of work, you realise how short life is."

Sahil cocked his head in a distinctly bird-like matter.

I hoped Ezra had taught him some self-control, or this would get messy. "Shall we get started?"

Mr Costello put on his glasses and picked up a single-sided page. "As executor of the will, I'll now read Rosalie Verma's Letter of Wishes and disclose the beneficiaries of her estate. All three beneficiaries of the will are here and present."

"I take it he doesn't mean me," said Echo. "I will presently retreat to the other side of the house to croon Celine Dion's 'All By Myself'."

Mr Costello cleared his throat. "Let us begin.

"I, Rosalie Verma, hereby appoint Mr Bernard Costello of Davidson, Costello & Son the executor of my estate. In the event of my death, this Letter of Wishes should be shared with the beneficiaries of my estate. My dear family, if my death comes to pass, know that I would not have spent my life any other way. Joshi, our life together was so much more than I could have envisaged that day you held a rose between your teeth on the university grounds and went down on one knee to ask me to be your wife. Before I met you, I had science, but I did not have love. And while science had been a driving force in my life, it is love which has truly changed me."

Mr Costello paused to wipe a tear from his eye.

"Your wife was a poet, Mr Verma. And a true beauty with her raven hair and full hips," he said. "I like to think if I'd met her as a young man before I lost my hair, I might have stood a chance."

"Steady on." Sahil flapped his arms. "That's my mother you're talking about."

"No need to worry," said Mr Costello. "She can't very well change her mind now, can she?"

Dad smiled weakly. "Rosalie liked gallows humour. How wonderful to hear her voice though she is gone."

"Then you'll love our latest innovation, Mr Verma. From next year, the soon-to-be-deceased will read their own Letter of Wishes in a pre-recording expertly made at our firm," said Mr Costello.

Dad recoiled. "Well, I am rather hoping not to lose any more family members."

"Where did Mum find your services again?" said Sahil.

Mr Costello lacked any self-awareness. "On page three of the Google search, I believe. She worked her way down when she required a solicitor immediately, and we were happy to help."

He pushed the plastic wallet across the table and snapped his briefcase shut.

I leaned forward. "Mr Costello, would you mind continuing to read the letter?"

"How silly of me. Of course.

"To mon amour, Joshi Verma, I bequeath my share of our family home on Tooting Bec Common, where we raised our family. Please never lose your love of painting, and when the time is right, find a new love of your own. Though I am no longer by your side, I trust you will use all your skills to help our children and never clip their wings, however painful you may find it. For what is life if we cannot soar?

"To my eldest child Sahil Verma, who has built such an extensive property portfolio. I am proud of you. Your interests lie in the tangible world, not the ephemeral. You chiselled your way forward in the world, but remember, your heart is equally important. To you, I bequeath my car and a cutting from my favourite rose bush to show you how far you have come and how far you can still go.

"To my youngest child Alisha, the dreamer, you are capable of so much more than you know. I'm sorry for all the times we stood in your way. I'm sorry for holding you back from what is rightfully yours. To you, I bequeath my books, the rights to my scientific research and a choker with an amber stone. You will find it between the seams of the world.

"Whatever sum remains in my accounts following the settling of my funeral expenses and related costs should be divided between STEMNET and Benoit's Patisserie in Kensington.

"In closing, I entreat you. Tend to each other faithfully so that you may find the answers that came to me too late in life.

"Your loving Rosalie.

"That concludes the letter," said Mr Costello. "Phew, that was heavy. I mean, searching Ancestry.com is one thing, but she went a little far with 'between the seams of the worlds', didn't she? Still, never fear. At Davidson, Costello & Son, we stand ready to hold your hand." He reached out a chunky fist across the table and wiggled his fingers.

We ignored him.

"In this folder, you'll find copies of Rosalie's testament and Letter of Wishes. We'll see to administering the estate, and you'll hear from us in due course." He shook each of our hands. "I wish you well and bid you adieu."

Dad rose to shake Mr Costello's hand.

"I will see this imbecile to the door," said Echo.

Mr Costello beamed. "The cat is miaowing at me to follow him. How delightful."

The door clicked shut behind him.

Sahil thumped the table. "She left money to a bakery instead of us?"

"We shouldn't think badly of her. She did like her cake," said Dad. "What I heard in that letter was love for us all."

"She left me the banger she died in, and a cutting of a rose bush. How is that love?" Sahil's flapping had become more and more erratic.

I shrugged. "The car was touched by a goddess."

Dad slumped and rubbed his hand over his face. "How could she ask me to love again? It just doesn't bear thinking about. Maybe she wasn't in her right mind. Take the mention of a choker with an amber stone. I've been doing mental gymnastics thinking about it. I never saw her wear anything like that."

The penny fell, but he wouldn't like it. "What stood out to me is the phrase 'between the seams of the world.' Ezra said that when referring to the Celestial Library. We know she'd been there, Dad. Remember? She had a book from there called *The Rose of Jericho*. I have to go there. I have to see what it is all about. I have to try and animate Tielbu there. It all leads there, don't you see? I've been too stupid to see it."

Dad stood up. "Did you not hear me last time, Alisha? I forbid it."

"You heard Mum's words. She said explicitly that you shouldn't stand in my way. For heaven's sake. I'm a grown woman."

The dishes in the sideboard began to shake, but he didn't notice.

"I don't care what it says in your mother's will. She's not here. I want you to grow, to find out more about your new identity, but it's too much of a risk going to the Celestial Library. Your grandmother died there. I can't lose you too. Will you just get that into your head?" He stopped, his arms spread wide for balance, his legs akimbo, like a drunk on the deck of a rocky cruise ship.

The house shook. Not just a little, but enough to make my heartbeat race.

"Oh my god," I said, "is that…"

A vase on the sideboard shattered on the floor.

We looked at each other in horror.

The house juddered to its very foundations, a rippling of brick, mortar and glass. A treasured picture of the Algarve fell off the wall, its frame shattering. The sound of smashing dishes came from the kitchen. A bookshelf full of encyclopaedias tipped forward, narrowly missing Sahil.

Dad shouted, "Get under the table. Now!"

He ran for the door, adrenalin making him quicker than his years.

I reached out to him. "Where are you going? Wait until the tremors stop. Echo will be fine. He's probably up a tree."

"My paintings." Dad charged out of the door past the rocking chandelier. "The portrait of your mother!"

Sahil cowered under the table. "Has he lost his marbles?"

I cursed long and hard enough to make my ancestors turn in their graves. "He's going to get hurt."

The sound of cracking lightbulbs and then popping filled my ears.

"Not if I can help it," said a nasal voice. A whirr of grey feathers flew past.

My brother's clothes lay in a heap on the floor. His trajectory was ragged, as if he didn't quite know how to fly in a straight line yet. He narrowly missed being sliced by the door.

"Whatever next?" I tore after him, a rush of blood in my ears.

The house rocked like a ship. Picture frames and books became projectiles. Screams in my ears from the street outside. The sound of falling objects became indiscernible. I was aware only of the hammering of my heart in my chest as time slowed.

I reached the studio after my dad and brother, and as I turned the corner, there Dad was, surrounded by canvases knocked from their easels.

He lay there, oh so quiet, beneath a fallen shelf heavy with art books.

His eyes were closed, and Sahil flapped on his chest.

My brother's green-tinged pigeon head moved side to side in panic. "Get help," he said. "Get help now."

11

I kept vigil at Dad's side while he waited his turn to be seen in a packed Accident & Emergency Department at St. George's Hospital. Three hours later, I crept out into the night under twinkling stars. Sirens blared across the city. A prayer group chanted in the middle of the car park. A young mother pleaded with her two young children to hurry up before they missed visiting hours.

A sadness settled on me. I dug out my phone and called Marina.

Her frantic voice came down the line. "How is Joshi?"

She'd known I was in pain across the miles. She'd texted me when the ambulance came for Dad. I wasn't sure if it was Marina being an empath or just Marina being a bloody good friend.

"He'll live," I said. "He has fractured ribs, a concussion and a gash on his abdomen, but nothing he can't recover from, thankfully. The doctors patched him and are sending him home. Echo's with him now. They're just waiting for his discharge papers."

She gave a sigh of relief. "That's good news. And what about you? How are you feeling? Your mum's will reading and then your dad ending up in the hospital is one tough day."

I kneaded my neck to ease the tension stored up there. "I'm utterly stressed."

"I'm not surprised. Let me treat you to a spa day when this is all over. How's Sahil bearing up?"

"He's gone AWOL. He's probably stuck in werepigeon form somewhere."

"I'll keep an eye out in case he turns up at the surgery." She giggled. "Although it was a lark seeing him flapping about like that when he's usually so sure of himself."

"You say that, but he's a liability. If I were you, I'd keep an eye out at your bedroom window. Now he's small, dark and can fly. Who knows what kind of voyeurism he'll get up to once he gets a grip mentally? You know what a thing he has for you. I'd keep your blinds shut if I were you."

Marina made a gagging sound. "Yuck. I'm happy to say I have my hands full with Robert. Literally. That man puts on quite a display of bedroom acrobatics. You know, maybe you and Ezra need to get your Moulin Rouge on. Who needs a spa day? That would relax you in twenty minutes flat."

The thought of being in bed with Ezra made my pulse race, but I kept my voice cool. "Err. We've kissed twice and had a bit of flirting. And a lot of aggro with his aunt. I think it'll be quite a while before I'm jumping into bed with him."

"Your loss. A wing woman has to try. A bit of attention from Robert has me beaming ear to ear. I finally got to put that new push-up bra to good use. Although I got to say, the underwire was so painful I whipped it straight off."

"I don't suppose the detective minded?"

She chuckled. "No, he didn't. It's just the thing to take his mind off his work. Speaking of which, he wants a word."

"Put him on then. Love you."

"Love you. I'll hand the phone over."

The line fumbled. "Alisha, remind me never to eavesdrop on you two again. I'm glad your father's okay."

"Thanks, Robert. What can I do for you? I should get back. I only came out for some air."

"It's a professional call, actually. The situation is worse than I thought."

I rubbed my temples. "You mean, the scientists are worried? Is there going to be another one?"

"At first, they thought the sensors were out. That there'd been a technical failure, you know? The state hasn't been investing as much as it should against natural disasters. You know how it is. Roads, schools and hospitals get the most investment. Governments should have a long-term vision, but there's no electoral benefit. The punters want to see the results there and then. So, politicians get blindsided until something like this happens."

"So, they need more earthquake protection in the future. Fortify our structures. Get some sirens or something."

"That's just it. It wasn't a technical failure. The machinery has been checked. They couldn't figure it out. The scientific community started backpedalling. Word is, the Prime Minister was raving mad. He's answerable to the people, after all. He stepped up to the podium outside number ten and told them it was an earthquake. He's been broadcast all over international media. But the scientists want the truth out. They won't be gagged if it happens again."

My stomach churned. "You're not going to tell me that it's the dark elves?"

"No, I told you before. There's no indication of the elves being that organised. But that didn't stop Phinnaeous Shine from walking into the Prime Minister's Office and telling him what he wanted to hear: a reason for the tremors."

"But that's crazy. The Prime Minister couldn't have bought it?"

"When a man is on the ropes, he'll buy anything."

"Phinnaeous Shine promised to solve the problem and sweetened the deal by providing a substantial donation to the Prime Minister's personal expenses in exchange for a free rein."

My tone was incredulous. "And the Prime Minister agreed?"

Robert's voice dripped with sarcasm. "What can I say? He's a class act. The way the Prime Minister sees it, if the earthquakes stop, he's home free. He gets the scientists in question to sign The Official Secrets Act, and then the country can move on. The wheels are turning fast on this one. It's shadowy stuff. No paper trails. Just nods and winks. Brown envelopes and secret handshakes. Phinnaeous Shine has already made a start."

"Whatever do you mean?"

"I mean that the elves are persecuted by the senate and Lavinia's forces. Elvish homes searched. Disappearances. An elf washed up on the banks of the Thames the other morning, just before the first run of the Thames Clipper. Luckily, the Shadow Squad got there first to pick up the body."

I sank heavily on a bench on the hospital grounds. Flinar flashed into my mind. "That's awful."

"Listen, I'm already crossing a line laying all this out for you."

"Then why are you?"

"Because it's my job to protect the peace."

"But there's not going to be any peace. The earthquakes aren't a natural phenomenon, and they aren't caused by the elves. So, both the Prime Minister and Phinnaeous Shine are chasing their own tails."

"Precisely, Alisha. It's a conundrum." Robert paused. "But it got me thinking. London is a secular city. Here, banks, restaurants and theatres are worshipped. Not gods. But there's been an unprecedented uptick in religiousness. People are spooked. The churches, mosques and synagogues of the city are overflowing. And our run-in with the sun god taught us that when there's more prayer, the gods of this city become stronger."

The world around me stilled. "You think the gods are behind this?"

"It's the only logical explanation. And you were key to stopping them the last time around. You might be featherweight, but you can definitely land a punch or two. Fancy another round?"

My pulse raced. "My dad just got hurt in an earthquake. I have an elvish friend. And I bloody hate bullies. You betcha I'm in. Where do I sign?"

"Er, mate, it's all off the books," said Robert. "Like, on the real down low. Shadow Squad style."

"I know, Detective. I'll be seeing you." I hung up but wasn't ready to go into the hospital yet.

My shoulders ached, and I felt all of my forty years. On a whim, I opened my camera app to check my face. My head said I was in my twenties, but the camera image made me wince. Having a scare did that. It aged you, or rather, it made you feel your age. I straightened my posture and sucked in my gut. A halo of frizz sat around my head, framing my bloodshot eyes and dry lips. I needed to hydrate and sleep and get to a kickboxing class or two to get my mojo back.

A huge furry thing loomed in the corner of my eye. I yelped and recoiled.

"It's only me," said Echo. "Or is it your reflection you object to?"

I slapped his rump, none too gently. "I thought you were a spider or one of Lavinia's bloody rats."

Echo grunted. "If that is so, the appropriate response would have been to pull out Transcender and slice a leg off. Not to scream like a girl."

"Girlie screaming can be very powerful, I'll have you know, Echo. It can propel babies down birth canals and scare off attackers. Think of it as a gathering of energy before we kick arse."

"Maybe if you're a banshee. Yours was a little lacklustre. Next time, I'd go for the sword instead."

"Noted. Dad all right?"

He inclined his head. "He's had enough painkillers to take the edge off and is sleeping soundly. Since I've never been to this hospital before, I spent my time scoping it out and marking my territory by leaving droppings in my favourite places."

I screwed up my nose. "That doesn't sound very hygienic. Next time, please remember a hospital needs to have sanitary conditions."

"In India, it is said pellets from a magical leopard are as lucky as a four-leaf clover. Some even suck them like boiled sweets," said Echo. "However, the hospital will no longer benefit from my bowels. I had to hightail out of there to avoid excessive fondling from the matron. She did a kind of pulsating movement on my belly that I think she learned from a vibrator." He jumped up on the bench next to me, and it creaked under his weight. "I was in half a mind to bite off her fingers, but I didn't want to ruin my appetite for tonight's hunt. It's not often we venture down to Tooting. The wind is carrying the scent of fresh meat." His whiskers twitched. "And something more divine."

I leaned my head against him and listened to the slow rumble of his chest. His fur was pillow soft and warm, despite the cool night. "I just talked to Robert Jameson."

Echo nodded. "I heard, druid. He might be a police offer, but he is an honourable man, and the argument he presented rings true. We are living in strange times when the Prime Sorcerer is in cahoots with a humdrum politician for nefarious reasons."

I was no longer shocked by the leopard's hearing. "You bought their story then? I thought you hated the elves."

"I do, druid. But my ancestors have always sided with the forces of good. I won't let my experiences sway me to back someone who does not deserve it. And then I remembered. Rajika Verma turned down Phinnaeous Shine's romantic advances. She was in her twenties then and had been struggling to animate the creatures her brother drew. This was before your father was born. Phinnaeous Shine promised her loyalty and more power than she could imagine."

"Dad told me she said no."

"She did. She didn't trust him." Echo growled. "And of all the people I have met during my long life, Rajika Verma was my guiding light. So, when you ask me if I believe the detective, I can tell you it reminded me I can't go wrong if I am led by what Rajika would have done. I am sorry for not standing by your side before, druid. I let an old enmity colour my judgement. But I'm ready to stand by your side now."

"Thank you, Echo."

"What do you want to do?"

"I want to sleep for a hundred years." I closed my eyes and nestled deeper into his fur. It was almost meditative, matching my breathing to his. I gave thanks to the gods that Dad had the care he needed. That the house hadn't crumbled. That I had my leopard. That the world was still beautiful despite all things wrong with it.

A purr rolled through Echo.

I straightened my spine and opened my eyes to find Gaia, Goddess of the Earth, standing before us on the sticky pavement, her cherubic face beaming. Her chiffon sari rustled in the night-time breeze. "I was wondering when you'd call me, druid."

I stood up and bowed my head, stuttering. "You have had a wasted journey, Goddess. I didn't call you."

Echo leapt from his perch and rolled over at her feet.

She tickled his snowy belly. Her voice was like mellow honey or bread and butter pudding, and everything was honest and good in the world. "Oh, I didn't come far. London is my city, after all. But you did call me, druid. You prayed, did you not, and gave thanks for your blessings on this bountiful earth."

"I did."

"Whose bell did you think rang in response?" She smiled with the patience of a mother talking to a child who hadn't quite caught the drift. "Mine, of course. It helps that I was listening. If I'm not, an offering comes in very handy."

I frowned. "You hear a bell when believers pray?"

Gaia swung her thick, black plait like a whip. Playful but somehow deadly. "It's more like a tug. As if someone is knocking me on the shoulder. Not all gods experience it that way, obviously. I believe Cupid experiences the twang of a bow on his heartstrings. And Apollo used to speak of the sense a white flag had been raised. And who knows what Loki of Asgard felt. He'd never give me a straight answer." She grabbed the folds of her sari and crouched down to Echo. "You are a sight for sore eyes, Chanakya Gunbir Hredhaan of Maharashtra."

Echo's adoring eyes had not moved from her face. He let out a pitiful mewling. "Goddess, I searched high and low for you. I yearned for your presence. I will abandon this druid forthwith and attend to your every need."

I did a double-take. "Hang on a minute. You just said you'd never leave my side, Echo."

He didn't take his eyes off Gaia. "That was before the goddess returned. If she desired it, I would throw you into a well and never look back."

"Traitor," I muttered.

Gaia gave us an amused look. "Now, now, I'm not here to steal away your leopard, druid. I am here to make amends after what happened with your mother."

My chest tightened with sadness and lingering resentment.

"I would like to invite you for a cup of masala chai in my favourite café. It is my daily ritual. Chai is always better when someone else makes it for you." She pushed a papery hand into her sari blouse and pulled out a clinking money bag. "My social security check just came through, and I thought I would spend a little on you."

I blinked. "I'm not—"

She held up a hand. "Wait. I know you are a little upset that I chose not to save your mother, but it is not every day a goddess invites you to a cup of masala chai. From all my travels and all my centuries, it is this tiny, unpretentious place across the road from Tooting Broadway tube station, squeezed between a fast food restaurant and a betting shop, that makes the perfect brew. Their masala chai is a milky, golden brown with cardamom, cloves, fresh ginger and a pinch of cinnamon. The leopard can join us if he promises not to leave his scent all over."

Echo purred in ecstasy.

I bit my lip. "I don't know, goddess. Maybe another time. My father needs me."

Her eyes flashed like the last throes of a falling star. "You refuse me, druid? After all I have done for you? Your father is in the hands of god's own NHS, and you have no need to worry. Mark my words, you will not survive the coming days without heeding my counsel."

Echo growled as if he was Gaia's protector and not mine.

My breath caught in my throat. "It's the sun god, isn't it? You're here to break it to me that he is back."

She sighed and sat on the bench. Then she placed her money pouch back in her blouse, pulling out a mint and offering me one. "He is still licking his wounds, but yes, child, he is back. Does the sun not rise? As much as I despair of his choices, the earth needs the sun. I didn't want to get involved. My place is in the shadows, but when your life was in danger, I rose against my kin at great risk to myself." She picked a dead leaf from a bush and rolled it between her fingers. It disintegrated, and the remnants floated away in the breeze. "The truth is that Ra's efforts to bring about suffering had the impact he desired. Prayer houses are full. Shrines are being set up by believers." She cast a warm glance at the prayer circle singing a familiar hymn in the car park. Her ears pricked at the chants from a mosque. "I feel my own strength increasing. The gods have been emboldened. They have yearned for this increase in power. They will keep on coming. We won the battle but not the war."

I wanted to trust her, but something niggled at me. "You speak like we're a team, but I've seen your power. You could crush me like an ant. You have power over the earth. How do I know the tremors aren't your doing?"

She swivelled to face me, and her anger hit me with the force of a tsunami. "Have you no faith, Alisha?"

"Sometimes faith isn't enough."

The rustling of the trees became thunderous, as if they had woken from sleep. "What a bitter disappointment. After all the miracles you have seen…Well, every soul has free will. I won't try to convince you. It is beneath me."

"I don't understand why you are leaving this up to me."

"God has always had his apostles, reluctant or not. Who says you're the only one?" She stood and patted my shoulder. "My masala chai awaits. I have three pieces of wisdom to impart to you, Alisha Verma. Not every battle is solved by escalating into war. Everything will unfold as it is meant to." She tugged Echo's ear with affection. Her eyes gleamed. "Goodbye, Chanakya. Stay away from the royal parks if you know what's good for you." She walked away in the direction of the main road. "Just one more thing, druid. Don't let your guard down with the vampire. I've warned you before about the undead. There is nothing the living should learn from them. Their corpses belong in the ashes, not walking the earth."

12

———————

The next morning, after checking with Dad that he had slept well and was recovering, I made my way to Fei Yen and Faeza's tea and occult shop, Shanghai Moon. It only took me down my street, across the zebra crossing and past an old Edwardian building called The Vicarage that I suspected was a swinger's club, given the glimpses of scantily clad couples in the windows and the sense of seediness that seeped out from it.

Shanghai Moon was tucked away on a side street, between a penny shop and a laundrette. A bell tinkled as I pushed the door open, and my two students looked up from the wooden counter. They were dressed in short, white lab coats, with their hair tied neatly in chignons at their nape. Fei Yen, the more ostentatious of the couple, wore bright pink lipstick. Rows and rows of transparent jars lined the shelves behind them, filled with all sorts of exotic leaves, pods and seeds, each marked with yellowing parchment of Chinese calligraphy.

"Alisha, there you are," said Fei Yen. "We spent the morning clearing up after the earthquake. We've just finished preparing the order for your dad."

I'd called them in the morning to ask for some Chinese herbal medicine to help him back on his feet. It felt odd for them to use my first name rather than Ms Verma, but only fair, given how much they'd opened up to me the night they rescued Flinar. Formality after that vulnerability wasn't right. Especially given I needed their help.

I hugged them. They were more than students to me now. They were friends. "I hope the damage wasn't extensive. What a shock that was last night."

Fei Yen sighed. "The city is reeling, Alisha. We can't complain about a few broken jars."

"And how about you, Faeza? It's good to see you back on your feet. I trust you are back to full health after our run-in with the rats?"

Faeza smiled. "Quick healing is one of the perks of being *hu hsien*."

"It's a shame we couldn't see your dad in person to assess him. It would've been much better to take his pulse and examine his eyes, ears and tongue before prescribing a remedy," said Fei Yen.

"I sent you a photograph of his tongue last night. Didn't you get it?"

"A photograph can't compensate for an in-person examination. Balancing the *yin, yang* and *qi* is a delicate process. You know that." Fei Yen wrinkled her nose. "What the photograph did tell us is that your dad has let his mouth hygiene go downhill since your mother's death."

"I'll get his dentist to look at that," said Alisha. "How much do I owe you?"

Faeza handed me a brown paper bag. "Don't be silly. It's on the house, especially after what Marina did for me. The instructions are in the bag. Make sure he continues with the prescribed treatment until his symptoms ease. There are no shortcuts when it comes to health." She grinned. "Unless you're *hu hsien*."

"I appreciate it." I looked around the shop. To the right, adjacent to a display of teas, crystals and what looked like voodoo dolls, was a painting of a landscape I'd never seen before. "Actually, there was something else."

As much as I missed Ezra and how his presence made my nether regions tingle in response, I hated being beholden to him. Hadn't he been the one who had suggested the Celestial Library as a solution to my Lavinia problem? Where was he then? My last attempt to animate Tielbu had been scary, but I'd made progress and was eager to try again. And if our hunch was right, once I had animated Tielbu, animating other creatures would be easier, and passing the trial would be a cinch.

Except I had no way of getting in touch with him. He seemed just to turn up when it suited him. Like I was Miss Available, and he was Mr Popular.

Or maybe it was that werewolves didn't seem to like mobile phones. They had their own way of calling each other. I'd asked, and apparently, Gunnolf preferred them to communicate the old-fashioned way and was averse to mobile phone contracts. They had biology on their side. According to Google, a wolf's howl could be heard six miles away, and werewolves were even more powerful. Ezra had promised to put me first, at least until the trial, but his disappearing act seemed hard to break.

Or maybe he didn't want to be answerable to me.

I got it. I wasn't his wife. My ex-husband had hated being answerable to me. He hadn't said it out loud, but I was pretty sure he regretted putting a ring on it. I could see it in his eyes.

Men were weird like that. They didn't mind being answerable to their bosses. But when it came to women, they kicked up a stink. Like a teenager sulking because their mum told them to clean their room. Even though their mum was right and their bedroom smelled of nuclear farts and old socks, and the stains on the bedding were embarrassing.

But Ezra wasn't the only person who could help me get to the Celestial Library. That was where Fei Yen and Faeza came in.

"What do you need? Some green tea perhaps or some lotus-scented tea lights or maybe a plush panda toy to cheer up your dad?" said Fei Yen.

I shook my head. "Oh no, that's not really his thing. It was really for me. You see, Ezra was going to help me, but he keeps disappearing on me."

Faeza's tone was gentle. "I'm sorry, Alisha. Wolves are devoted to their family. Perhaps you're not quite his family yet. How long has it been since you've seen him?"

I frowned. "A day or two."

"A lot changes in a day or two," said Fei Yen. "We know this city like the back of our hands. But the streets are whispering to us. They say the seekers have been mobilised against the elves."

I gripped the paper bag more tightly. "Ezra wouldn't do that. He's a good man. He saved my life not so long ago."

Fei Yen sighed. "He did. But orders are orders, especially for wolves, and maybe he doesn't have the courage to say no. This feels like a witch hunt, like in Shanghai. The elves are at the mercy of the senate. There's panic on the streets. Lavinia's forces show no mercy. Flinar almost came to a sticky end last night. It was blind luck he could harness his black hole magic to come here."

I held my breath. "You saw him? Is he okay?"

Fei Yen nodded. "He's rattling with fear. We let him hide in our store cupboard. But then the rats started to sniff around. Flinar didn't want to put us in danger again, so he escaped through the back window. We've not seen him since."

I crossed my fingers. "No news is good news. He's probably holed up somewhere."

"Or maybe he's lying in a ditch. We warned you, Alisha,"

said Faeza. "The senate cannot be trusted. If the British state harmed civilians, there would be an uproar. The police, judges and journalists would step up to defend humdrums. Within minutes, people on Twitter would raise banners and hashtags in support."

"Do you know what happens when peculiars are harmed by the senate?" said Fei Yen. "Absolutely nothing. There is silence. Because the senate is the judge, jury and executioner. It is the treasurer, the education, and the holder of the keys to the palace. It can wipe our magic and minds if it chooses, and nobody would stand against them."

I bit down on my lip. "So you won't help me?"

Fei Yen and Faeza spoke as one. "We didn't say that."

"You must decide your own path," said Fei Yen.

"Do you choose, like us, to stand outside the remit of the senate? Unsanctioned but free of their control?" said Faeza.

I shook my head. "I don't. I choose to pass my trial. But I choose to help the elves and stand against the senate, where they have fallen foul of their own laws. The Judge's Law. The delicate power balance between co-existing peculiar communities must be protected."

Fei Yen sighed. "Then I suppose I should give you this." She reached under the counter to bring out a brown leather strap with a slim holder at one end. "It's a baldric to hold your sword. Can't have it getting into the wrong hands."

I turned it over in my hands, then reached inside my jacket for Transcender. I slipped the sword into the pouch. "It's perfect. I can't thank you enough." I looked up. "But I'm afraid I need one more thing. I need you to tell me how to get access to the Celestial Library."

"Well, that is easy," said Fei Yen. "We haven't lived for centuries as *hu hsien* and increased our knowledge of Chinese herbal medicine without access to ancient texts. There is not only one way of reaching between the seams of the world, but our way is the easiest. What you must do is choose an auspicious day and step through our gate."

I frowned. "You have a gate?"

"Oh, it's not a normal gate. You can teach us about the English language, British culture and kickboxing, but we can tell you still have a lot to learn about the Otherworld," said Faeza. "The library is an evolved being made of more than bricks and mortar."

Fei Yen ruffled through a calendar on the wall. "Mmm, that will do the job quite nicely. Come back tonight. Luckily for you, it's May Day today, known to the druids, of course, as Beltane, one of the eight Sabbats, marking the halfway point between the spring equinox and the coming summer solstice."

"Of course." I had no idea what was going on. A druid with no idea about my culture's calendar: the minute I was out of there, I would pull up my Google search box.

Fei Yen came back to the counter. "The festival of Beltane will make your passage easier. The library will be more amenable to druids tonight. Added to that is the fact that you are a descendant of a Custodian. I'd wager you'll slip right through the gate."

"It will be as easy as sliding on a pair of gossamer stockings," said Faeza.

I had no idea that anyone wore stockings anymore apart from in S&M role play, but I nodded along. "Hang on a minute. I'm invited to a coven dinner tonight. I didn't want to go, but I can't get out of it."

Faeza swallowed hard. "Well, you'll have to come along afterwards, then. Just make sure those rats don't follow you."

13

My heartbeat was a hummingbird in my throat as I walked into the history cabin at Wildwoods. It was crucial I got the better of Orpheus today. His ability to mindread jeopardised my plan to animate Tielbu at the Celestial Library. If he found out, it was only a matter of time before Lavinia came knocking. I had an idea of how I could pull the wool over his eyes, but it wouldn't be easy, especially since I was the kind of girl who wore my heart on my sleeve.

Orpheus strode in, impressive in his Wildwoods robes. His chiselled face was like granite, with no sign of warmth. He pulled out a chair and lowered himself into it without taking his eyes from my face. "And so we meet again, Alisha. Let us hope that today's history lesson will be less dramatic. Tell me, what strides have you made in your training since the last time we saw each other? Your brother tells me he has discovered his werepigeon side. Although, judging by his internal monologue, his ego is a little fragile. And Helio tells me that Marina did good work in the bestiary."

I nodded. "She is getting better at controlling the flow of emotions."

"How about you, Alisha? Your emotions are raging today."

"Get out of my head, Orpheus."

"Only very few people can shield their thoughts from me, Alisha. It takes years of practice, and many just don't bother." His eyes darkened. "I, on the other hand, have years of practice in delving into the thoughts of others. It's as easy for me as—"

"Peeling a banana?"

He jerked. "Your mind is a gutter, Alisha. Will you stop referencing phallic objects?"

"I was doing nothing of the sort." I grinned. What I had learned was that throwing in the odd curveball for Orpheus could throw him off track. Today was as good a day as any to practice. I jumped to all the phallic objects I could think of: cucumbers, carrots, bratwurst, ice lollies, cacti, willy straws, the sell-out rabbit vibrator from my local corner shop…

"Can you stop that?"

"Oh, I can go all day," I said. "The question is, can you?"

He grimaced. "Your immaturity is toe-curling. I've never known anything like it."

"Then you haven't lived." I switched tactics and thought of iced buns, melons, lemons, Alex's favourite blow-up doll and Robert DeNiro's strap-on bra from *Meet the Fockers*.

Orpheus flung back his chair and stood up. "What is wrong with you, woman? You are a demon."

I smiled sweetly. "I am a druid, and I am eager to learn. How about we call a truce, Minister? You stay out of my head, and I'll stop polluting your fragile sensibilities."

He sighed. "I imagine it's the only way to get any work done with you in this mood. The purpose of today's history lesson is to talk about ancestry. Ancestry plays a large role in the Otherworld. That is to say, ancestry and genealogy can make the difference between being a slug or a lion."

"Well, that sounds a bit harsh."

"Or being a werepigeon or a shapeshifting sorcerer."

"My goodness, I hope you didn't give my brother this speech. You would've crushed his already fragile soul."

"I don't tell my pupils what they want to hear. I tell them what they need to hear," said Orpheus. "I am the Minister for History and the Today, not the minister for holding hands."

I looked at his white, paper-thin skin. The man needed some Vitamin D. "I imagine your hands are quite cold."

"You can mock me, druid, or you can pay attention. That is if you do want to pass your trial."

"All right, grumpy pants. Teach me."

"As I was saying, ancestry has an impact on what kind of peculiar you will be." Orpheus continued smoothly, with no need to inhale or exhale and a voice that was sharp all around the edges. All business and no humanity. "The most, dare I say, desirable peculiars are the result of the same kind of peculiars mating."

I spluttered. "Bloody hell, does that mean my brother has to find a werepigeon?"

His stillness creeped me out. He was either still or moving faster than light. The man had no middle gear. "The conclusions are not mine to draw. It is my duty only to share the wisdom of the senate, especially when pupils of marriage age are being initiated into the Otherworld."

"I've got to say, Orpheus. I don't think you need to worry about that. I got marriage out of my system a long time ago. And I'm not looking to do it any time soon."

"Then you will remain childless?"

My shoulders drooped, but I kept my voice steady. "My ex-husband and I tried for a baby, but it wasn't meant to be. It's probably a good thing. I couldn't imagine sharing custody with a tool like him. The doctor said I have a minuscule chance of carrying an embryo to term, even if I were to get pregnant. I have this condition, you see. Amenorrhea. It means I don't get my period."

He winced. "I don't need all the details, druid."

"What? I thought vampires liked blood?"

Orpheus flushed with embarrassment, and I chalked that up as a win for me. "Blood from the veins, not from the nether regions."

"You're the one who asked me to share."

He nodded slowly. "Alisha, I trace the genealogy of all the students in my class. It is often a way to make breakthroughs in their understanding of themselves and their talents. Your case is no exception. If your parents had not shunned Wildwoods, you might have come to this realisation sooner. As it is, your parents were too focused on their mundane lives. Imagine spending all that time in a humdrum laboratory, slaving over a stove or worrying about what your next car purchase should be when all this power coursed through your fingertips."

I frowned. "You are wrong, Orpheus. My father might have been wrong, but my mother lived the life that had always been intended for her. She was born to be a scientist. No magic ran through her veins."

His thin lips curved upwards. "Do you really think a virgin peculiar such as you could befriend a goddess and go up against the sun god if you were ordinary?"

I lifted my chin. "I'm not ordinary. I'm Rajika Verma's granddaughter."

"My research proves you are more than that, druid. Your grandmother didn't know it, of course. I remember her. She was powerful, yes. But she was also romantic. She believed love surpassed all. It was why she wouldn't bed Phinnaeous Shine. He wouldn't have wed her. They were the same kind of peculiar. But as his mistress, she would've known power beyond all her dreams. But a loveless union was something she couldn't envisage. Years later, when your father met Rosalie, it's why she didn't stand in their way. She recognised true love, despite Rosalie's shortcomings as a humdrum.

Despite her knowing that, if Joshi married a humdrum, his allegiance to the Otherworld would be weakened."

"She was right."

His lips twisted. "Oh, the twists and turns of history. If Rajika had lived, I am certain she would've found out what I uncovered, and we would not be sitting here today. I would not be teaching you about the bones of the Otherworld. Your family would be one of the most powerful families the Otherworld has known."

My pulse raced. "Spit it out, Orpheus."

"It took me hours to piece it together. It's when I found out your mother was born in Brittany that the penny dropped. When I found your maternal grandmother's name in the journals of Jules Renard, it finally clicked."

"What did?"

"Why did your mother leave France?"

I thought back to the threads of conversations I'd had with Mum over the years. "She came to the UK as a student. Her village was too small for her to pursue her passion for science. She got a scholarship from a London university, and that's where she met my father. She didn't look back."

"Do you ever see your mother's family?"

"She barely had anyone left. She didn't have fond memories of the place, so she made her life with my father. The rest is history."

His heavy brows furrowed. "The ghost of history always surprises us in the present. Today is one of those days. You don't have amenorrhea. I would bet my favourite coffin on it."

"How could you know that? Have you been snooping around my doctor's records?"

"Your mother wasn't a humdrum at all. I think your mother's side stems from a community of virgin priestesses. Not all were virgins, and not all were priestesses, but legend says it was a powerful place."

"Surely my mother would have known that?"

"Not if the druid practices had died out. According to Renard's journals, the few holding onto their heritage were simply thought of as lunatics. They lost their homes and, after a time, were simply known as the village idiots."

My spine tingled. I didn't believe it for a second, but it was a cool origin story.

"Do you know what this means, Alisha?"

"I'm sure you're going to tell me, Orpheus."

He leaned forward. The dark-chocolate and sweet-cherry scent of his beard oil assaulted my senses. "It means that you and your brother are the culmination of two druid lines, one French, one Hindu. That's a potent mix. It's a mix that the senate approves of. And it explains why you are so intriguing."

I fidgeted, tempted to bring out my shopping cart of phallic objects. This was getting way too intense. "Well, hooray for that. Hasn't changed whether I can have children, though, has it?"

He paused. "Who knew we would have something in common? I, too, am childless."

I patted his hand. "I'm sorry to hear that."

"I'm a vampire, Alisha. We can't create life."

"I forgot. It's been a while since I watched *Twilight*."

He rolled his eyes. "The vampire in *Twilight* has a child. I quite enjoyed the movie, especially its depiction of sleeplessness. The concept of vampire baseball was quite a revelation and is something I'd be keen to establish at Wildwoods if the leprechauns didn't ruin everything with their stubby legs. However, when the child was born, I gave up my commitment to the saga."

I gave him a thumbs up. "Orpheus, who knew you were a movie buff? I'd pegged you for an opera-only kind of bloke."

His eyes glinted. "*La Bohème* is rather marvellous. I think we have more in common than we both thought, Alisha."

I screwed up my face. "Like what?"

"We are both childless. We have both seen *Twilight*."

"I hate to break it to you, Orpheus, but that's a grand total of two things. One tiny and one huge. I reckon, given the Law of Probability, I'd have as much in common with any old Joe off the street."

He pretended to stake himself in the heart, and I warmed to him a little more.

"You know, you're not so bad. I thought you couldn't stand me, and here you are, trying to spend time with me. What's the deal, stiff?"

"Please don't call me that again. Perhaps it's just as well I'm not your mentor." He sighed. "Let's just say that your potential intrigues me. Particularly the possibility that a childless woman can animate lifeless objects. Are you any closer?"

I thought of Tielbu's reptile skin quivering under my fingertips.

Orpheus smiled.

I clenched my fists. "Hey, I thought we had a deal for you to stay out of my head."

"Oh, I've been in your head all this time, druid. I warned you; it is not easy to outsmart me." His eyes flashed. "My contemporaries will be very excited to hear of your plan."

I looked at my cuticles, trying to feign disinterest, but thoughts rattled through my brain like a runaway train: my annoyance with Ezra, my fear of Lavinia, my rage at the senate for targeting the elves, my longing for Tielbu and my hopes of reaching the Celestial Library.

He smirked. "Both your thoughts and your racing heartbeat give you away, druid."

I took a deep breath. "What do you want, Orpheus?"

"I want you to sit next to me at tonight's dinner."

"That is all?"

"That is a start."

14

———

I rang Dad. "Are you sure you don't want to come to the dinner party tonight? We can swing by and pick you up."

"No, no, I'm fine. You go and have a good time. I need my rest, and Alma next door has offered to bring me some lasagne. My appetite is better. In fact, my mouth's watering just thinking about it. Bay leaves are her secret ingredient, you know. She's as talented in the kitchen as your mother was."

"You sound so upbeat." I didn't tell him about Mum's ancestry. No need to burden him or anyone else with Orpheus's ridiculousness. The man had probably been sniffing the glue of all those ancient book bindings. Next, he'd be telling me he had access to Marcel Proust's or Anais Nin's journals, too.

"I am upbeat. A brush with death will do that to you. I'm lucky you and Sahil were there to call the ambulance. Sure, the house took some knocks, but nothing that some tender loving care won't fix. The way I see it, the tremors were a reminder not to lose my faith. A man can lose his way if he drifts from his faith."

"So you're okay with my choices?"

"I wouldn't go that far, but I'm trying not to get worked up about it. Just in case my old ticker can't take it."

"Enjoy Alma's lasagne, Dad."

"Thanks, love."

I put the phone down and went to my wardrobe, tossing clothes onto my bed until I finally found something I could feel powerful and comfortable in at Lavinia's party. A niggling sense of dread permeated my stomach at the thought of the evening ahead. Getting ready tonight felt like putting on armour, especially my control pants. Those things gave me a peachy shape, but damn, they were like a medieval chastity belt. I was determined to scrub up well. No doubt, the witches tonight would dress to kill. Hell, I wouldn't put it beyond them *to* kill. I hadn't forgotten the knockout punch Ravynne's truth serum had delivered the last time I was at the coven flat. Wily Lavinia would be on the lookout for any hint I was untrustworthy, and this time Elvira wasn't around to soften her coven sisters' more ruthless instincts.

"Echo, will you just stop crooning and leave me to get dressed in peace? You're worse than a toddler."

"Party pooper. I was just trying to be helpful. Don't you appreciate the party soundtrack I'm providing? 'The Love Shack' is an excellent mood maker. In my experience, it is impossible to listen to without shaking a rump."

I picked up a cotton bud to fix my eye makeup. "That rump-shaking made me ruin my eyeliner, but it wasn't as bad as you doing Jay-Z's rap in 'It's a Hard Knock Life.' I shudder to think what the neighbours made of that. They probably think I'm on acid because no normal person makes that noise."

While he wandered off, I fussed with my hair, pulled my long hair over one shoulder and put a leafy, vintage silver hair clip on the other side to add some glamour.

The sound of gushing water came from the bathroom.

I popped my head around the door. Claw marks marred my new shower curtain, and wee trickled down it.

"Echo!" I rushed forward to shoo him out. "For the millionth time, you don't need to mark territory here. There are no other leopards to compete with."

"But there are wolves." He gave me an appraising look. "You have never looked so beautiful. Except perhaps on your wedding day to that imbecile. Still, I can hear your heartbeat from here. Erratic, like that of a gazelle being chased across the savannah before I tear its throat out. You could give tonight a miss, you know."

I sighed. I could have called with an excuse. Dad's injuries were common knowledge, and it would not have been farfetched to say I needed to play nurse. But the dinner at Lavinia's was an opportunity for unprecedented access to the Sorcerer's Senate, and I wasn't missing the chance to flush out some intel about the tremors and whether Phinnaeous Shine was as sordid as the detective and the foxes believed. Plus, this was the perfect foil for the plan I had hatched with Echo.

"No, we're not backing down," I said. "How about we just go through the plan again?"

"As you wish, druid. The plan is for me to roam the wilds of London using my superior nose, ears and speed to work out whether the gods are indeed behind the tremors. All while you are dining with the senate. I am not to engage the gods or give away my presence without consulting you." He huffed. "Thereby allowing you to swoop in and take all the glory."

"Echo," I said. "It's not about the glory. I want us to work as a team. I don't like sending you out without backup, but Fei Yen and Faeza are too worried about you devouring them to go on a mission with you alone."

He turned his nose up in the air. "Well, this is going to cost you a freezer full of premium steaks. Plus some caviar if I don't make an acceptable wild kill tonight."

"I wouldn't expect anything less." I gave myself one last look in the mirror and slipped on some silver sandals.

Echo gave an appreciative growl. "You look more and more like your grandmother every day."

"I wish you could come with me tonight."

With Dad recuperating at home, I counted on having four allies at the party: Marina, the detective, Sahil and Ezra, if he bothered to show up at all. And then there was Orpheus: handsome but cold-blooded and stiff as a board, with dead, emotionless eyes. But underneath it all, I suspected he just needed a hug. If it floated his boat to sit next to me, I wouldn't refuse. Of course, it was an extra bonus if keeping him busy meant he would keep my plan from Lavinia.

I looked at the clock on my bedside table. Marina and Sahil were early.

"Are you going to get that, druid, or would you like me to be your butler?" said Echo.

I threw a pillow at him, tucked the picture of Tielbu into my bra and went to open the door. My mouth went dry.

There stood Ezra. His usual tousled, chin-length hair had been slicked back. An uneven tan clung to his skin, deepening his warm moon glow to a golden sand. His snugly fitting tuxedo accentuated his taut chest, slim hips and rock-hard thighs. The moonlit runs with his pack apparently kept him in shape. He held a bouquet of flowers in his hands.

I wanted to sound authoritative, but my words came out in a stutter. "What are you doing here? I'm capable of getting to Lavinia's by myself."

"I thought it would be a nice gesture to pick you up. I brought you these." He handed me the sunflowers.

I raised an eyebrow. "This isn't a prom date. We're going to your sneaky aunt's house for dinner with a nest of vipers."

"You've had a hard week. I thought this would lift your spirits. If you don't like them, we can give them to Dotty a few doors down. Judging by the state of her grey knickers on the drying rack she always displays, I reckon she doesn't get much company. *She* might like some flowers." His eyes roamed over me, taking in the slinky, azure blue dress and the strappy, silver sandals I'd chosen. "You look amazing, by the way."

My stomach somersaulted. "Where've you been?"

Grey eyes implored me. "I can't tell you, Alisha. It would put you in danger. Are you going to let me in?"

I walked ahead of him into the flat, hoping that his wolf's nose didn't catch the scent of Echo's liberal marking of the new shower curtain. "It's the elves, isn't it? Were you tracking them down as part of your seeker role? What have Lavinia and Gunnolf got you doing?"

He took my hands. "Nothing. I told you I'd focus on you, and I've kept my promise. When are you going to realise I'm on your side?"

"How can I? You're never there when I need you. Maybe it's because of your parents dying so young or you never trusting anyone wholly. Or maybe it's the teleporting thing. You can just disappear. In fact, disappearing comes to you as easily as breathing."

Ezra held up his hands defensively. "Easy. What's going on with you?"

Echo slinked into the room. "Perhaps she needs a poo. I have noticed her habits aren't as regular as mine."

We both swung around in unison. "Shut up, Echo."

I turned back to Ezra. "When are you going to be open with me?"

"When I know you won't fly off the handle." His thumbs caressed my palms. "I found it, you know. I found the Celestial Library."

"You did?"

He nodded. "It was tricky, but I made it to the door. I finally managed to hold onto the threads of it. The Custodian wouldn't let me in, though. I don't blame her for being cautious. There's a tonne of concentrated power in the library, and she doesn't let any old peculiar in. I would have come sooner, but I've been trying to puzzle it out."

"Actually, I found my own way in."

"You did?"

"I did. I'm going there tonight after the dinner at Lavinia's."

Ezra whistled. "I didn't think the student would surpass the mentor so soon. Impressive, hellfire. The question is, are you going to let an old man hang onto your coattails?"

"You can't come. It works for me tonight because it's Beltane."

His brow furrowed. "Bell, what?"

Google was my friend.

"May Day. A Gaellic festival important to druids. Think maypoles, bonfires, dancing and fertility rituals." I grimaced. I guess that last bit wasn't meant for me.

A mischievous look danced in his eyes. "Now you're really making me want to go."

"Well, you can't."

He sighed. "It makes sense, now you mention it. Gunnolf once told me that his only entry to the Celestial Library was on the full moon, and when he passed the threshold, his wolf became submerged, even when he tried to call it forth."

"Passage for me will be easier because I'm Rajika Verma's granddaughter."

Echo purred. "Finally, you appreciate her majesty."

We turned on him. "Shut up, Echo."

"No need to be so tetchy. Rajika Verma never raised her voice at me, and she let me eat all the pet dogs I wished," said Echo.

I rolled my eyes. "She was obviously a better woman than I."

"So we agree," said Echo.

I bent down to scratch his ears. "It's time for you to go

forth and do wondrous things tonight. Be clever, but more than that, be subtle. No singing and no eating pets."

He puffed out his chest. "I'm honoured to be of service."

I headed for the open back window.

"When the mice are out, the cat will play."

"What was that about?" said Ezra.

"I'll fill you in on the way." I picked up my phone to send Marina a text. "Dad's too tired to come. I was going to hitch a ride with Marina and Sahil."

"And now? Can I escort you to Baba Yaga's? A belle like you shouldn't turn up to the ball in a vet's van. It's much more appropriate for you to arrive in a werewolf's arms."

My traitorous body told me to go with him. I stepped into his arms, and the scent of spice and nuts filled my nose. "Was I ever going to say no?"

He smiled and murmured into my ear. "Those sandals make me want to take you straight to the bedroom."

"Soon. If you're a good boy."

Ezra grinned and hooked his arms around the small of my back.

I clung to him. The world slipped away in swirls of monochrome as we shot into our future.

15

The sensation of teleporting wasn't quite like flying. It was more like being suspended in a vortex, clinging on, waiting to be ejected at your destination point. No wind whipped through my hair—I would have welcomed that. It was just me in Ezra's arms, holding my breath. I kept my eyes shut and tried not to think too hard about the physics of it. About how teleporting wasn't like a plane. There hadn't been engineers poring over plans down to the smallest calculation. There hadn't been test flights and scrutiny and government backers. I put my life into Ezra's hands simply because I fancied the pants off him. I'd made life-changing decisions on far less information, but they hadn't resulted in me being flung about the atmosphere like a projectile in a pinball machine.

When we arrived outside Baba Yaga's Gym in Wimbledon, the sunset was an orange glow on the distant horizon.

I stepped out of Ezra's arms, releasing my grasp on the silken lapels of the dinner jacket.

His eyes drifted to my chest. "Er, you may want to…"

He turned away to spare my blushes.

My breasts had sprung out of their optimal position in my dress. Oh, the shame. I jiggled them back into place and adopted a falsely bright tone to hide my humiliation. "We might be in for a bit of drama tonight, but at least it's not a spin class. They are the very definition of sadomasochism."

Lavinia's gym, with its white script on a green sign and its window front displaying dumbbells of various sizes, was couched in darkness.

I peered inside. "Are you sure we got the day right? It's awfully quiet in there."

"The coven guards its secrecy fiercely. It might seem quiet out here, but inside, it'll be a completely different scenario." He knocked lightly on the glass door.

"They're never going to hear that." Dread pulsed through me. "Maybe we should just go."

He gripped my bare arms. "Listen here, Alisha. The rats are going to be here any second. Since Orpheus knows your plan, we're in the shit. But it's salvageable. We just have to get through tonight. Sit next to the vampire to keep him sweet, but don't trust him. Don't trust my aunt. In fact, don't trust anyone who isn't me or you haven't known all your life. I'll be watching. If your tap your chin, I'll come and rescue you."

"My chin?" I thought my last wax job had fixed the errant hairs, but maybe not if Ezra had honed in on it. He was a wolf. Did that make me a pig? *Not by the hairs on my chinny, chin, chin,* sang my head.

Orpheus was in for a treat tonight if he delved into my mind.

The door opened, and we looked down to find an upright rat wearing a bowtie and a tiny waistcoat.

Ezra gave a gentle smile. "Good evening, Maurice."

The rat bowed. "Good evening, Ezra. Good evening, druid. Please follow me."

We walked in darkness past the glossy reception desk, bubble gum walls, pink tub chairs and the mirrored studios.

Floor lanterns holding jasmine-scented tea lights glowed at the bottom of the stairwell that led to the coven flat. My sandals sank into the carpet as I followed the rat springing from stair to stair in front of me, with Ezra close behind me. The rat leapt up to the top step and placed his left forefoot on the handleless door at the top of the stairs.

As the door swung open, a wave of noise—classical music, raucous chatter and clinking glasses—crashed over us, so much so that I took a step backwards. Ezra's warm hand on my back seeped through the material of my dress, compelling me to keep going. We followed the rat into the opulent inner sanctum of the coven, with its embossed wallpaper, clashing colours and imposing chandeliers that would have looked at home at The Ritz. The coven's umbrellas lurked in every corner, a reminder of their power. Rats skittered between the guests, bearing trays of grapes and cheese and wine and champagne. From a distance, it was clear that the senate had turned out in full force.

Ezra bent down to accept a flute of champagne from Maurice, the rat, but I refused. I'd learned my lesson last time.

"Heads up, incoming," said Ezra.

His aunties approached, sashaying over in a rustle of taffeta and silk and chiffon, looking more like sirens than family.

"Nephew." Red-haired Isadora wore a black evening gown and gloves that set off her hair to perfection. She took his hands. "If only your mother were still with us. She'd be so proud. And Alisha, I do hope your father is recovering well. How good of you to tear yourself away from nurse duties to grace us with your presence."

Ezra gave a tight smile, his skin tan against his crisp white collar. "Aunties, aren't you magnificent? The centuries have no impact on your beauty."

Lavinia tossed her head of silver curls and cackled. "Oh,

stop it, Ezra, or I'll send you to the rats in the basement for a spanking."

"Just like old times," drawled Ezra.

"Whyever are you emptyhanded, Alisha? Did the rats not offer you a drink?" said Lavinia.

I grimaced. "I refused it. It's hard to forget the green smoothie last time I was here. The truth serum's a little hard to forget."

Lavinia gave me a hard smile. "Don't be silly, dear. This is a party. Besides, it's not like you have anything to hide. Besides, Ravynne had no time for potions today. She spent all day buffing and polishing and curling to look like that. She's no catfish."

Ravynne waved at Ezra from across the room, and he grinned at her.

I bit down hard on my lip, tempted to kick her to kingdom come.

Lavinia patted my arm. "No shortcuts or falsies for her. Beauty takes work, you know."

She knew I was wearing control pants. There was no other explanation for her tone.

"Druid," said Chandra. "The last time we spoke was the night we lost Elvira. Let's hope this time you're more of a good luck charm."

Elvira's loss still stung me too, but the witch didn't have to rub my nose in it. I decided to play it saccharine sweet rather than spoil the mood so early in the evening. Sometimes a velvet glove was better than a sledgehammer.

"Speaking of good luck, your skin looks wonderful," I said. "What a glow. You must tell me your secret. I'd kill for it."

Lavinia thrust her conical, pneumatically impressive chest out. "Oh, we did kill for it. Pilates can only do so much good. We needed a dozen collagen potions and the blood of a goat to bounce back from that spell on the sun god. But let's not ruin a perfectly pleasant evening. I can't wait to hear about your progress in animating the dragon. I've barely been able to think of anything else."

Her sisters exchanged glances.

I rambled on like a train threatening to come off the rails. "It's quite a crowd."

Lavinia sighed. "I was rather hoping Roger, Raphael and Andy would come, but alas, they are too busy preparing for Wimbledon. Although I did cast Roger a little spell to help speed up his serve. I have a soft spot for the way that man wears a suit. He could ask me anything, and I'd be putty in his hands."

Isadora leaned in conspiratorially. "My sisters have bedded at least one tennis player in every generation. It's one of the perks of living in this neck of the woods. And you know the most surprising thing?"

I shook my head.

She tittered. "Not all of them wear tighty-whities."

Lavinia looked over our heads. "The last of our guests have arrived at last. The empath is going to give the Prime Sorcerer a heart attack in that get-up. She looks as scrumptious as his succubus house slave."

Off they went, in a cloud of hairspray and sweet perfume, to greet Marina, Robert and Sahil.

Marina had missed the memo and dressed like she would for a rock festival, with a PVC skirt and bustier, together with a spiked collar. Judging by the look of disquiet at the bowtie-clad rat, Sahil was having problems leaving his humdrum side at the door. Only the detective looked as cool as a cucumber in his threadbare tux.

"Relax," said Ezra. "Your heartbeat sounds like the drummer from Rage Against the Machine."

"I'm trying." I glowered, trying to avoid Orpheus's glare from across the room. By the looks of it, he'd opted to leave his robes at home. Instead, he wore a sleek suit and white shirt. "Any chance you can wrangle it so Marina is sat next to me? Since you're on first-name terms with the rats. I'm going to vomit with anxiety otherwise."

He gave a curt nod and strode away, leaving me alone like a fly in a spider's web.

With the scene clear, Orpheus approached and bowed with stiff civility. "This is an unfortunate place to have your friends desert you, druid. May I escort you to dinner?"

I gulped and looked longingly at my friends. Then I tucked my arm into his. "I'd be honoured."

His eyes narrowed. "Then let the evening unfold just as each of us wishes."

16

I had to give it to them. The Drach sisters and their rat familiars knew how to stage a party. We followed them into the dining room, where a magnificent oak table and burgundy upholstered chairs had been prepared for dinner. The centre of the table had been decorated with an arrangement of orchids and dahlias, church candles, gleaming cutlery and napkins. In the corner, a harp played of its own accord, the strings plucked as if by a ghost.

I nodded at senate members as Orpheus guided me to our seats. He didn't bother with niceties. True to his word, Ezra had arranged the table so I was wedged between Marina and Orpheus. He sat between his Aunt Chandra and her coven sister, Ravynne, who had done such a devious job with the truth serum.

Thank you, I mouthed at him.

My best friend's arms closed around me, and I swung around to hug her.

She whistled like a yob on a building site. "You look like a warrior princess."

"And you look like a rock chick from the seedy part of town."

Marina's eyes twinkled. "Mission accomplished. I may be an empath, but I'm more goth girl than Mary Jane."

I patted the seat next to me. "You're here, next to me."

"Perfect. I was hoping to play footsies with Robert all night, but since he is sandwiched between man-eating coven sisters, you'll have to do."

Diagonally opposite me, wedged between Lavinia and one of her coven sisters, Sahil jittered with nerves.

I gave him a thumbs up.

"Your brother's in bad shape tonight," said Marina. "His aura is off. I tried to get him to open up on the way, but he wasn't having any of it. Closed up like a clam."

There was a scraping of chairs against the concrete floor as we all took out seats.

Orpheus raised an eyebrow and leaned closer to me. "This sort of thing makes me want to stake myself in the eye. But the rats can cook, and it is usually easier to bend Lavinia's will than to say no. I've always found it illuminating where Lavinia chooses to seat me at the dinner table. There was a time I would be in the centre. But now, like you, I find myself next to the kitchen."

"I quite like this view, actually." An army of rats could be seen dressed in tiny white coats and chef hats, stirring, chopping and plating up exquisite wares for our consumption. It was like Ratatouille on acid, an assembly line of skilled rodents. "A good thing the worktop in there isn't porous. Rats are incontinent, apparently."

"Yes, they are," said Marina cheerfully. "They use urine to mark routes and territory. I'm pretty sure we'll be ingesting some tonight unless the witches have gone to the effort of house-training them."

Orpheus sighed. "I am very picky about what and who I eat. There will be no bodily fluids in our dinner tonight. The coven rats are better trained than a dog at Crufts."

"Good to know," said Marina.

"It's all part of Lavinia's show of power. And she does like to revel in it. When you're as old as us, you realise that love, talent, beauty and happiness are all fleeting. Humdrum power, too, is fleeting. There are too many variables. Stock markets, housing values, divorce settlements." He raised a sardonic brow. "But for peculiars, power is easier to hold onto than other desires. An army of rat spies and chefs. Cauldrons and spells. Aerial acrobatics on umbrellas. That woman is drunk on her sense of importance. Her very own aphrodisiac."

I stared at him open-mouthed. "Why, Orpheus, who knew you could talk in more than monosyllables about anything other than history?"

"Perhaps I'm not the person you think I am, druid." His eyes gleamed. "Of course, I know exactly who you are. For example, I know that you have no desire to be powerful. I'm not sure if that's to be pitied or lauded."

Marina leaned in. "Interesting how the non-coven women have been pushed to the sidelines. Who's the woman with the cat-like glasses next to Rayna Willowsun?"

"That's Margola Silver, the Minister for Information," said Robert.

"Men are allowed here by invitation only," said Orpheus. "When we enter the inner sanctum, it's all eyes on us. At least the ones currently in vogue. We're the prize, the toy, the entertainment. Female guests are the add-ons, not the main meal."

"Charming," said Marina. "So much for the sisterhood."

Phinnaeous Shine sat at the head of the table in a top hat. To his right was the werewolf alpha Gunnolf in a shirt that had been ironed for once. Just along was Helio, the Bestiary Minister, whose translucent wings fluttered in tandem with his expressive hands. There was Cillian O'Meara, the leprechaun Finance Minister, rubbernecking at the jewels and artefacts decorating the room, which I had assumed were fake until I saw the gleam in his eyes. I sucked in my breath at the sight of what could only be an angel with dirty wings and long, stringy blond hair. He reminded me of Kurt Cobain, and judging by the looks on the faces of the coven witches, he had exactly the same effect on them. I pulled my eyes away.

Orpheus rolled his eyes. "That's Erelim. Minister for Diplomacy."

"He's an angel."

"Erelim is an angel in physical form only. He's a tricky scoundrel, but then what would you expect from a diplomat?"

"Why are his wings so sooty and tattered? I imagined his wings would be more cloud-like, you know?"

Orpheus cocked an eyebrow. "Everyone's fallen nowadays, druid."

Lavinia occupied the central seat at the table. She stood, tapping a spoon against her champagne flute for attention.

The room quietened.

"Welcome, dear guests. Although dark times are upon us, I am grateful you've taken the time out of your busy schedules to break bread with us tonight. The rats have been toiling all day to cook us a feast that will delight our senses and sate our bellies. There is one who is not here tonight. Our darling Elvira was taken from us too soon and in the most heinous circumstances. But she, too, would want us to drink and be merry." Lavinia took her seat, smiling benignly at her guests.

As if on cue, the rats filed out to stand behind us, one for every guest, each balancing an aperitif and a starter of what looked like baked goat cheese with roasted pears and rocket salad.

Sahil physically recoiled.

"My darling werepigeon," said Lavinia. "Once you get used to the rats, you'll find they are as good as any concierge, chef or street fighter you'd find anywhere in the world. And their salaries are so cheap. A chunk or three of Appleby's Cheshire cheese or Red Leicester keeps them happy to follow orders."

The rats leapt onto the table with our starters, like gymnasts—aware of every body part from their tails to their whiskers. I looked on in awe as Marina gasped in delight.

"They are not so adept at serving soup," said Orpheus. "I should know."

I took a bite of my salad. "You know, it's actually quite nice sitting next to you when you're not delving into my thoughts."

He pushed his food around his plate, waiting for the rats to return to the kitchen. "I'm playing nice. It occurred to me after your revelation at our lesson that I need to ask something of you, Alisha. Do you think you can give it to me? Just a small favour."

"A favour? So can I refuse?"

Orpheus dropped his voice. "It wouldn't be wise, druid. There are plenty of those here eager to get their hands on your dragon. This request would be the cost of my silence. It would be so easy for me to open my mouth in this company. There are so many here waiting for you to slip up." He paused. "But I am also a useful ally."

My voice was cold. "What do you want, Orpheus?"

Beside me, Marina stilled. She squeezed my leg under the table.

"I'm a proud man. I don't ask a lot of anyone. If you find the Celestial Library, I need you to get something for me."

"Why can't you go yourself?"

Dark eyes that I couldn't read. "I have tried many times, but vampires are an embodiment of death. And death doesn't belong in something heavenly. Sometimes, death occurs inside the library, as with Rajika Verma. But death can never enter from the outside. The library's defences don't allow it."

"What is it you want?"

"In 1564, the theologian John Calvin died. At the time of his death, he had a chest in his home that contained all his worldly treasures. During Calvin's lifetime, many men had hunted for pieces of the cross of Christ. The cross had been found by St. Helena during her pilgrimage to the Holy Land in 326."

I frowned. "This isn't a history lesson, Orpheus."

His heavy brows snapped together. "Patience, druid. The cross was lost in the folds of time. Some theologians claimed the blood of Christ made the cross indestructible. So over the years, fragments of wood started to be sold as relics, and the relics multiplied until nobody knew what was real and what wasn't."

"But you started talking about Calvin's treasure chest."

"That I did. He had said that if all the supposed pieces of the cross were gathered, they would fill the cargo hold of an entire ship. When he died, a piece of the cross was found."

I gasped. "He had been hiding it all along?"

Orpheus nodded. "He had. That remnant, druid, is stored in the Celestial Library. And I would very much like you to obtain it for me."

"Why me?" I bit my lip, drawing blood.

His eyes followed the motion of my tongue. "Because I know you have a way to get inside. And I know you don't want me to spill your secrets."

Marina scooted under the table to retrieve a napkin and leaned across to give it to Orpheus, her hand lingering on his. "Would you look at that? You dropped your napkin, Minister."

He accepted the napkin with a curt nod. "So, do you have an answer, Alisha?"

I didn't want to make an enemy of him. I had already slighted him by choosing Ezra as my mentor over him. I lowered my voice to a whisper. "I don't like being threatened, Orpheus. And we're not friends, so I'm not doing you a favour for free, regardless of your threat to tell Lavinia of my dragon plans. What will you do for me in exchange?"

"I won't rig the magical trial in your favour or influence the vote," said Orpheus.

I flung up my hands in protest. "I wasn't going to ask you that."

A smirk. "Weren't you?"

I sighed. "Okay, maybe it crossed my mind. But a thought isn't a crime."

"I like you, druid, against my better instincts. That's why I'm going to tell you this as compensation for services about to be rendered. Your werepigeon brother has set something stupid in motion. I'm surprised it didn't happen sooner, given the state of his internal monologue. I had hoped he'd come to terms with his new self, but his jealousy of you riles him into poor decisions."

My blood cooled. "What has he done?"

"He is a changed man. If you value your relationship, you need to act now. Otherwise, it bodes ill for the future."

I stole a look at Sahil. "He what? What's he done?"

Orpheus rolled his eyes. "I might be a mind reader, but I don't know everything. Your brother's brain is a swamp. You don't want to know what he thinks about the empath. Especially in her outfit tonight."

Marina leaned forward. "I heard that."

"I suppose I have to give you something else in return for this titbit of information?" I said.

"No, that one is for free, as a sign of our friendship. Watch your back. He is not the man you think he is." He paused. "So, are we agreed?"

Ezra's eyes bored into me.

Talk about abandoning me in the viper's nest. "If I agree, there is no guarantee I will succeed."

"How right you are, Alisha. Nothing leaves the Celestial Library without the Custodian's permission. You will have to persuade her. But I will know if you failed or are deliberately thwarting me. Your thoughts will tell me. This will be our secret, druid." He pulled a card from his suit and pressed it into my palm. "Bring it to my den, not to Wildwoods."

"Watch out," said Marina. "My ears are burning. Someone's talking about us."

Lavinia raised her voice from across the table. "Would you look at that? Look at Orpheus and the druid in their cosy tête-à-tête. It's enough to make the rest of us feel left out. How selfish, Orpheus. You must share her with us. Tell us, druid, what do you think of our endeavours against the dark elves?"

I could feel Ezra's hackles rise from across the table, and I'd not even touched my chin yet.

The words came out before I could stop them, despite Marina's goth-girl boots kicking me under the table. "I think you've turned your might on the wrong people. You've already crushed the elves once before. They are not responsible for the tremors. You're as bad as bullies in a school playground. Or drunken louts in a pub who target someone just because they look different."

I could hear a pin drop. The rats stopped scuttling in the kitchen. The harp paused. Mouths stopped chewing, and cutlery was laid gently on plates. Blood rushed to my ears as all eyes turned to the Prime Sorcerer for the inevitable explosion. What I wouldn't have given to have Echo crooning a pop song to break the ice.

I scratched my chin.

Grey eyes held mine.

Phinnaeous Shine finished his mouthful, and when he turned to me, his eyes burned with passion. "Your accusation reeks of ignorance, druid. The Sorcerer's Senate embraces difference. Just look around you. You would do well to stay out of matters which don't concern you. The big guns are at the table. You're nothing more than a mewling lamb. Your grandmother would be turning in her grave."

I shrivelled with embarrassment. Would no one jump to my defence? My friends and even my brother remained quiet.

Orpheus coughed. "The dark elves are indeed a blight, Phinnaeous. But we cannot discount the theory of another reason for the tremors. My vampires have been trawling the city in the dead of night, as is their habit, and they have seen unnatural things. Herds of cows and deer moving in great swells across the city. Great wails coming from the caged beasts at London Zoo and in small holdings. One reported seeing a two-legged goat in Richmond Park who raised a top hat at him. Could it be that our intelligence has led us astray? Facts are more important than fiction."

The Prime Sorcerer slammed down his cutlery. "Hogwash, Orpheus. Besides, you know as well as I do that history is as much about the stories we tell ourselves, not about facts. I'm surprised to see you spout this nonsense. The Otherworld is only strong because we use all the advantages we have. In a few weeks, the elvish networks will be so destroyed they will struggle to even host a tea party, let alone launch an attack on an institution like Wildwoods." He turned to Robert. "The outcome of this war is practically signed, sealed and delivered. Isn't that right, Detective Jameson?"

Robert coloured. "Quite right, Prime Sorcerer. The Prime Minister is counting on it."

I smarted at the detective's cowardice and glowered at him. "You are destroying elvish lives, Prime Sorcerer. And for what?"

Lavinia banged the table.

"Enough! I won't have this insolence. I'm disappointed, Alisha." Her eyes glinted.

I wondered if this was what she'd wanted all along. To see me fail the trial because she had lost so much more than she had gained when we made our deal to defeat the sun god.

"You are one of our brightest initiates, Alisha," said

Rayna. "I suggest you consider your next moves very carefully."

"Hear, hear," said Helio, the bestiary master. "You have so much to contribute to this fight. Not since Kraglek have we had the prospect of such a magnificent creature in our sights. A dragon would be my crowning glory."

Anger coursed through my veins. Tielbu wouldn't be theirs.

"You'd be wise to keep your mouth shut, druid," murmured Orpheus.

Ezra raised a glass. "I propose a toast to our new initiates. May they cover us in glory."

"May only the worthy pass the trial," said Phinnaeous.

"May they obey our rules," said Gunnolf.

"May they be the allies we deserve," said Lavinia.

I held Ezra's gaze, and we drank.

When Lavinia came around to murmur in my ear, her voice was hard. "I was wrong to trust you, druid."

I stuttered. "You weren't wrong, Lavinia. Together, we saved lives."

Cold fingers gripped my shoulder blades, but judging by her eyes, it was my throat she wanted. "I gained nothing. The vial of my nephew's blood didn't work."

I bit my lip. "You could ask for another. He is family, after all."

"You fooled me once. I won't fall for it again. No one denies me what I covet. You will pay for your deceit. I lost Elvira and the respect of my coven sisters. I won't be so quick to get into bed with you again. Bring me the dragon, or you will be sorry."

17

———

A main meal of stacked roasted aubergine, sautéed potatoes, tiramisu for dessert and a cheese board worthy of Buckingham Palace followed my outburst. I kept my mouth shut. Marina's hand on my knee, Ezra's tight smile and Orpheus' stony expression made sure of that. Once the ordeal of the coven dinner was over, Robert, Marina, Ezra and I slipped out into the night. Only Sahil stayed behind, buoyed by my public flogging and having far too much fun with the minor coven members to leave the party once the alcohol had eased his anxiety. Judging by the tentpole in his trousers as we left, he was feeling much more of a frisson than fear.

Ezra kept his silence until we piled into the front bench of Marina's van, which she'd parked on a side street. He was too clever to speak out beforehand. London had many rats, but the rats in Wimbledon were the most prolific of all, and the majority were loyal to the coven. What was more, I had just shown the head of the London coven that I was not on her side. The Minister for Defence knew only one mode of thinking. If I wasn't with her, I was against her.

"Well, at least we got out of there in one piece. Holy moly, the emotions were high in there." Marina turned the key in the ignition. The engine spluttered to life. "Rob?"

"Yes, sweet cheeks?" said the detective.

"Thank you for not assuming you'd drive."

"No problem. This beauty is your baby."

Marina grinned. "Don't you forget it."

Ezra swivelled to face me, his thigh pressed against mine. "Sorry to break the harmonious vibe in here, but I am so angry I could murder you, Alisha. What part of 'don't rock the boat' do you not understand?"

I winced. "Well, a good thing you didn't teleport me out of there. Judging by the look on your face, I would have ended up at the London Dungeons."

"A blessing, if you ask me," said Marina. "She would have puked all over you with all that goat cheese, burnt aubergine, cream and potentially rat piss floating around her stomach."

Ezra tore off his bowtie and opened his top button to reveal his charm necklace. "I'm not joking, Alisha. That was not good in there. You need votes to pass the trial. That means you need allies. The problem is, every time you open your mouth, you end up making enemies."

"Huh," I said, skewering Robert with a scathing look. "At least I had the balls to speak my mind."

"That's not fair. What was he supposed to do?" said Marina.

"It's called playing the long game, sunshine," said Robert.

Ezra bristled. "What did the vampire want? He was whispering in your ear all night."

I stiffened.

"Are you going to tell him, or should I?" said Marina.

I shrugged. "He wants me to convince the Custodian to let me take him a stake from the cross of Christ from the Celestial Library. If I don't, he'll tell them my plan to animate Tielbu away from the grasp of the senate."

Ezra cursed long and hard. "You've got to be kidding me.

It's one thing, you going to the library tonight and animating the dragon, but two things can't happen. Orpheus can't get his hands on the stake, and your dragon can't fall into senate hands. You make sure when you animate that thing that you tell it to fly far away from here."

Warmth spread through me. "So you think I can do it?"

He gave me a black look. "You can do anything you set your mind to. If Phinnaeous Shine thinks you're a mewling lamb, he's mistaken, and it will cost him."

Robert rubbed his hand over his face. "Why would Orpheus want a piece from the cross? It's not my area of expertise, but an old sod knows that vampires fear holy relics."

"Actually, that's not true. They wouldn't be thrilled, but they can take a splash of holy water or a cross being shoved in their face," said Ezra. "But this is different. A piece of wood from the true cross, on which the son of God bled, would do real damage. So the question is, really, unless Orpheus is a hoarder of historical artefacts in his own right, why does he need such a deadly weapon?"

I held onto my seat as Marina flew over a pothole. "Maybe that's it. History *is* his jam."

Marina drew in a shaky breath and kept her eyes fixed on the road. "I know why. I felt it when I handed him his fallen napkin at dinner. Orpheus wants a piece of the cross because he wants to end his life."

I frowned. "That's ridiculous. An arrogant, self-serving beast of a man like that is having too much fun making other people miserable to take his own life."

"You're wrong, Alisha. It wasn't just tonight. I've sensed his sadness in my history lessons too. He's always droll, often obnoxious and sometimes downright scary," said Marina. "He is never happy or even content. He's in pain. I sensed it when I touched him tonight. That fragment is his exit out of the world."

"Holy shit," said the detective. "I'm pretty sure I don't have a duty of care to a suicidal vampire, but it's still enough to break your heart. Not mine, obviously. I'm as tough as nails, but like, your general observer would find this a sorry state of affairs. He needs to buddy up with someone, you know, so he can spill his thoughts and find peace."

Ezra gave a mirthless laugh. "That is the most ridiculous thing I've ever heard. Firstly, a centuries-old vampire finds peace by kicking the bucket. Secondly, if he opens his mouth to the senate, the ancient laws don't mess about. There's no workplace protection. He'll be kicked off for being unfit for duty. And if what Marina says is true, I'm pretty sure being a senate member is what's keeping him going."

"Well, then maybe he should talk to the other vampires in his den," I said.

"Those arseholes? The tiniest show of weakness, and they'll stick him in a coffin at the bottom of the ocean," said Ezra. "No, we stick to the plan. Find the library and claim your identity as an animator by bringing the dragon to life. Make sure you assign him a purpose when you do. Remember, his will is tied to yours at the moment of birth. The vampire can take care of himself. We're not going to make his problem better or worse. We're going to preserve the status quo."

I took a deep breath. I didn't like being told what to do. He had a point, but he wouldn't be in the field making those decisions. "Okay, so I have my orders. So it's time to give you *my* orders."

The copper flecks in his grey eyes danced. "I knew you were trouble."

An object flashed in the corner of my eye, coming at us like a bat out of hell.

I gripped the seat tightly as we chugged along. "What on earth? Stop Marina, that's...that's..."

I squinted into the darkness. It was in the middle of the

road, straddling the dividing marker. It raced towards us, smaller than a car but bigger than a motorcycle.

Marina held her course, not slowing down, putting us on a collision course.

"Slow down, you lunatic," I said. "Pull over!"

Maybe it wasn't mechanical. It had a golden glow. A gracefulness of form that was familiar.

Marina pulled over to the kerb and rolled down her window. "It's Echo. Hey, Echo, over here."

Echo slowed his pace, and his glow subsided, revealing the rosettes on his coat so familiar to me. He padded over to the window. "Open the back of your van, Marina Ambrose. I came this way, hoping to find you all. I have much to tell you, but the ears out here are many."

The van groaned with his weight as Marina settled him into the back, cushioning him with blankets. She closed the doors and returned to the driver's seat while the rest of us swivelled to face Echo.

"What did you find?" I said.

He sank his head onto his paws. "I roamed the streets of the city. It was a night of respite from Lavinia's forces. Nothing was untoward, so I accepted the invitation of an old man, who gave me a tin of sardines. In thanks, I didn't eat his sausage dog. I talked my way into an elvish drinking hole and listened to their tales of woe. A group of pussies invited me to join them on the banks of the Thames for an evening of revelry, but I rejected them because I am a protector of the Vermas first and foremost, and the tremors had wounded Rajika's son."

"Are we any nearer to the point?" said Ezra.

"Nope," said the detective.

"Ignore them, Echo," soothed Marina, keeping her eyes on the road.

Emerald eyes glistened. "It was in the Royal Park of Richmond I found him. Disheartened that I hadn't been able to find any clues, despite my superior assets compared to a lowly detective—"

"Watch yourself," said Robert.

"I decided to buoy my spirits by hunting the deer in Richmond Park on my way here to meet you."

I jutted out my chin. "Gaia told you not to go there."

"But did she, Alisha? The goddess knows how to play me like a violin. I think she meant to nudge me in that direction without becoming embroiled in matters herself." He gave a throaty purr. "It feels good to be used by her."

Robert smirked. "The leopard sounds like a teenage boy."

Echo's growl reverberated in the van. "I was doing your job, Detective. You see, as well as over six hundred roaming deer in Richmond across a thousand hectares, I stumbled across the epicentre of the tremors—a being whose music called to me. Who would not be drawn to a rendition of *We Will Rock You* on the flute? It's very impressive, given his missing thumb."

I gave him a blank look. "The flute?"

Marina slammed on the brakes. "Pan, as in god of the shepherds and flocks, chaser of nymphs and lover of musical instruments?"

I flew forward.

Ezra pinned me back against the seat.

"Pan, the horny dude who also goes by the name of Faunus?" said Robert. "He's no threat. He settled down. He used to be a porn site owner. He has a thing for mating animals. But now he's a royal gamekeeper and a board member at Battersea Dogs Home."

Echo nodded. "He's quite a strange fellow when you meet him. His clothes reminded me of an English gentleman's, all cord and buttoned-up tweed. Except he had a forward-leaning body, with skinny calves and strong thighs that gave him a ridiculous air. He had pale green eyes and a mop of thick, brown hair. Worst of all were the horns that protruded from his head, covered only by a tatty top hat, which fell off when he saw to the fire. Not forgetting his missing thumb, of course."

My pulse accelerated. "I remember Pan from my parents' stories. He's half divine, half animal. That dualism runs through his personality. He's cheerful and playful one minute and devious and terrifying the next. He likes both disorder and harmony, depending on his mood. He's a trickster god. A god of panic. Which Pan did you meet tonight, Echo?"

"It was a delightful half-hour in his company. Luckily, I hadn't harmed his flock yet, although I had been eyeing some juicy rumps. He was tickled that I shared my given name with a beautiful nymph he used to know. He played his pipe and confided in me that Ra's exploits led to him regaining some of his old strength."

I grimaced. "Pan's strength is legendary. Him getting stronger is not a good development."

Echo growled. "I met a god who is tired of blending in. A god who has reclaimed the thrill he gets from causing panic. A god who agrees with Ra that human suffering causes panic."

Marina frowned. "But how is he making the tremors occur, Echo?"

"By moving the flocks as one, of course. Pan controls them all: the deer, the sheep, the geese, and the goats. It is effortless for him. A simple run of notes on his flute, and they do his bidding, sending tremors through the earth. He revels in the chaos and the panic. The ensuing loud noise of crashing buildings and urgent sirens excites him. He doesn't mean to kill or maim, but this destructive side of him is as much a part of him as the caring side of his flocks. He grows stronger from the prayers of the fearful and grieving. He is enjoying himself for the first time in centuries. He told me himself, from his own lips, just before I came here. He's not going to stop without reason."

Marina sighed and started up the van again. "But why isn't Gaia doing anything about it?"

I folded my arms in anger. "Why does Gaia do anything? She's a law unto herself. And here we are, stuck in the middle of this again."

A wolfish growl met my ears. "I've given up scolding you for flouting the Magical Constitution. There will come a time when you will reap the consequences, but it is not for me to police you. But one thing is set in stone. You promised me that you'd put the trial first, Alisha."

"He's right," said Marina.

"No," said Robert. "He isn't. You lot may not be police officers, but you can't stand back and do nothing about this. It's us, or it's a whole lot of innocents harmed. Will you have that on your conscience?"

Ezra glowered, and nobody said a word. The silence was punctuated only by the splutter of the engine.

"I'm not backing down on this, Ezra. We just can't. I won't," I said. "But tonight, I'm going to meet my dragon, and nobody is holding me back from that."

The tension in his jaw eased, and he sighed. "Okay, hellfire. We'll do it your way. Get your dragon, secure your destiny as an animator, and then we'll find a way to appeal to the trickster god's gentler side."

"Be careful, Alisha," said Echo. "The Celestial Library can be a dangerous place."

Marina drew to a halt outside Shanghai Moon. "It's decided then. Go kick some butt, Alisha. Echo can stay at mine tonight."

I nodded and kicked off my strappy sandals. Then I pulled out my hair clip and left it on Marina's dashboard before tying my hair in a ponytail with a hairband knocking about the van.

Marina gave me a knowing smile. "Uh oh. She means business."

Ezra and I climbed out.

My bare feet hit the asphalt.

Marina's rainbow head leaned out of the window. "Call me."

They drove away, bumping along the uneven street.

Ezra sighed. "Since I can't come with you, do you want me to walk you inside?"

I leaned into his chest for a brief moment. I almost spilt the beans about Orpheus's concerns that Sahil had done something stupid, but I held back. We already had so much on our plates. My brother would have to wait. "Nah, I got this."

"Okay. Good luck, Alisha." He kissed the top of my head and teleported away, leaving me standing in the deserted street, wondering if I had bitten off more than I could chew.

18

Pungent smoke from an incense burner curled through the air as I walked into Shanghai Moon at half past eleven. Fei Yen and Faeza, in matching chequered pyjamas, rushed over in a fluster.

Faeza ushered me towards a small round table. "You're cutting it fine. In half an hour, Beltane will be over, and your passage to the Celestial Library will not be so certain."

"I'm sorry," I said, pressing a kiss on both of their cheeks. "I got here as soon as I could."

Fei Yen frowned. "Why are you barefoot? Have you had trouble with the rats?"

"No, actually, they were delightful tonight if I block their incontinence out of my mind. The bare feet are more because I can't run in high heels." I looked at their tiny feet. "And I'm pretty sure you don't have trainers in size 6 for me to borrow."

Fei Yen shook her head. "I'm afraid we wear children's shoes. A consequence of foot binding. You have your father's picture?"

I nodded and craned my neck to look around the shop. "Are you hiding the gate in plain sight?"

"Something like that." Faeza cleared away a stack of gloopy Chinese takeaway boxes from the table. "Take a seat."

We sat, three women around the table, one in an evening dress, the other two in pyjamas. On the table were a simple lamp and a stack of tarot cards. A midnight blue curtain hung from a circular rail on the ceiling. Fei Yen pulled it over the rail, enclosing us in the soft velvet folds, which glittered with silver sequins that looked like stars.

"Take some deep breaths, Alisha, and remove the frown from your face," said Fei Yen. "While you look quite the picture in that dress with your dirty feet and the scowl, you do not come to the cards with a fighting disposition. You come with a softness."

I filled my cheeks with air and blew out what I could of my stress, although, to be honest, it would take a day with a masseur to really get anywhere. "This isn't what I was expecting."

Fei Yen snorted. "If you are going to succeed in the Otherworld, perhaps it's time for you to clear your mind of expectations. They will only hold you back. Now take some deep breaths."

I resisted the urge to roll my eyes.

Faeza picked up a deck of cards bordered in gold. She shuffled it with the ease of a casino croupier. "In my hands are twenty-two Major Arcana cards and fifty-six Minor Arcana cards across four suits: Cups, Pentacles, Swords, and Wands. I'd like you to tap the deck to spread your energy through them."

I tapped them, and a frisson of anticipation made me shiver.

"Now I need you to ask an open question that will get you closer to the library," said Faeza.

"Sounds easy enough," I said. "Will I make it inside?"

Fei Yen rolled her eyes. "That's just about as closed as it gets."

"Way to put me at ease."

"It's okay, Alisha. Just try again," said Faeza.

"How about…how can I get into the Celestial Library?"

Faeza chewed her lip. "Better but not quite there. It's a little self-serving. The library likes its visitors to be pure of heart."

"Gah, hang on." I slowed down my breathing and closed my eyes. Then it came to me. "Where is the hidden opportunity in a druid visiting the Celestial Library?"

"Yes, I think that might be it." Fei Yen's eyes shone. "And just in time. Hurry, Faeza, Beltane is almost over. We have mere minutes. You'll have to go with a three-card spread, not the Celtic Cross."

Faeza nodded. She cut the deck by dividing it into several piles and then folded them into one again. Then she spread the cards across the table with an artful swish of her hand. "Choose three cards, Alisha. Quickly."

I scanned the cards, my heartbeat hammering. Their backs were satin black with rounded edges. Three floated towards me. I reached out and touched them. "Those ones."

We all leaned forward as Faeza turned over the cards.

"The Two of Cups," she said. On the card, a barely clad man and woman exchanged cups in a ceremony. "This card implies balance, respect and honour. You have the opportunity for new partnerships if you are aware of your talents and strengths as a couple and trust one another to do what you are good at."

"Hurry, my love," said Fei Yen.

Faeza turned over the next two cards in quick succession. "The Ten of Pentacles and the Wheel of Fortune. Oh, Alisha, Alisha. Only your intuition will tell you if these are auspicious cards or not."

On the second card, an old man sat beneath an archway leading to bounteous vineyards. At his feet sat his family. The final card depicted an enormous wheel covered in symbols of the zodiac. A sphinx that reminded me of Wildwoods sat on the top of the wheel. A devil on the bottom.

"My intuition is currently as useful as a lump of rock," I said.

She patted my hand. "The Ten of Pentacles speaks to your ancestry and your future. Your family roots have set you in good stead, and you should have no fear. The wheel symbolises that greater forces than us are at work here. The same forces that govern the changing of the seasons. But the wheel is no cause for fear. It symbolises the relentless forward motion of time but also renewal and growth." They gathered the remaining deck and put it to one side, leaving the three cards I had chosen facing upright. "These are your cards, Alisha, but only one is the gateway. This is your journey now. Choose the door."

I gulped.

"Quickly, Alisha," came Fei Yen's frantic voice. "The window of opportunity is almost gone. Thirty seconds until the clock strikes midnight."

I lunged forward and touched the Ten of Pentacles, thinking of the mum I had lost and the grandmother I had never truly known. I gasped as icy cold travelled up my arm and spread to my whole body, giving me nipples as hard as bullets and stiffness to my very bones. I clamped my eyes shut as fear clouded my mind.

"Breathe," came Fei Yen's soothing voice from far away. "Trust in the universe."

The cold was everywhere. My eyelids, my bum cheeks, my ears and my nose. Everything was so cold it hurt.

Then, somehow, just as Alice went through the looking glass, I went through the tarot card. In that fleeting second, I sensed the turning of the Earth, the heat of the sun, and the death of distant stars. But it was Neptune that called to me, the windiest planet in the solar system.

Part of me wanted to let go, to be lost in the folds of the

world without the need to think or strive or do the laundry. Still, even as I considered it, I knew my loved ones needed me, and I needed them. I was as likely to let them down as I was to eat a whole bag of doughnuts without regrets.

I drew on the strings in my mind and pulled my question close to me. *Where is the hidden opportunity in a druid visiting the Celestial Library?*

Something snapped, and I catapulted forward, too cold to even tremble.

A sudden stop. A warming of the temperature.

I opened my eyes. I was in a great hall bathed in golden light, with white marble pillars threaded with pink veins. A fireplace had been lit in the corner next to two armchairs. It crackled and spat and beckoned me with its glow. I approached it, shaking like a leaf, and sank into an armchair. The blue tinge to my extremities struck me with horror, as if my fingers and toes had been frozen deeply. I was too afraid to check that my bra still held the picture of Tielbu, in case my fingers snapped off before they thawed.

As I considered my options, a strange scratching sounded across the stone floors. A woman wearing a three-quarter-length trouser suit approached. She had a grace about her, from the silver threads in her shoulder-length dreadlocks to the calm in her brown eyes and the sheen of her tawny skin. She wore lashings of mascara and metallic eyeshadow the same shade as the blade runners strapped to her thighs.

A calm descended over me. My intuition told me she wasn't an immediate threat. Well, my intuition and the fact she was carrying gifts which could only be meant for me.

"Welcome, druid," she said with a sad smile. She handed me a hot water bottle, a fluffy dressing gown, slippers for my feet and a cup of sweet, milky tea.

I relaxed into the dressing gown, realising with a start that it was warm, then eased my toes into the slippers. Then I hugged the hot water bottle to me for a moment, placed it on my lap and took a slurp of the tea. Warmth spread through me, and I started to feel more like myself.

"Thank you," I said. "How did you know how I like it?"

"I know lots of things, Alisha Verma. I am the Custodian, after all. I even know that you prefer your tea without sugar unless you are overly tired or have been through an ordeal, in which case you like two heaped spoons of brown sugar."

"How wonderful. Can I stay here forever?" I frowned. "I didn't mean that. Although it is nice here." I blinked, and endless rows of books appeared: leather-bound, pocket-sized, gilded, hardbacked and spiral-bound. "I mean, really nice."

"Oh, this is just the pre-chamber." She sat in the other armchair and crossed one leg over the other so her trouser leg rode up to reveal scarred skin underneath. "First, we must deal with formalities. You came through the tarot?"

I nodded and took another slurp of tea. "I did."

"It was made easier because it is Beltane. The first of May."

The colour had returned to my fingers. "That's right."

She leaned forward, and though the fire spat embers her way, she did not flinch. "And because your grandmother has been here and your mother before that. That is why you came in so easily. Third generation rights. Although that hasn't always worked out so well in the past."

I punched the air, and my tea slopped dangerously against the edges of my cup. "I knew it. I knew Mum had been here."

The Custodian regarded me with narrowed eyes. "Regardless of your gene pool, your visit will end abruptly unless you pass the test."

"Did my mum pass the test?"

A grunt. "Well, of course, she did. She had the wherewithal to bring me a signed first edition. A marvellous addition to my collection, I might add, and a gutsy ploy. She was an impressive woman. I am sorry for your loss, by the way. But for those who fail the test, there is no guarantee that you will be able to return from whence you came."

I sat bolt upright. Now that I was warm, I really didn't want to risk the journey again. Not yet. "My friends didn't tell me that."

"Why would they? Fear would only have made the pull of the dark greater." The Custodian paused. "Regardless of your natural advantages, it's not easy to find your way here. Many have failed before you. Tell me, druid, how did you hold on?"

"My leopard's supply of steak needs replenishing, and I am the woman to do it."

"It is an unusual reason but a valid one." She tapped her knees. "We will begin."

The flames of the fire leapt higher. It blazed, casting shadows deep into the room.

I put my cup aside.

"First, we test your druidness. The library itself is a living organism with likes and dislikes. Just as humans are picky about who is allowed into their inner circle, the library, too, has requirements. For example, it won't lend to people who bend the corners of pages or break the bindings of books. It has a particular dislike for people who leave bogies on pages, which is why a certain Bestiary Minister is never allowed through these doors again."

I wrinkled my nose. "Eww. That's disgusting."

"Since you have entered on Beltane, we will ascertain how druid you are." She raised an eyebrow. "Nobody likes cultural appropriation."

I thought of Orpheus's insistence that I was the product of two druid lines. "I have it on good authority that I am quite druid."

"Then you won't mind answering these questions. Are you a Bard?"

I shook my head. "I am not."

"Can you play any folk instruments?"

"Er, no."

"Not even the banjo?"

"No."

"How about a mandolin?"

"Nope."

"Not even a kazoo?"

I hung my head.

"A sitar?"

She frowned. "Well, that's a disappointment. The sitar is my favourite."

I looked up. "My parents have one gathering dust at their house."

"That's hardly something to boast about. I was hopeful when I saw the tone of your skin that you might be a sitar virtuoso, with you being Indian."

"I have both French and Indian heritage, actually. And I haven't asked you if you can rap just because you are black."

She laughed. "I like straight-talkers. Not many of them left these days." She stood up, and her blade runners tapped against the floor as she strode to the mantlepiece. "Hang on, just let me get the implement."

I didn't like the sound of that. It sounded like some sort of sixteenth-century torture device. "What implement?"

"The one that tells me if I can take a chance on you." She picked up a small oblong object from the mantlepiece and came to my side. "Say ahh."

"Is that hygienic?" I said, just to register some sort of protest. I opened my mouth anyway.

She held it under my tongue, and the clouds cleared from her face. "Just as I thought. One hundred per cent druid. Which means no elvish or vampire blood."

I baulked and drew my head back. "That didn't seem very hygienic. Why are you against elves and vampires?"

"For two very different reasons. This is the Celestial Library. Death doesn't belong in something heavenly. And the elves are a difficult people. All people have both good and bad in them, except the elves too often have let their good side be submerged underneath the darker side of their natures. Whether that is their fault is another matter entirely." She sighed. "Still, it is time for the final obstacle. We must ascertain the purity of your heart."

"How can we possibly do that? Do I pinkie swear? Or do the Scouts' Promise?" I shuddered. "Or must I take a truth serum?"

"Are you always this melodramatic? There is only one way for us to test your heart, and that is by introducing you to Nightfall."

"Nightfall?"

A clacking of hooves echoed through the great hall. My heart clamoured when I saw an enormous black stallion approaching. He whinnied and snorted as he trotted over to the armchairs, and when he reached the Custodian, he tossed his mane and bowed before her. She laid her forehead against his. He nuzzled her, and she laid a gentle hand on his muzzle.

"To pass the test, all you need to do is ride Nightfall from here back to the end of the hall."

"But he's not even wearing a saddle."

Nightfall turned his head towards me. When his demeanour changed, I almost wet myself. I would have preferred to do endless pelvic floor exercises than to ride him. God knew my bladder could have done with a bit more control. He bared his teeth. His ears were forward like he was some sort of Soviet spy actively monitoring me. He surged forward and nudged me.

I recoiled. "He looks a bit demonic if you ask me."

"Alisha, he's in the Celestial Library. Trust me, he's not demonic."

I grimaced. "Oh, I don't know. He looks pretty villainous to me. Is frothing at the mouth normal for him?"

The Custodian sighed. "This is your test, not Nightfall's. Unless you are giving up?"

I shrugged off the dressing gown and my slippers. I'd only ridden a few times before—on family holidays when the horse had been trained to follow a course regardless of who was on its back. This was going to be a whole different ballgame. I took a deep breath and approached Nightfall.

He whinnied, his tail swishing.

"Do you have any carrots? I think I can get him to follow me."

"It's ride or die," said the Custodian.

"Like literally?"

"Your guess is as good as mine."

"That's comforting." I held my hand up to calm Nightfall, whose tail had now reached a frenzy.

He towered over me, his coat so glossy that, without a saddle, I feared falling off. That was if I even made it up there.

"In your own time." The Custodian's voice dripped with sarcasm.

I looked behind me at the armchair.

The horse followed my every move.

I leapt on the armchair, hitched up my dress and sprang onto Nightfall's back, using my strong kickboxing legs to hold on for dear life as he bucked, leaning forward to keep my centre of gravity low.

"Easy, Nightfall." I patted his flank and murmured against his skin. "I'm not going to hurt you."

His ears turned sideways, and the bucking stopped. But I still had no idea how to get him to move in the right direction. I couldn't cling on in a stationary position forever. Not to mention the large expanses of skin I was exposing in an outfit utterly unsuited to this task.

I clamped my legs tighter and windmilled backwards so one arm could reach Nightfall's rump. I was an animal lover. I wouldn't have used a whip even if I'd had one.

Instead, I lifted a hand, my heart racing, and sent a gentle breeze up his arse.

I shrieked and catapulted forwards, slipping and sliding and cursing. The sound of thunderous hooves filled my head: twenty metres, ten metres, five metres from the end of the hall. The books were a blur beside me, and I wondered what would happen if my life ended here, in this limbo place my loved ones couldn't reach.

Nightfall jerked, his hooves now sliding against the floor, his motion slowing.

I took my chance and slipped from his back, twisting as I fell. Horror filled me as I took in the void beyond the hall. The fear in the whites of Nightfall's rolled eyes cut me to the core. I hit the deck and ignored the blunt pain in my forty-year-old back. I raised my hands, called the wind to me, and created a buffer between horse and void. I held it until he regained his footing and then released it. Only then did I collapse onto the floor, utterly spent.

The horse trotted over to me and nuzzled my hair.

I'd need a salt bath after that knock, a whole load of paracetamol and a chiropractor, but at least I'd made a friend.

The Custodian loomed over me. "Bravo, druid."

"I passed?"

A serene smile flitted across the Custodian's lips. "You chose Nightfall's welfare over your own. I'd say that proves your purity of heart, and the library agrees."

"Well, that's a relief." I tugged my dress to preserve my modesty.

"Did you really doubt yourself? Isn't it odd? Women can be as glorious as the night stars but waste time navel-gazing. And yet, flawed, crusty, self-congratulatory men never once consider that someone else might be better placed to pick up the sword."

I looked at her feet. "Is that how you got those? By picking up the sword?"

The Custodian tutted. "That's not something you ask a person on the first encounter."

I flushed. "I'm sorry. I don't even know your name."

"Most people call me by my title. But before that, I was called Calypso Archer."

Now the test was over, I searched her, looking for pointy ears, wings, fangs or hairy body parts. Anything to give me a clue as to where she fitted in the Otherworld. "May I ask what kind of peculiar you are?"

"My dear druid. My talents are many, but they are not peculiar. Come. Time passes quickly between the seams of the world, and you will want some sleep before the day dawns. We find ourselves poised at the threshold. Soon, you will tell me why you have come, but first, your reward for passing the test. You do wish to see the library? All you have to do is open your eyes."

I sat up and groaned. "They are open."

"No, I mean *really* open them."

19

———

I blinked, and the great hall transformed. The walls vanished, and the pillars sank into the ground. The floor surged until it reached farther than the eye could see. I sucked in my breath.

Paintings of angels and cherubs danced on the ceiling in the flickering light of stars and planets. The bookshelves existed still, but they multiplied in number and rose higher still, endless reams of wisdom and love and entertainment between those bindings. Behind us, the fire roared still, primitive and true. The armchairs, however, had become iron thrones with high backs and gilded ridges, and I frowned, thinking how plush the seat had seemed underneath my bottom. Feathers lay under my feet. I wondered if this was a room of tricks or true desires.

Nightfall gave a neigh of goodbye and cantered off into the distance.

Calypso smiled. "You didn't think the library would reveal its true image without you passing the test, did you? Even in the throes of battle with the dark elves, it kept most of its secrets."

I stood, groaning at my aching muscles, then looked around in wonder.

She strode ahead like an impatient guide at a museum. "Do follow. The Celestial Library is not the only moving library in the world. There are physical libraries that are passed down through households, of course. Then there are libraries in the minds of passionate readers, who are just as likely to offer a quote as they are to kiss their mothers. There are libraries on e-readers, entire worlds that fit into a jacket pocket. That's a special kind of magic. There are libraries on rickety wheels that offer a lifeline to poor communities. I especially like those. Oh, and libraries in little boxes at the end of driveways. Not the most glamorous sort but an exemplar of generosity. And finally, rather ridiculously, there's the main library at Indiana University, which sinks an inch into the ground each year because engineers failed to account for the weight of all the books it would eventually hold." She paused. "All those libraries are worthy places, but they are not quite like this one."

I didn't know whether to look up at the angels and planets or sideways at the bookshelves, where I spotted Gaiman, Angelou, Hawking, Austen, Hemingway, L'Engle, Nin and a curious tiny book from 1913 called *Don'ts for Wives* by Blanche Ebbutt.

Calypso grimaced. "Sadly, I'm a custodian, not a curator."

"It's a wonderful collection. I did English Lit at university, you know." For some reason, I craved her approval.

She raised an eyebrow. "There are many other languages with valuable literature apart from English, Alisha."

"Oh, yes, I completely agree." I flushed and stared at the shelves. "There's no particular order. It's not alphabetic or based on genre or even on colour. How are you supposed to find what you want here? Is there a catalogue?"

"Don't be silly. The best reads are discovered by accidental browsing," said Calypso.

"But what if I wanted to read something in particular?"

"Well, then you close your eyes, of course, picture what you want and walk the way the universe pulls you."

A shiver ran up my spine. "That sounds dangerous."

"No worse than crossing the street in London." She gave me the eye. "Now tell me, druid. You are allowed to take one item away from the library. What is your request? Perhaps the first draft of *The Handmaid's Tale* or *Jekyll & Hyde*? Maybe Frida Kahlo's journal interests you more. Or John Travolta's script from *Pulp Fiction*?" She rubbed her hands in glee. "No, I don't think that's quite it. How about an interactive set of *Harry Potter* books? No? Then maybe a copy of *Faustus* once read by the devil himself?"

I took a deep breath. "Actually, it's not books I am after today."

Calypso's brow furrowed. "An English Lit graduate who does not wish to borrow a book?"

"I'd like to read everything in these walls, but sometimes need has to come before desires." Anxiety exploded in my stomach. "I thought after coming all this way, I'd be able to take as much as I wanted."

Calypso grunted. "Like a spoiled child in a sweet shop? I'm sorry, druid. It doesn't work that way. What you take from the library, the library will require back in some form, whether now or at a later date. In a more beautiful world, of course, dealings with the Celestial Library would be less transactional. But this is not a beautiful world. It is a world of monsters."

I gulped. "That's a bit bleak."

"I like to think it's truthful. How can we stand in a place of knowledge and not speak the truth?" She pressed her lips together. "Make your request pure, druid, or the library will exact a price from you greater than you wish to give."

My mind raced through my options. Ezra had encouraged

me to focus all my energy on animating Tielbu here. But he was unfamiliar with the Celestial Library.

How could I turn down the opportunity to return with something wondrous?

Orpheus wanted the remnant of the cross for himself, but he was possibly suicidal. While I didn't want to be responsible for his death, I didn't take his threat to reveal my plans to the senate lightly. Except if I animated Tielbu in the library, the senate wouldn't be able to get their hands on him anyway. Even if Lavinia heard about it, it's not like I had anything to lose. Her trust in me was already broken. So Orpheus was shit out of luck.

I frowned. I could ask for the choker necklace from the will, the one Mum had said I'd find in the seams of the world. The Custodian had confirmed Mum had been here, so it only followed that my hunch had been right. Although maybe it was selfish to come all this way and ask for something of value only to me. Hadn't my very own grandmother laid down her own life in this place for the good of others?

"You seem to be torn," said Calypso.

Something niggled at me. Echo had confirmed that Pan was behind the tremors.

I jumped, sending feathers wafting up. That was it. "I need an artefact, not a book."

Her eyebrows shot up. "And what makes you think we hold artefacts here, druid?"

"I may be new to all this, but I've been listening in my history lessons. I have gone unheard when teaching so many of my own lessons that I always listen when the tables are turned." I paused. "I need something to convince a powerful being to lay down his weapons."

Calypso sighed. "That is never an easy task. You have two options. You can overpower them or convince them of the error of their ways. Neither is easy. Follow me."

She strode on, faster on her blade runners than I could keep up with.

I scampered after her, dirty and tired but with growing certainty that I was right to ignore Orpheus's needs and my own.

The run of bookshelves ended, and Calypso turned into an arched doorway made of oak. She whispered three short words in an unfamiliar tongue, Welsh or Gaelic or something altogether unknown. The door creaked open, and she stepped over the threshold. "Are you coming or not?"

I followed her in with a darting gaze.

The room was small, with low light and a cool temperature. On the floor was a thick rug that muffled the sound of our feet. I inched forward to get a closer look. Brass tables lined the walls, topped with red velvet pillows which displayed wares as if this were a high-end jeweller.

Calypso turned to face me. "There are a small number of vaults like this dotted around the Celestial Library. They are never in the same place. They move like blood cells around a body in a never-ending but random cycle. It's a system put in place by the very first Custodian."

"My grandmother?"

She folded her arms. "I've lost count of the number of times I've been asked that very question. Rajika Verma was the seventy-eighth Custodian. She was an impressive person, but it's tiresome when everything is attributed to her."

I winced. I'd obviously touched a nerve.

Calypso waved a neatly manicured hand. "Each vault contains a number of objects stored separately from the main collection. They are varied in nature, donated by or stolen from heroes and heroines across history. Here is a Girl Scout sash that imbues the wearer with an extraordinary sense of practicality. How do you think Mary Poppins was able to get those Banks children in line? Over there is a telephone that can call anyone, dead or alive."

My heart hammered in my throat. I definitely would be back for that one.

"And over there," said Calypso, "is a key that will fit any type of lock of any type of door or window. We're very careful about who we lend that one out to. There's Shakespeare's quill that makes any struggling author a master playwright, Hemingway's typewriter, of particular value to those who struggle with brevity, and a lens once belonging to Galileo, for those poor at directions."

I frowned. "Isn't that what sat navs are for?"

"Yes, druid, but they always need updating." Calypso walked over to the far corner of the room, where a tightly woven straw bag rested on a cushion. "This is what I think you are looking for: the bag of storm winds gifted to Odysseus. It is a bag of cunning as well as great power because your opponent will not know you are carrying a weapon when they look at it. And as a wind druid, you are well suited to wield this power. It will only be yours momentarily, but it will allow you to carry your opponent far away so that he may never cause harm again." Her tone sharpened. "However, I must warn you, Alisha, that a weapon like this should not be used lightly to solve an argument between men."

"And what if the person in question isn't a man?"

Calypso frowned. "Is he an animal?"

"Half animal, half god, I think."

Her head jerked in surprise. "Do not bite off more than you can chew, druid. The laws of the universe are many. Some are written. Others are convention. Many more are unspoken. It seems to me that you like to bend the rules. Just don't break them, or even your allies won't be able to come to your aid."

The dim lights in the vault turned up a notch and then faded once more as if they had a faulty connection.

"Well, isn't that something?" said Calypso. "It turns out

that the library would like me to bend the rules this time in honour of your grandmother, who once served here." She turned on her heel, crossing to the brass table on the far side, from where she picked up a small piece of wood.

I recoiled, thinking it was the remnant of the true cross and that the universe was telling me to fulfil Orpheus's request after all.

Calypso turned the wood over in her hands, taking great care not to damage it. "I should really wear gloves when handling this. It's cypress wood, found amongst the plains of Mount Ararat where the borders of Turkey, Armenia and Iran intersect."

I peered closer. "Am I supposed to know what it is?"

She huffed. "It's a piece of the bow from Noah's Ark."

"*The* Noah?" There was a nursery around the corner from my flat called Noah's Ark. She was probably talking about that one.

Calypso rubbed her temples like I was giving her a headache. "Of course that Noah. Which other Noah goes by one name only? This artefact might not seem like much, but it has a gentle power. It reminds the holder of their better natures. And believe me, druid, lasting success comes only when you appeal to a person's humanity. Generosity is always more effective than barbarity. Whether you choose to heed my advice is your choice."

I'd heard that advice three times now. From Dad, who had said, *a man can lose his way if he drifts from his faith.* From Gaia, who questioned my own faith and had told me that *not every battle is solved by escalating into war.* And now from the Custodian. *Generosity is always more effective than barbarity.*

"I don't know how to thank you."

She handed me the artefacts.

The bag weighed nothing at all. The wood, too, was so light it was easy to think I was coming away with some fancy dress knockoffs.

"You may take both items, druid, although you may use only one. Borrowers may use artefacts for seven days unless they have a special exemption. On the seventh day, I will collect the items from wherever they are in the universe."

This woman couldn't be cooler.

I wanted her job. The view. The books. The secrets. I wanted to be her.

"If that is all, druid, I will ask Nightfall to take you to the void. You are not the only visitor here tonight."

I swallowed hard. Now didn't seem the right time to ask her for a favour. "Actually, there is the small question of a dragon."

20

Calypso led me out of the vault and locked the door shut behind us. She frowned. "A dragon? There has not been a dragon on earth for many moons, Alisha. Unless you are talking about a fictional one? Smaug from *The Hobbit* perhaps, or Viserion from *A Song of Ice and Fire,* now rather commonly known as *Thrones*?"

I set down the artefacts on a shelf. The picture of Tielbu poked me. "I have something in my bra."

"I'm not the sort of person who responds to being propositioned, druid. I prefer to do the propositioning myself."

My cheeks flushed. "Oh no, you misunderstand. I'm seeing a werewolf, and before that, I had a humdrum husband, who is now an ex-husband, and to be honest, I really should have given myself more time to be alone. So, you see, I really wasn't propositioning you."

She shoved her hands in her pockets, taking her coolness level up to a whole new level. I was pretty sure Marina would find her irresistible.

Calypso pursed her lips. "I don't know whether to be offended or relieved, but we move on."

"Is it true that what happens within this library cannot be seen by anybody on Earth, even gifted peculiars?"

"Not only is that true, but not even those from other planets can see what occurs here. Why do you ask, druid?"

I reached for the picture of Tielbu.

Realisation dawned across her face. "So you have even more in common with your grandmother than I thought. What is it you need from me, granddaughter of Rajika?"

"I need a safe space to animate my dragon. I've been close a few times before. I can feel him underneath my fingertips, but I've never quite had the courage to see it through." I looked around the central space, where the ceilings had opened up again and the planets shone above in the vast void of space. "My gut says that my dragon would quite like to be born here, amongst the stars. What is more, he will be born free, not a slave to those on earth who want to use him. I don't have a child, so I have no idea what it is to be maternal. Maybe the dragon is the closest I'll come to that emotion. All I know is I feel a great sense of responsibility to him. He wouldn't have to stay here, but if this could be the place of his birth, I would be very grateful."

"This is no place for a dragon. Just imagine what his fiery breath would do to my books." Calypso scrutinised me far longer than comfortable. "But I, too, value freedom. I will grant you your request if you grant one for me."

"What do you want?"

"I wish for a day where you swap places with me, and I can roam the world without care or responsibilities."

A day to roam this library without someone looking over my shoulder. Hell, yes. I almost bit her hand off. "Done."

"Then pick up your artefacts, druid, and be quick about it."

She raised her hands like a conductor, and the Celestial Library responded. A shuttering sound occurred, a twisting, a closing, and suddenly the bookshelves vanished, and only bare shelves remained. Calypso whistled low and long and in cantered Nightfall, satin black against the feathery floor. She leapt as he approached, bouncing high off her blade runners and landing cleanly on his back. He whinnied in greeting.

"What are you waiting for?" She leaned down for the artefacts, then again to haul me up behind her, my pelvis tucked in close against her bottom. She rode hard towards the fireplace as the library closed behind us, and a series of locks and bolts echoed in our ears.

This was exactly the kind of dramatic but gentle erotica that made Marina horny. It just made me terrified.

"Phew. That was close," said Calypso as we reached the fireplace. "I hope my other visitor holds his nerve until I get back."

I unpeeled myself from her back, jumped off Nightfall and reached for the artefacts. "Sorry to break it to you, but I'm pretty sure they've pissed on the floor."

"Well, never mind. Clean-up is not part of my job," she said. I was really starting to covet her job. She rode Nightfall to the farthest corner of the room. "It's time to find your courage, druid."

My stomach churned. I laid aside the bag of Odysseus's winds and the piece of Noah's Ark. The air was still and quiet, apart from sighs coming from Nightfall. I blocked out both horse and mistress and unfolded the crumpled picture of Tielbu. I knew him, even though I hadn't yet met him. He'd been with me all my life, so this wasn't like conjuring a stranger. It was conjuring a friend.

A few cleansing breaths later, I was ready to begin.

I trailed my fingers over the page. The flames from the fireplace cast shadows over Tielbu, making him more fearsome than in my childhood stories.

I looked into his gentle, amber eyes. I didn't know if it was the otherworldly strangeness of the Celestial Library, the knowledge that nobody could find us here or the lingering presence of my grandmother, but I formed an instant connection. What I wouldn't have given to have her lead me through this process, but she was long gone. I willed myself to carry on, despite my sweaty palms and quivering limbs.

The lines of the painting danced underneath my fingertips. They shimmered in the half-light, stretching and pulsing like veins. The dragon's thoughts were my thoughts. Or perhaps my thoughts were his thoughts. He was confused and excited, just as I was.

Rings of smoke floated into the air from the page. No, from his nostrils.

It shouldn't have been possible, but it was.

I pushed aside all rules of reality from my brain, concentrating on making the dragon's flesh real, coaxing him off the page with fingers that instinctively knew what to do. His wings stretched off the page, and I couldn't believe my eyes.

The Custodian gasped behind me.

I held my breath.

The dragon's wings solidified before my eyes, bat-like, with the bone structure visible through thin skin. The iridescent blue of the painting oscillated like it was a body of water: blood and cells and fire and heat.

I reached into the page and pulled like I was a midwife delivering a baby. Like this was the deepest meditation of my life.

Tielbu emerged.

He had a round, scaly head with large nostrils and sunken, amber eyes that meant me no harm. Four horns protruded from his head. They were white and tiered, with the two smaller ones at the front near his angular ears. His breath was hot and rancid, with teeth that reminded me of tombstones. He had a long neck, scaly and turquoise like the rest of his body, and a long tail that ended in a sword-like edge. Four slender limbs carried his muscular body, each one ending in sharp, black talons. He was as large as a two-storey house.

My heartbeat thundered as the page disintegrated between my fingers and fell to the ground in embers.

The dragon landed with a thump on the floor under the starry, planet-filled sky of the Celestial Library, and he was the most beautiful, awe-inspiring creature I had ever seen. He retracted his wings and lay in a dazed heap.

Nightfall screamed and galloped away into the dark, shuttered library.

"Tielbu," I breathed.

The dragon tilted his head.

"Mummy?" His voice broke my trance. It was raspy. And needy.

I almost lost all bladder control then and there.

"Well done, druid," said Calypso. "New things always take bravery, and you have excelled yourself many times over tonight. That is not a sight I will ever forget, and for that, I thank you. But now, you must leave."

"What? How?" I said, breaking my eye contact with the dragon at last. She could have let us hole up there for the night. I mean, I felt like I'd just given birth. A cup of tea and toast to recover my energy would have been nice.

Calypso grimaced. "You leave by riding him, of course. That should up your chances of reaching home, and at least you won't be cold this time. Although, a newborn dragon could be pretty erratic. Oh well. Just think of the gateway from which you came. Don't lose focus. I'd hate to have to collect your body, too, when I come for the items you are borrowing."

I gulped. It'd been hard enough riding Nightfall. How on earth was I supposed to ride Tielbu?

"Ride him, druid. Leave it too long, and the bond will wear thin."

I frowned, realising I hadn't thought this through. I'd been so focussed on animating Tielbu and hiding his birth from the senate that I hadn't considered where he would go next to remain under the radar. "But where is he supposed to go?"

The dragon made a rumbling sound in his throat.

I looked at him in alarm.

"That isn't my problem, druid. Did you think you could bring a creature to life just to oil the wheels of your talents and then walk away from him? He is part of you now. It's not like you can release him into space."

"No, of course not." My eyes darted from her to the dragon and back again. I was going to need Marina's help. Hell, I was going to need all my friends. "I'll think of something. I will. Could I have a backpack, at least?"

She kept her distance but pointed to the iron throne. A luminous MC Hammer rucksack hung off its arm, emblazoned with the slogan 'Hammertime'.

I cringed.

"You didn't think a hot water bottle, dressing gown and slippers were all this room was capable of providing, did you? I had front-row tickets to that concert, I'll have you know. MC Hammer headlined, supported by TLC, Boyz II Men and Jodeci." Her eyes had a faraway look. "What a night."

I took small, tentative steps to the iron throne so I didn't unnerve Tielbu. I retrieved the rucksack, placed the artefacts inside, put it on, adjusted the arm straps and clipped on the waistband. "I guess I'm as ready as I'll ever be."

She gave me a wry smile. "I wish you luck, Alisha Verma."

My shoulders were tight as I approached the dragon. Beads of sweat broke out on my upper lip and underneath my breasts as I neared him. Usually, sweaty underboobs were a sign of forty-year-old buxom me weathering a hot summer's day, not the need to mount a flipping dragon.

I steeled myself, remembering how Tielbu from Dad's

stories would never harm an innocent. And he had called me Mummy, so that indicated he probably liked me.

The dragon gave a gentle roar as I approached.

I gritted my teeth and drew closer.

His amber eyes narrowed, and his head turned to face me, nostrils snorting smoke.

"We're going home, Tielbu," I said brightly. "You're going to take me, and then Marina is going to know what to do. You're going to love her as much as you love me."

He lifted his head as if he understood.

I hoped it wasn't to turn those sharp canines on me. I took my chance and clambered onto his scaly back, slipping and sliding across the great expanse of reptilian skin that felt like worn leather, only bumpier, like the scaly underside of a rhododendron leaf.

Tielbu stood up in surprise, turning in a circle and extending his wings.

I shrieked, trying desperately to hold on. My dress had bunched around my waist, and my legs were splayed outwards in a wide-legged straddle, except this was no horse.

Calypso raised her voice above the rush of blood in my ears. "You'll need a better grip than that."

I rolled my eyes. "That's helpful. Thanks."

I shimmied higher up his body, towards his neck. Between his wings was a little dip. I settled myself in it in a jockey position, bum up in the air, centre of gravity low.

"What now?" I asked.

"Think of the gateway," she said.

The floor fell away, and we plummeted like stones in a well.

21

───────

"Oh, my god." Fear clouded my vision as I hung on for dear life. "We're going to die."

How tragic for Tielbu to come to life and then die with me here without fully realising his potential. Forty-year-old me had at least done some cool shit these past few months, and before that, my life had been pretty decent, if you didn't count my gambling ex. Even in the dying throes of my marriage, at least I hadn't been in freefall.

Unlike now.

We fell through the night sky with no chance of survival. Tielbu's hulking body gave me some protection from the cold, but the iciness penetrated my body all the same. Maybe that was why he didn't flap his wings, though each was expanded to a span of five metres. We plummeted, getting closer to death with every passing moment. I had no idea how dragon mummies coached their offspring to fly. My legs seized up in their jockey position, and it was all I could do to hold on.

All coherent thought threatened to leave my brain as hysteria set in.

I'd only managed to animate a flightless dragon —clever me.

Yet, even in the depths of that darkness, against the reptilian skin of the dragon and the deathly beauty of the night, it was my loved ones' faces I saw. Dad, pale against the sheets in his hospital bed with his wiry, unkempt moustache. Rainbow-haired Marina in her rock-chick party outfit. Echo crooning one of his favourite songs. And travelling through the cosmos safe in Ezra's arms. I had to get back to them.

I was done with the freeze response.

My options were fight or flight.

I lifted my hands, numb with cold, moaning as I channelled wind to the dragon's wings. I didn't know if this was all in my head or if I could control my fate and the dragon's, but I tried all the same. I gave it my all.

The dragon roared.

His wings began beating at last.

I collapsed against him, all spent, and pictured Shanghai Moon. There, against my closed eyelids, I conjured curls of incense smoke and rows of teas and, within it, the round table and the tarot card from my reading: the Ten of Pentacles, with its archway, vineyard and elder surrounded by family.

My consciousness slipped away, and I laid my fate in the hands of the universe.

A TUMBLING. A crash.

Some viciously spoken Chinese words that could only have been cursing.

A wail. "She brought the dragon with her. Was that her intention?"

"Who knows? She is like a toddler learning its first steps. A bringer of carnage but lovable."

I lay sprawled and shivering on a hard surface.

Hot breath on my legs warmed me. The heat spread up my limbs and to my flank.

Someone wrapped a blanket around me. "Did she have to land on the table? It's not like we can ask her to pay for the damage on her teacher's salary. Why would a young woman wear such huge knickers?"

The dragon growled with such intensity that my blanket oscillated. He shifted his bulk, and glass shattered.

"We have bigger problems than Alisha's knickers. We should call the vet. She will know how to control it."

"Perhaps his arrival is auspicious."

"Dragons are destroyers."

"They herald great change."

"Perhaps we should tie it up before it fully recovers. If we can get close enough. We might stand a chance as foxes."

The dragon grumbled, but he sounded as dazed as I felt. Thank the stars.

"Maybe we should run for it. A dragon doesn't just sit pretty. They are apex predators."

"We can't leave Alisha here. They eat humans, you know. Night class is nothing without her."

I opened one eye and then shut it again. I wasn't ready to face reality.

"She is pretending to be unconscious. See, just like a toddler. Next, she'll want us to play peekaboo."

A shadow fell over me. "Wakey, wakey, Alisha. It's time to clean up your mess."

I sighed and sat up. "Hi Fei Yen and Faeza. Surprise. I made it."

The dragon turned his head my way. Wounded amber eyes that needed me.

Fei Yen slapped her forehead. It was the biggest break of politeness I'd ever witnessed from her. "Not a good surprise, considering the chaos you have brought with you."

"You can scold her later, Fei Yen. She must close the gate." Faeza fumbled in the pocket of her pyjamas for the Ten of

Pentacles. The card, which had been in pristine condition, was now curled and blackened at the edges.

I stared at it. "What must I do?"

"Burn it, of course," said Fei Yen.

My eyes widened. "With dragon breath?"

Faeza snorted. "No. We are in a populous city of millions of people. We are also standing in the home that Fei Yen and I care very much for. No dragon breath in here. Use matches."

She handed me some from her other pyjama pocket, impressing me with her organisational skills. But in her mood, I decided not to compliment her in case she bit my head off.

The dragon tried to get up, but I was certain he'd take down the ceiling if he did.

I put up my hands. "No, no, Tielbu. You must stay with your belly to the ground, or you'll destroy their home. No getting up and no opening your wings."

He grumbled and collapsed his weight onto his slim forelimbs. Then he crept forward in a belly shuffle.

Immediate danger over, I turned back to the tarot card. I didn't need eyes at the back of my head to track Tielbu's progress through the shop. The sounds of chaos gave it away. I held the card up and set light to it, letting it smoulder in my fingers before using my power to suppress the flame. A pang of sadness flared in my stomach. Who knew when I would see the Custodian and the Celestial Library again?

Fei Yen swung in my direction. "Now that the ritual is complete, it's time for some home-truths."

I smiled. "That is an excellent word, Fei Yen. Well done."

Her delicate eyebrows knitted together. "You're not a teacher at this moment. You are a very naughty student. You brought a dragon to our shop. This is our home, not a playpen for dangerous exotic creatures."

The dragon upended a crystal display with a resounding clatter.

I winced. "I'm sorry. I was out of my depth up there. I was winging it."

"We were afraid he was going to breathe his fire on us and turn us into charred husks," said Fei Yen. "But we are in one piece. For now. Dragons are volatile creatures."

Truth be told, he didn't look volatile, judging by his body language: relaxed muscles, retracted wings and slightly forward-leaning ears. He was clumsy but content. His long tail swung as he snorted and sniffed the shop with all its exotic wares. He had taken a particular fancy to a bucketful of what appeared to be magic mushrooms.

Faeza took the mushrooms away, careful not to turn her back on the dragon, and disappeared into the back of the shop, returning with a hot mug with a lid and what looked like a portion of duck pancakes in a metal dish. She gave Tielbu the duck pancakes and pressed the mug into my hands. "Drink up. Hot tea without milk will give you energy and lower your stress hormones. The snack will keep the dragon busy while we decide what to do."

I accepted the tea gratefully. The sweet scent of pumpkin and aniseed washed over me as I flicked open the lid of the mug. I slurped it down in one go like I'd gone days without water, then set it aside. "I'll pay for the table and the broken items, you know. I wouldn't leave you with this mess."

Fei Yen nodded. "We'll send the bill to your flat."

"How long was I gone?"

"Forty minutes, tops," said Faeza.

I looked at the clock in amazement. "That's impossible."

A rumbling purr came deep from within the dragon. Apparently, the duck was going down well.

"Time passes differently in the Celestial Library." Faeza tore her gaze away from Tielbu, who picked at the duck pancakes and seemed to take up at least half of the shop, even sprawled on his belly. "What happened to you, Alisha? It looks like you've been through the wars. Your dress is ripped to shreds. And what is the rucksack on your back? You didn't travel with that. What is hammertime?"

"You can't touch this," I said.

Faeza frowned.

We didn't have time to explain pop culture references. I decided to leave that for the next night class. "Never mind. Before we get to the rucksack, we need to call Marina because I'm pretty sure the dragon isn't going to sit prettily for much longer. I should let Dad know too. Tielbu is his creation as much as mine."

"Fair enough, but you should change into a spare set of our pyjamas because your father has had too many scares recently to be frightened out of his wits by you looking like that," said Faeza. "A daughter should always care for her father's feelings. Unless he is an arsehole."

"Faeza," I said. "I had no idea you had a potty mouth in English."

Fei Yen smiled at her wife. "She has a potty mouth in many languages. Let's call your people, Alisha. Just promise that when this is all over, you will get back to being the night class teacher we love so much."

22

———————

W e squeezed into Shanghai Moon: six adults and a
dragon.

"I never thought the day would come when I'd see a
dragon in Shanghai Moon," said Marina.

Faeza grinned. "Then you underestimated the power of
our humble little shop. Everything is possible here."

Luckily, Marina had the foresight to leave Robert at her
flat baby-sitting Echo. Not that I would have minded the
detective joining our meeting. It was more that Echo's
presence always added to the unpredictability of a situation,
and we currently had much more unpredictability than I
could possibly stomach. The quick wash in Fei Yen and
Faeza's bathroom hadn't been enough to rejuvenate me.

My heart craved a pen, a crossword book and an empty
room.

My mind knew we had to solve the problem of Tielbu and
quickly.

My body wanted Ezra there and then, with cream on top.

"Let me get this straight," said Ezra. "In less than an hour,
you found your way to the Celestial Library, gained both the

library and the Custodian's trust and borrowed two magical artefacts?"

"Uh-huh. But the question is, what were you doing at Marina's place? The last I knew, she was racing off with Robert and Echo, and you had teleported away."

Grey eyes shone. "You wanted the world to stop for you just because you weren't in it? Or are you jealous of Marina and me spending time together?" He glanced at Fei Yen and Faeza. "What is it with the three of you wearing matching pyjamas?" He grinned. "I dig it."

I made a Herculean effort to focus, despite my tongue tangling. "No flirting right now. Can't you see what's in the room?"

Tielbu lumbered towards us, his tail swinging like an axe, hacking down a display of aromatherapy posters.

Ezra didn't miss a beat. "I'm trying *not* to see him. I'm torn between exasperation and awe. You've done something amazing, but I hoped you'd keep the dragon hidden away a bit longer. You've made it a thousand times harder to pull the wool over my aunt's eyes by bringing him to the city so soon. She's still in the throes of her madness against the elves."

My heartbeat accelerated. I needed my friends right now. I couldn't pull off a dragon heist across London without them. "You will help me, though, Ezra? And if Lavinia asks you outright about the dragon, will you lie for me?"

His voice lost its hard edge. "Look, you've put me between a rock and a hard place. I don't want to declare outright war on my aunts if I can help it. And as Justice Minister, Gunnolf is gunning for the elves too. I'll help you, Alisha, but I'm not sure I can lie for you. The pack bond is so strong that my alpha would know anyway. And opposing my aunts never ends well."

It hurt that he wasn't putting me first, but maybe that was asking too much, too soon.

But I had to protect Tielbu.

"Will you two stop bickering and look at this magnificent creature?" Dad teared up. "I thought I saw my mother do astonishing things, but this is right up there with her greatest feats."

Marina's jaw had slackened with wonder. "I don't think I've ever seen a creature so magnificent. Not even the tortoises on the Galapagos Islands or the penguins at Boulders Bay. I can die happy now I've seen him."

Ezra sighed. "After all your doubts, Alisha, you managed to animate a dragon in a strange place without any of us holding your hand. I've never trained an initiate quite like you. You'll pass the trial with flying colours. That is if you don't turn the whole senate against you by waving a much-coveted dragon under their noses and then denying it to them."

"Then we have to hide him quickly, before anyone notices and before Lavinia or Gunnolf puts you on the spot."

The dragon half-heartedly clawed a display of calligraphy with his black talons.

Ezra stared at him. "He's not very driven, is he? I mean, in the stories of old, a dragon would be rearing up against its enemies, burning them alive, plucking villagers from their dwellings and dropping them from a great height. This one is almost aimless. More sloth than dragon."

"He's concussed," said Marina. "I expect he took quite a knock falling into the shop. But look at his eyes. It feels like he's following our conversation."

I winced. "Yeah, about that. I might have forgotten to give him a purpose as I was animating him. In all the stress, it kind of slipped my mind. But I think his lacklustre scouting in this shop is because I told him to be careful."

Ezra turned on me. "Dammit, Alisha. You can't be serious. A purpose might have prevented him from being manipulated by the senate, and you even failed to do that. We went over this. It's how it's been done for centuries.

Animators assign purposes at the moment of birth. Now we have a deadly weapon that is a blank slate. I could kill you."

Tielbu lunged at Ezra with a roar.

Ezra flinched and teleported a safe distance away.

"It's okay, Tielbu." I laid a trembling hand on his dry, reptilian skin. It couldn't have been more different to stroking Echo.

"I'd say right now the dragon's instincts are to protect Alisha," said Marina. "As for you two, you might be in love, but you sure know how to be at loggerheads."

I frowned. "We are not in love."

"You can't pull the wool over an empath's eyes," said Marina. "So unless you want this city to fall to pieces, zip it. No one says a word unless you put dragon care at the top of the agenda. Do you want my professional help or not?"

Fei Yen and Faeza grinned.

"She is awesome," said Fei Yen.

"We should invite her for takeout," said Faeza.

Marina gave them a quizzical look.

"We don't cook," said Faeza. "But we'd learn for you."

Ezra snorted. "That sounds like a booty call if I ever heard one."

I rolled my eyes at him. "Marina's right. We need to focus on the dragon."

Marina neared the dragon, taking her sweet time, and when she was a few inches away, she picked up a piece of duck that had been a victim of Tielbu's poor table manners and placed it in front of his talons.

Tielbu surged forward on his belly and retrieved it. His tail swung around.

I gasped. "Watch out!"

Marina jumped back, narrowly avoiding being slashed. "I'd quite like to keep my body intact, thank you very much, Tielbu. My Merck Veterinary Manual isn't exactly going to help work out his needs, and we don't have time to go through folklore or Grimm's Fairy Tales for inspiration. Despite his full-grown size, he's like a newborn. He doesn't know how to exist in this world, and he doesn't have a mother to teach him."

Tielbu swung his horned head towards me. The word came out as clear as day. "Mummy."

Marina's eyes widened. "He can communicate with words?"

"This isn't the grandchild I expected," said Dad drily.

Ezra gave a heavy sigh. "What I see is a weapon that just became even more valuable."

"Fictional dragons eat humans, but let's hope it doesn't come to that," said Marina. "I think since he's a newborn, he'll take his cue from us about eating. I'm a bit reluctant to feed him live sheep, and I really like lambs." She pressed her lips together. "He definitely needs more space. I don't know what to suggest, apart from maybe letting him loose in Richmond Park and letting him eat Pan. That would kill two birds with one stone."

I raised my eyebrows. "Er, Pan's immortal, Marina."

"Oh yeah, I forgot. My bad."

"I watched a documentary on bearded dragons recently," I said. "They eat live food. Crickets, mealworms and ringworms, that sort of thing. They also eat veg and leafy greens. A hipster menu. You know, sweet potato, lettuce, kale, parsley."

"That's like comparing a tadpole to an alligator," said Ezra. "Look at those canines. He needs meat."

Marina brightened up. "I know. I have this friend who is into picking up roadkill. He gives saving them a go, but more often than not, it's too late. Like, these deer and squirrels and pigeons are properly squished. It's really sad. I'll get him to hook us up for Tielbu. Plenty of fresh water also, please. And be prepared for the amount of waste he's going to excrete. It's not going to be pretty."

Fei Yen and Faeza groaned.

"You have an hour to move him," they said in unison.

I turned pleading eyes on Dad. "How about your house, Dad? You've got plenty of space."

Dad shook his head. "Uh-uh. What would the neighbours think? We can't get a glamour from the witches because they can't know he exists. Even if he did have a glamour, word would spread amongst peculiars within seconds. My house isn't becoming some sort of magical peep show."

"I wish we could be more generous. As foxes, we have a few hiding places around the city, but none is big enough to house a dragon," said Fei Yen. "We work hard at keeping our boundaries. You know how it is. Everyone wants to take an inch."

Faeza winced as the dragon lumbered forward to sniff a sticky patch on the floor. "We're truly sorry. We know what it is like to be outsiders, but we need to think about our well-being. We don't bear the dragon any ill will. But there is only so long our neighbours will chalk his roaring up as the sound of a passing freight train, and we have a shop to run. If we can help to move him safely, we stand ready."

Dad peered at Ezra's charm necklace. "Are any of those trinkets you wear around your neck of any use?"

"Afraid not, Joshi," said Ezra with a hard smile. "Dragon-charmer isn't really something that comes up often. But there are some woods I know. They could work as a hiding place just until the dust settles. The woods are off the beaten track and border the motorway, so any noise the dragon makes will be masked by the sound of the cars. There are no houses for miles."

"The woods where the wolves run? Next to your farmhouse?" I asked.

Ezra frowned. "Hell, no. That would be serving him up to Gunnolf on a platter. There's no way I want to reignite a war between the witches and werewolves. It was bad enough when they were warring over me."

"Okay. Other woods then," I said. "Only, how on earth are we going to get him there?"

Marina frowned. "I could tranquillise him, but I'd be taking a wild guess on how much I'd need and how long he'd stay down. It's not like he can fit in the back of my van anyway."

"There's no way I'm teleporting him," said Ezra. "That was hairy enough with the leopard. And we can't go to the bestiary master for help, or the dragon will end up in captivity like Kraglek. Whatever else, he is bonded to you, Alisha. You could ride him to the woods, couldn't you?"

Marina perked up. "That would be awesome."

"With all the CCTV in this country? Or do you think I could just ride up until we have cloud cover and hope not to show up on flight radar? Look at the size of him. You haven't even seen him fully stretched out. It's not like he'd be mistaken for a seagull or eagle. There'd be geeks with binoculars talking about UFO sightings within minutes." I cringed. "Riding a dragon isn't like taking up horse reins. I have no idea how to guide him. It's not like he'll follow sat nav directions. It's a shot in the dark."

Dad nodded. "I don't know about the rest of you, but I'd rather my daughter didn't fall to her death."

"As far as I can see, we have two choices," I said. The dragon's unblinking amber eyes followed my every move. "We call Gaia or Orpheus."

Ezra groaned. "Neither vampire nor goddess can be fully trusted."

"Orpheus might be demanding, but I think he's on my side, and his abilities could come in handy," I said. "If the dragon is seen, he has the ability to wipe the episode from the minds of witnesses. But he is quick to anger. It must be a vampire thing. And he's going to be livid that I didn't bring him the stake." I sighed. "If we can't have a glamour from the witches and we don't want to risk Orpheus's anger, maybe Gaia can turn him into something that Lavinia wouldn't even bat an eyelid at."

Dad beamed. "So, do I finally get to meet the goddess?"

"I guess so, Dad."

The jars in the shop rattled.

The dragon lifted his head, fixing an intense gaze on the spot behind me.

Ezra grimaced. "Alisha, bringing in Gaia doesn't always calm things."

I shrugged. "What other choice do we have?"

The rattling grew more insistent. Light fittings swung.

I gripped Dad. "Pan's at it again. Take cover, everyone."

The dragon let out a roar so fierce I jumped out of my skin, but all eyes turned away from him and onto something or someone behind me.

My body quivered as I spun around.

"I thought you'd never call, druid." Gaia's eyes flashed with annoyance. "How rude of you not to introduce me to the dragon straight away. Worse still, you wanted to call a vampire ghoul to your aid instead of a goddess. If it were any other age, I'd put you across my knee and give you a spanking."

23

Gaia was a sight for my troubled heart. Not her beauty —although I had often known her to be beautiful—but her soothing presence. Ezra was sceptical about the gods, but in the time I'd known Gaia, I'd come to realise she didn't just make plants grow. She had the same impact on creatures, human or not. That was why it had seemed like a betrayal when she'd not intervened to save Mum. I hoped she'd make a different decision about Tielbu. The Goddess of the Earth was all about life, after all. If she couldn't provide camouflage for Tielbu, at the very least, then she wasn't fit to be a goddess.

Tonight, her hair hung in limp strands down her back as if it had been oiled. Her skin was free of makeup, and she wore a simple, short-sleeved nightdress that fell to her calves. Like any woman past middle age, she'd taken the time to put on a bra before leaving her house. The toenails on her bare feet had been painted fire-engine red.

I bowed my head in greeting and then met her shining eyes. "Goddess, I hadn't yet uttered a prayer to call you or made an offering. How did you know to come?"

A benevolent smile deepened the creases on her face. "Oh,

I've been tuning in and out now that we're friends, druid."

She turned her eyes to those gathered, beaming at the sight of Tielbu.

Fei Yen and Faeza executed perfect bows with their hands pressed together.

"Goddess, welcome. Can we bring you some tea?" said Fei Yen.

Gaia beamed. "No, thank you, foxes. I had my chai tonight. Otherwise, I'd never sleep."

Marina curtsied. Ezra gave a wry smile.

Dad came forward and knelt at Gaia's feet. "Goddess, we meet at last."

She nodded at him. "Hello, Joshi, son of Rajika Verma, pitied by the leopard, broken by Pan's earthquake."

I frowned. "You knew? You knew Pan caused the tremors?"

She snorted. "Of course I did. There are not many things on God's green earth I don't know. But I also told you I try not to get involved in these things. The backlash is sometimes not worth the reward. Besides, I quite like Pan. He's not all bad, although sometimes he does bad things."

A ripple of annoyance ran through me. "You often point me towards danger when you are infinitely more powerful. Like sending an ant into a bullfight."

"You forget, druid. When the heavens crumbled, the power of the gods was rendered finite. So it's more like sending an ant to fight a monkey. Maybe you should listen more carefully. Like other humans, you only hear what you want to. What I said was danger is sometimes best avoided. A mind can do more damage than a sword 99.9% of the time. Why else do you think old women so often have the last laugh?" Her eyes sparkled. "Isn't this just a wonderful pyjama party? Now move aside so I can make the acquaintance of this wonder." She strode forward to meet Tielbu, showing not an ounce of fear.

He purred as she inspected him.

"Just marvellous." She opened his mouth and knocked on his teeth, unafraid that he might burn her with the fire that surely lurked within him. Next, she trailed her fingers down the length of his scaly body, like a trainer inspecting a racehorse. Then she picked up a translucent, bat-like wing to examine the bone structure underneath. When she had finished, she returned to his horned head with a nod of satisfaction. "Seeing him reminds me of the days when the Earth was young and teemed with creatures long forgotten. You wouldn't have received this gift from the universe unless you'd shown great selflessness, druid. It seems we have chosen well."

"Forgive me, goddess. What do you mean by *we*?" said Dad.

Gaia's eyes twinkled with mischief. "You misheard, Joshi, son of Rajika. Your human ears are no doubt full of residue. An affliction left over from when Adam was made of clay."

I clasped my hands together. "Goddess, is it possible for you to transform the dragon into another creature? I know it's a big ask, and I know you have to be careful about how much power you expend. But I wouldn't ask if it wasn't important. Without your help, the dragon risks being used in a war against the elves."

All eyes turned to Gaia.

She paced across the debris-ridden shop floor as if it were a stage, enjoying the attention. "I could do what you ask. I suppose I could transform him into a Komodo dragon. They are lizards, of course, but close enough in biology for it not to be too much of a stretch. Or maybe a dragonfly would be preferable? Petaltail dragonflies were around in the Jurassic age and are quite spectacular at aerial acrobatics. Or perhaps a black dragonfish. The males of the species are nothing special, but the females have long black bodies and fang-like teeth, plus light-emitting organs dotted about their heads and bodies. We could release him into the Thames. It could be a good fit if we changed his sex."

"Much as I love Tielbu in his current form, all three options would be much easier to transport and nourish than a dragon," said Marina.

"So, will you help us?" I said.

Gaia smiled. "No."

Behind me, Ezra groaned. "Bloody typical."

Gaia threw him a look of disdain. "Watch your tongue, werewolf, or the heavens will smite you."

Dad nodded at Gaia. "Well said, goddess. The men she brings home do make me wonder."

I gave a nervous laugh. We were running out of options. "Why won't you help us?"

"Because, my dear druid, why should the dragon—or you, for that matter—hide your light under a bushel? Your enemies should respect you. Not because you wish to cause bloodshed. Because without respect, there is no progress. You are no longer the druid woman with power over the wind. You are the mother of a dragon. The rider of a dragon. At least for today. My advice to you is to keep the dragon just as he is and hide him in plain sight. Take it from a goddess who hides amongst humans. It is far easier to hide in plain sight than one would think. A walking stick, a few grey hairs, a basket of grubby laundry...There are so many ways to convince someone that the dragon is harmless." Her eyes twinkled. "He could be a movie prop, say, or a statue or part of a grand festival. No one is going to think he is real. And if they do..." She shrugged. "Everyone else will think they are crazy. The average mortal mind just can't keep up."

I slumped down against a wall, defeated. "Forgive me, goddess, but that is shockingly unhelpful."

"Is it? The path is yours, Alisha, not mine. You must decide how to proceed. As they say, the date of your birth and death are written. Everything in between is your choice." She smiled. "Your choice to borrow those items from the Celestial Library was an interesting one. I can sense the power in the rucksack from here. Are you hiding a holy item in there?"

I chewed my lip. "Perhaps."

Gaia's eyes shone. "Is it from one of the prophets?"

I nodded. "One of them."

"Abraham's staff?" she said, approaching it.

My heart thudded. I wanted to trust her, but she was so wily. "Nope."

A look of frustration passed over her face. "Moses's basket?"

"No."

She giggled as Tielbu blew rings of smoke into the air, making the rest of us splutter. "Very well, druid. You may keep your secrets." A distant look entered her eyes. "My other work calls. One of my rascals is knocking on my front door as we speak. It may be the middle of the night, but my home is always a safe haven. I never liked the concept of latch-key kids. I'm the neighbourhood grandmother who feeds anyone who comes to my door and offers them a listening ear. I dare not keep him waiting. When youth crime goes up in London, I always feel a pang of guilt that I didn't bake enough cookies." She touched my back, and healing warmth pulsed into it, where I had cracked it against the floor of the Celestial Library during my test with Nightfall. "I wish you and the dragon well, Alisha Verma."

***

FEI YEN and Faeza dragged boxes from their storeroom and carefully unpacked them on the shop floor. Out came two colourful, lightweight dragon heads and two long serpent-shaped bodies on poles made from bamboo hoops and rich fabric. The yellow, gold, red and silver costumes shimmered in the twilight.

"Londoners are used to diversity on the streets of their city. This may not be China Town, but the people of Balham are kind. And often drunk. Dragons bring good fortune and prosperity. This will work," said Faeza.

Fei Yen nodded. "We will do a dragon dance across the city to your woods, werewolf. Faeza will wear the head of the first dragon, with Alisha and Ezra manoeuvring its rear. Tielbu will be sandwiched in the middle. I will lead the final dragon, with Marina and Joshi making up the body. We've just got to hope any passers-by think he is an exquisite costume. The goddess is wise for guiding us in this direction."

Ezra rolled his eyes. "The goddess is out of her mind."

"Who are we to doubt her?" said Dad.

I sighed. "Well, I guess we'll have to give it a go because the dragon is not the only problem on my list."

Melancholy amber eyes stared at me like he understood every word.

I'd have to be more careful about how I talked in his presence.

Faeza picked up a red dragon head. "Our aim is for the spectacle of the two outer dragons to mask Tielbu. It takes years to learn how to do a dragon dance with skill. For today, we will be a roaming dragon with wave-like movements. Just make sure the body keeps in time with the head."

Marina tied up her hair and sniggered. "This is going to be a car crash."

"Yep," said Ezra, grey eyes brooding. "I'm more a stand-at-the-bar-and-drink kind of guy."

"If we make it to the woods, my roadkill supplier is going to land us with a feast fit for a dragon," said Marina.

"This is the most fun I've had since Rosalie died," said Dad, picking up the green dragon's body. "I don't care if I have to be a dragon tail. I don't ever want this night to end."

I picked up the body of the red dragon. "At this time, the

streets aren't going to be heaving. But we will be bumping into cleaners, nightclub revellers, transport workers, bouncers and bar staff." I approached Tielbu. He made space for me between his front limbs, but I had too much of a healthy respect for his sharp talons to get too close. "If you can understand me, please just copy our movements. We don't want anyone to notice you. There are rats and people and witches and fairies and worse in this city who would do you harm. Stay close. Stay on the ground. And under no circumstances breathe fire."

Ezra raised an eyebrow. "Like that's going to help, hellfire. Come on, let's get this over with."

I fetched my rucksack—ignoring Ezra's inquisitive glance —and we sorted ourselves into our teams. Faeza, Ezra and I headed up the procession in the red dragon. I coaxed Tielbu to follow me. Fei Yen, Marina and Dad brought up the rear in the green dragon.

There could be no comparison between the real and the fabric dragons. Tielbu was much larger, even when we held the fabric dragons aloft. His sunken eyes, protruding horns and scaly, turquoise skin made a mockery of our costumes. No artist or designer could have emulated the horror of his bone-crunching teeth. But still, we continued with our plan in the hope that both humdrum and peculiar eyes would be fooled by the mundane exterior of our world to give the possibility of a dragon credence.

Out, out into the cool early morning air, where the night was lifting, and the streetlights still shone. Out, out into the grimy South London streets with a magnificent dragon in tow, into a world where men still hunted animals for their skins. Out, with the dragon unfurling his cramped limbs and standing tall between us. Out, with my heart pounding and Ezra stiff with nerves in front of me, to spirit a dragon across London to deep dark woods at the edge of the M25.

24

We crossed the city from Balham, heading northeast towards the woods. The streets should have been empty, but we came across pockets of people praying, their eyes shut in fervour. I spotted placards resting at their sides, blood red on white.

The end is nigh. Make your peace.

God dooms the unfaithful.

The tremors are God's anger brought to life.

I frowned. "What's going on?"

"It's the tremors," said Ezra. "The folk here think it's a sign of the end of the world. There are reports of atheists asking to be baptised overnight. Of priests having to turn strangers away from confession. Prayer houses are full to the brim with all-night mass. It will only make Pan stronger."

Still, our dragon dance didn't have a dedicated audience. We jolted and bumped and dragged the costumes through the streets, led heroically by Fei Yen and Faeza. Ours wasn't a fluid dance or imaginative one, but there was something special about it all the same. About the ripples in the red dragon, aided by my wind powers. About the feeling in the green dragon, aided by Marina's empathy.

The six of us had come together to sneak Tielbu to safety, even though the dragon dance was out of our comfort zones. If we'd been part of a parade in China Town, we would have drawn ridicule for our lack of skill, but at the early hour, we delighted passers-by too tired, preoccupied or stoned to look too closely. We danced down endless streets until the red and the green dragons achieved a rhythm of their own. Tielbu ambled along, snorting and sniffing overflowing bins. He followed me, less obedient duckling than distracted teenager on a school trip.

"Keep up," I urged, my arms aching from holding the prop aloft.

There was a sense of freedom about attempting something so brazen. Like riding the tube without a ticket or skinny-dipping in a public lake.

In a way, it made me feel alive.

Which was weird, given how close we were to discovery. How one false step could blow our plans to kingdom come and endanger us all for our duplicitous plan.

A four-year-old with a mop of ginger hair drew up alongside us at a zebra crossing. "Look, Mama. It's a dragon."

"Uh-huh," said his bleary-eyed mother. "Give the nice dragon a wave."

Next came a homeless man sheltering in the doorway of a charity shop, whose eyes followed us the length of the road.

"All right, mate?" said Marina.

He gave her a stained-tooth smile. "I'm still dreaming, love."

In Peckham, stoned students joined our parade for a few blocks, congratulating us on our lifelike blue dragon.

Gaia had been right. It was difficult to upend a prevailing reality, even when the evidence was in front of humdrum noses. They were much more likely to assign mundane explanations to extraordinary events.

Ezra was so close I could touch him, with his tight arse in

his tux trousers and his grey-streaked hair curling over the white of his collar. I didn't touch, though. I wasn't a creepy old git in a pub. I gave his tapered hips and strong arms the odd admiring glance as we worked together to keep the accordion movement of the green dragon in motion. Our dragon dance took place without a drumbeat, which meant we could converse. I let my guard down and stopped focusing on Tielbu. I forgot he had understood my words and that I should be careful about what he heard.

"This is the most surreal mission I've ever been on," said Ezra. "You continue to turn my life upside down, hellfire."

I poked the small of his back. "Is that a good thing?"

He grinned. "Well, it isn't boring. Who knew middle-aged women would be such a handful?"

"In more ways than one." I teased.

Faeza tossed us a look over her shoulder. "Stop talking. Keep moving, you two. You have as much rhythm in your bodies as a pair of snails."

Ezra waggled his eyebrows at me as he manoeuvred the midsection of the green dragon in a wave movement.

I giggled. "If only there weren't a god meddling in this city again, a maniacal senate and a morbid vampire, I might just be prepared for a certain werewolf-wizard to swoop me off my feet."

Ezra's tone sobered. "I didn't peg you as an MC Hammer fan. What is it you have in that rucksack, Alisha?"

I sighed. "Odysseus's bag of winds and a piece of cypress wood from the bow of Noah's Ark."

He froze, disrupting the dance. "Bloody hell. You're going to take on Pan."

I bumped into his back. "I am."

"Keep moving!" said Faeza. We hadn't even reached the banks of the Thames yet.

"What's going on?" called Marina from under the green dragon.

Ezra ignored her. His eyes narrowed. "What if he kills you?"

Behind me, the dragon growled.

I shushed him and turned back to Ezra. "I don't think it'll come to that. And I'm so tired of people underestimating me."

Our eyes locked. "We are trying to protect you."

"Then stand by my side."

"Dammit, hellfire," said Ezra. "You're stubborn as hell."

"I'd rather die fighting than standby while innocents are in danger. I'll take on the god. And if he turns his fire on me, I'll think of something. Or you will."

The dragon roared, and this time no chugging trains or spluttering buses could obscure the sound.

Nor could the costumes we carried mask the fact that he was real. Not when I'd lost control of him in the middle of the waking city. One minute, he was safely sandwiched between the red and green dragon. The next, he raised his head and stretched his translucent wings. We watched, gobsmacked, as he left our ranks and flew across London.

I wasn't sure how it happened or what spooked him. Whether it was the sense that I was in danger or that I wasn't in control. Animals did that. They took control if you lost it, and I was no alpha. I wasn't even a mother. I was just a druid woman out of my depth.

I prayed Lavinia's rats had their eyes downcast. I prayed nobody would look up. That if they did, they would see the dragon and think him to be an aeroplane. Or that they were in the middle of a mental health crisis. Anything but the truth. Because, dammit, I was days away from my magical trial, and it was a really bad time to be singlehandedly responsible for outing the existence of peculiars to all of humankind. There could be no punishment large enough for such a screaming faux pas. I would die of shame, even if they let me live. Unless a city-wide *Men in Black*-type neuralyzer was actually a thing.

I'd have to ask Orpheus, after all. Not that he'd help me once he found out I didn't fetch him the stake from the cross like a good little doggy.

We dropped the costumes and tracked the dragon's progress across the sky. Only when he disappeared from sight did we turn to each other in horror.

"I'll teleport after him," said Ezra. "Except we don't know where he went."

Dad was downcast. "Don't worry, Alisha. We'll get him back. The goddess was wrong."

"I told you religion always messes things up. Science is much more reliable. I'll get my tranquilliser," said Marina, ashen-faced.

"We need to get back to the shop," said the foxes. "It's almost opening time, and the dragon caused much damage."

Marina's mobile phone buzzed. "Robert? It's not a good time."

His voice came through loud and clear. "Mi5 chatter is going into overdrive. Apparently, there's a dragon sitting on Big Ben. You lost him, didn't you?"

Tielbu was in Westminster, atop arguably the most famous landmark in the country. Perhaps it was the chimes of Big Ben that drew him as the clock struck six in the morning. He was cleverer than I'd given him credit for—less mewling babe at my breast than a toothy, flame-throwing alien that was probably ravenously hungry. I had no idea how malleable or deadly he could be in the wrong hands. Instead of worrying about where we'd hide him, I should have taken the time to understand him better.

It couldn't have been any worse. Or so I thought.

I took a deep breath as Lavinia pinged me a text message.

You animated the dragon. You have until 4 p.m. to turn him over to me. I'll have the rats prepare a carrot cake and coffee to celebrate. L.

"What we need is damage control from Orpheus," I said. "But first, you're taking me home, Ezra. Transcender is in my knicker drawer. If I'm going to face a dragon, a vampire and a god, I need to be at my most powerful."

25

By the time Ezra had teleported me home, I'd looked like Hagrid from *Harry Potter*, in my too-small pyjamas and flip-flops loaned from the foxes, with my hair frizzy from the night's ordeals and my ridiculous rucksack on my back. I changed into joggers, a T-shirt and trainers in five minutes and dragged a brush through my errant hair. Then I opened my knicker drawer and pulled out the baldric Fei Yen had fashioned for me, together with Transcender. I stashed them in the rucksack, along with the items from the Custodian.

For too long, the sword had been hidden in either my knicker drawer or under my jacket. But it was about time to stop hiding who I was in Otherworld company. They wore their wings, fangs and claws openly, so why couldn't I bring Death's sword? I was counting on the fact that the mere sight of the sword would make people think twice before messing with me.

We stood outside Orpheus's gentleman's club in Charing Cross. Even here, the impact of the tremors was evident in the number of shows cancelled in the theatre district. The sets of *The Lion King* had been damaged, and the lead from *The*

Mousetrap was still in the hospital after being crushed by a rocking chair.

We stopped at a newsagent so that Marina could string some bulbs of garlic around her neck, and I could neck a can of Red Bull. If I couldn't get my beauty sleep, then caffeine would have to do. I'd sent Dad home to rest with the promise that I'd call him if he could help. In actual fact, it helped more to have him out of harm's way being clucked over by Alma next door. I didn't want him to end up in the hospital again. That left Marina, Ezra, me and Echo, who sprang out of Marina's bedroom window into a chestnut tree to escape when Robert was on the phone to Marina.

"You abandoned me to a humdrum. I will never forgive you." The leopard honked with laughter. "It is for this reason the universe has ridiculed you. You are the only peculiar to have achieved the most magnificent feat and most absurd feat of your life within hours of one another. You both created and lost a dragon. This would not have happened had I been by your side. Instead, you turned me over to a babysitter. I suggest, given my good relationship with the vampire, you leave this part to me." He turned his nose up in the air. "And you, Marina Ambrose. I thought you were my friend. You high-tailed it out of there with the werewolf without a second thought for me. Next time you need me to consult at your practice, I won't be so willing to give up a night's hunt to help you."

"I'm sorry. Truly. You are part of the team, and we were stupid to leave you behind." Marina stroked him, her finger tracing the rosettes on Echo's coat.

He purred deep in his throat. "Keep doing that, and maybe you will be forgiven after all."

Ezra muttered. "A dragon on the loose in London, and the leopard is making it all about himself."

Emerald eyes gleamed. "I heard that, dog."

"Come on, you lot." I climbed the Edwardian-tiled steps

to Orpheus's club. "We have no time to lose. It's time to face the vampire and beg for his help. Who knows what to expect in there? If this is a gentleman's club in the sordid sense of the world, we'll need to be extra careful. Between morbid, angry and hungry vampires, it's going to be fraught in there."

"Gunnolf's been here a few times at Orpheus's invitation," said Ezra. "My red-blooded alpha was quite disappointed there weren't any strippers."

Echo purred. "Be on your guard. A vampire's lair is dangerous even to their friends."

I nodded. "Marina, you're our litmus paper. Any early warnings would be welcome."

She was still in her PVC skirt and bustier from the night before, but somewhere along the way, she'd lost her spiked collar. Her goth-girl makeup had softened through the night, and her space buns had unravelled to leave her turquoise, pink and purple hair free-flowing.

"You can count on me." She crossed her fingers and rubbed the four-leaf clover tattoo on her wrist.

"Marina, you do realise the garlic isn't going to help to ward off the vampires?" said Ezra.

She scowled. "Leave a girl her myths."

The building was a three-storey Georgian affair, made of a white stone with pleasing symmetry, multi-pane windows and pilasters at the entrance. Heavy curtains and nets marred the view of the inside. The business card Orpheus had given me held only a single line of the address in a stark font on a white card. On the back of the card was a request to knock seven times in quick succession on arrival.

"Here goes nothing." I rapped on the door seven times.

A window slot opened. Black eyes regarded us.

"Name," said a brusque voice.

Echo stepped forward, but he was too short to be seen by the man. "Chanakya Gunbir Hredhaan of Maharashtra, at your service. We wish to meet with Orpheus Might, Minister for History and the Today."

"Show yourself."

Echo leapt into the air.

The black eyes blinked. "Again."

Echo growled and leapt again.

"We don't let animals into this club."

"I'm not an ordinary animal, you imbecile," said Echo.

A pale hand shoved the man unceremoniously to one side.

The door clicked open, and a woman with tumbling red hair appeared. Her black silk negligée emphasised her pale skin. "Apologies for Vorigan's bad manners. Welcome. I'm Oana. Orpheus told me to expect a druid and her friends. I didn't know it would be so soon."

I nodded. "Thank you, Oana. We need to see him straight away."

She gave a quick nod. "Follow me."

We followed her into the club, where green Chesterfield sofas and mahogany coffee tables filled a dimly lit room. Cigar smoke curled through the air, despite the early hour, and a record player played jazz in the corner. Laddered bookshelves and paintings took my breath away, and my eyes lingered on what could only be a Renoir and a Constable. Vampires lounged in various states of undress. One sipped a tumbler of thick, viscous red. I tore my eyes away from him to focus on Oana.

"There are eight of us who live here. Vorigan, who you met earlier, Orpheus, Quillan, Seskel, Aurel, Xanthe, Bianca and me. Bianca was the last to join our clan, but even she is over seventy years old, although she looked closer to her thirties when Orpheus turned her. Normally, women wouldn't be welcome in a gentlemen's club without an invitation, but Orpheus changed the rules back in the 1970s."

I gulped at the intense gaze of the scrawny, strawberry-blond vampire, who had set aside his tumbler and stood to join the tour. Nothing worse than an unknown vampire at our backs in a dark mansion.

Oana led us down a corridor with lanterns on the walls. "The bedrooms are in the basement. The rest of the building is comprised of three floor-to-ceiling libraries, a billiards room, a boxing ring, two bars, a chef's kitchen, a day room, formal dining room and a casino. We currently have three hundred people on the membership roll, with a waiting list triple that. A mix of the literati, politicians and old money. There's a strict dress code during club hours, of course, which are from two in the afternoon until two in the morning." Her lip curled. "We also have rules about not snacking on the patrons during those hours."

The scrawny vampire approached us from behind with a suddenness that made Marina squeak in terror.

"Piss off." She swung around as he sniffed her neck.

Blue soulless eyes like chips of ice.

Without thinking, I raised a hand. A gust of wind flung him back against a painting.

He snarled and came at both of us, fangs bared.

Echo growled and leapt at him, but the vampire was quick, quicker than my hands could react.

"He's hungry," said Marina, trembling with fear.

Oana's voice was a hard rebuke. "Enough, Seskel. Orpheus will be displeased."

Seskel ignored her, his body a blur as he advanced.

My hands tingled as I raised them, unleashing a column of wind that surprised me with its velocity and strength. It swept the vampire along the hallway, taking lamps, side tables and pictures with it. The wind rang in my ears.

Beside me, Ezra cursed.

I didn't stop to check what came next. I slipped off my rucksack and pulled out Death's sword, prepared to cut him down like a tree. To hell with politeness when a deadly vampire had my best friend in his sights. But a mould of dust lay where the vampire had fallen.

The lights failed, not one by one, but rather all at once, sucked into a void.

This time, I didn't need Ezra to tell me that he'd used his moon charm.

Ezra whispered in my ear. "The female vampire will not let that go unanswered. Orpheus's scent is not much further. I will teleport the women to him."

Echo roared, sending a shiver up my spine. "Go ahead. I will deal with this one and be right behind you."

Ezra cupped our elbows none too gently.

The ground disappeared from beneath our feet. I opened my eyes to a cavernous study with a marble slab for a desk and austere black shelving. Marina coughed up phlegm next to me.

"Are you okay?" I said.

She grimaced. "Just another man who can't take no for an answer. Is he alive?"

Ezra kissed his moon charm. "Deader than he was before. Thanks to you."

"Oh god, that's terrible. I didn't mean to." My heartbeat raced.

I caught the now-familiar whiff of beard oil before I noticed Orpheus. Dark chocolate and sweet cherry. He was nestled in an armchair reading a book of Siegfried Sassoon's poetry. And he only had eyes for me, despite the fact the three of us had teleported into his study without warning.

"I take it you had some trouble on the way?" said Orpheus.

His hair was damp from the shower. His attire—bare feet, an Oxford university sweatshirt and joggers—took me by surprise, but it shouldn't have. Most Londoners were still asleep at this hour, after all. I could hardly expect him to wear Wildwoods robes in his own club.

Ezra snorted. "Your man almost had us for breakfast."

We jumped as a body thudded against the door, and a dragging sound ensued along the corridor.

I gulped. "Orpheus, I think I...the vampire, Seskel. He's a pile of ash in your hallway. And Oana and Echo are battling it out by the sounds of it. She was quite cross that I staked her friend."

"He was a lech, though," said Marina helpfully.

"It took us under three minutes to work out who the wildcard is in your clan." I grimaced. "Was."

Orpheus held my gaze. "Why do you think I asked you to come here? I was hoping something like this would happen. He's been a thorn in my side for a while." Then he put down his book and sped to the door so fast he blurred. He opened it and grasped both Echo and Oana by the scruffs of their necks like they were puppies and not formidable in their own right. He barked a command. "Leave us, Oana. And tell Vorigan to clean up what remains of Seskel. The druid did us a favour. He'd become a liability."

Echo shook off Orpheus' grip and prowled into the room, spitting and clawing at his own tongue. "An untasty opponent is the worst kind of enemy." Emerald eyes settled on Orpheus. "A wonderful abode you have here, but your roommates leave a lot to be desired."

I snorted. "I bet those vampires don't wee in corners."

Echo inclined his magnificent head. "Touché, druid. Not every creature is so generous. I didn't need rescuing, Orpheus. I could have put her out cold. Well, colder. But I need someone to scrape the vampire off my tongue."

Orpheus's thin lips lifted in a hint of a smile. "It is not you I was worried about, Chanakya. You are a skilled warrior, and vampires tend only to feed on animals when there are no other options nearby. In case you haven't noticed, we are in the heart of London."

"I knew I was right to like you," said Echo. "Now that I have arrived, we may proceed."

I sighed. "I really am sorry, Orpheus. My strength surprised me. I'm still learning."

"Well then, it was good training for you, Alisha, because the Wildwoods trials are always dangerous," said Orpheus. "Truth be told, you've probably done me a favour. Seskel should have known new peculiars are off-limits. At least until the trial has passed. There are plenty of humdrums who are hooked on vampire venom and allow feeding in exchange for the high. All vampires are unpredictable, but I've never met one with such an insatiable hunger. He was a liability and would have long been called to justice by Gunnolf, had I not foolishly intervened on his behalf. Even a month or two in his coffin failed to persuade him to be more law-abiding." He frowned. "But I see now that is not the only thing you are here to apologise about. What disappointment do you have in store for me, druid?"

My chest tightened. "I could not do as you asked. The stake from the cross remains in the Celestial Library."

Black eyes narrowed. "Would not or could not? You reached the Celestial Library, somewhere I am unable to reach. I, a historian. I, a book lover. I, who crave new experiences and meaning. And you deny me."

"It's not her fault." Ezra stepped forward, his voice laced with a growl. "You expect too much from an initiate."

Orpheus stood up. He was taller and slimmer than Ezra. Not as muscly. But at that moment, he was stronger and fiercer. "Quiet, werewolf. You are here as an escort, nothing more."

"I am here as her mentor, Orpheus. And I tell you, she did the right thing."

"There is no such thing as the right thing, wolf. There is only the question of who benefits," said Orpheus.

Echo snaked between the two men, breaking their dance

of cocks. "Focus, children. There are other pressing matters at hand."

Orpheus stared from one to the other, a nerve in his jaw twitching. "Yes, I see now."

I bit my lip and blurted it out before he could read more of our unfiltered thoughts. Better coming from my mouth, so I could frame the news advantageously. "We need your help, Orpheus."

He snapped. "Speak plainly, Alisha. To gain my trust, your words and thoughts must match. Embellishments are for lesser men than me."

"I am in trouble. I have broken the Founder's Law. My dragon has settled on Big Ben, and without you, the Otherworld will be exposed. Will you help me?"

The vampire grew still. "That is both an impressive and a stupid predicament."

Echo nodded. "Indeed. Who knows what havoc the dragon is wreaking as we speak."

"Actually," said Marina. "Robert is texting me a running commentary. No news organisations are involved yet, and sleepy Londoners are too busy looking at their phones to look up. But he reckons we'll be in trouble as soon as the tourists enter the equation or the dragon roars or eats someone."

Ezra's voice dripped with sarcasm. "No pressure then."

Orpheus's eyes darkened. "Nothing in the world is for free, Alisha. You did not help me. Perhaps your mentor has forgotten to teach you the value of reciprocity. It oils the wheels of the Otherworld and the humdrum one too."

Marina stepped forward. "Or perhaps the reason you want to die, Orpheus, is because you have forgotten that friendship doesn't come with conditions. That help doesn't always require a favour in return."

Orpheus turned on her. "You dare spout the secrets I keep hidden from the world, empath?"

He clenched his fists and flew towards us, then past us,

sweeping his arm across his desk. A stack of textbooks, an inkwell and a carafe of red wine flew across the room, ending in a sorry mess on the floor.

A cracking of bones and a small, gut-wrenching moan that matched the horror of his morphing into a different creature. A stretching, a clawing, a writhing, and suddenly Ezra wasn't Ezra anymore. No more calm, clear eyes, soft lips and stubble. No more broad shoulders and chiselled jaw. No more tousled, grey-brown hair or a roll-up hanging from his lips. Instead, a copper-brown wolf, with a silver chain suspended from his neck, bared his teeth at Orpheus.

"Oh. My. God," said Marina.

"The wolf is smaller than me," said Echo. "I like this."

Ezra growled and came to stand sentinel between Marina and me.

"Relax, wolf," said Orpheus. "My anger is rooted in frustration, not in vengeance. Do you know how difficult it is to end an immortal vampire's life, especially one as strong as me? I have been buried in a coffin at the bottom of the Atlantic. I have travelled to the North Pole to be frozen in ice. I have been entombed in brick walls and welcomed being staked more times than I can count. And still, I am here. Still, I exist."

"I won't be responsible for ending your life, Orpheus. Like Marina, I believe in saving them. Unless I'm backed into a corner and am defending myself or my loved ones."

Echo sighed. "She even defends the lives of poodles. It's very inconvenient."

I chewed my lip. "Maybe you need more reasons to live, Orpheus. You are a man of learning. A man who craves new experiences. What historians would choose to die when a dragon has been birthed for the first time in an age?"

Orpheus hesitated. "I have never seen a dragon before."

I smiled. "There are plenty of new things in the world to see. And it turns out I can create them off the page."

"Are you promising me a lifetime of new experiences, Alisha?"

I shook my head. "No, I'm promising you that, even without my involvement, the world offers more to an immortal vampire than you have realised. No one experience is ever the same."

He raised his eyebrows. "You are an insufferable optimist, druid."

"I'm starting to find out that vampires are insufferable pessimists."

Orpheus rolled his eyes. "You have yet to tell me what is in the rucksack."

I grinned. "Just another few marvels for you to experience, Orpheus. Now, are you ready to help hide a dragon from the world?"

"I will come, druid, but I will not publicly act against the senate." He shuddered. "Now, if the wolf will stop posturing and change into his true self, we might be able to salvage the situation."

Echo honked with laughter. "We will also be able to judge the size of his nether regions."

26

We stood in a circle: Ezra, Orpheus, me, Echo and Marina.

Ezra, back on two feet, was in a grumpy mood. "I'm not holding the vampire's hand."

I skewered him and Orpheus with my most disdainful teacherly look. "You know, you both wanted to mentor me. Would it be impossible for you to get along for the purposes of saving this city and its people and creatures?"

Echo purred. "They tolerate each other. You cannot expect them to like each other."

"The leopard is wise," said Orpheus. "I must look at whether there is a Wildwoods vacancy for him."

"Actually," said Marina, "he already has a job consulting at my surgery."

"Who needs to mark territory when I have already made a lasting impression on the humans around me?" purred Echo. "I have not shamed my ancestral line."

I sighed. "I'll swap places with Orpheus. Make sure you're holding Echo as we travel."

"Take a breath," said Ezra. "Now."

We teleported. This time I kept my eyes open. Ezra was

pale and thin-lipped with concentration. Charing Cross to Westminster might have only been a few tube stops away, but I could tell taking so many of us through the void cost him. We clung onto each other, me between Ezra and Orpheus, travelling in this unnatural way, our bodies squeezed and stretched through space and time, flung to our destination. I didn't dare think what would happen if we let go. Who Ezra would save or where the untethered amongst us might end up.

Being in the Otherworld was an act of faith.

We emerged out of the monochrome world into the light, where the Houses of Parliament sat on the north bank of the Thames. Westminster Bridge had been closed to traffic and pedestrians after the damage sustained in the tremors. The Palace of Westminster stretched before us in the early morning dew, honey-coloured limestone carved in an intricate gothic style with the clock tower at one end. A homeless man gawped at us as we caught our breath and slicked off Echo's drool from our clothes.

"Oh broken world. Can you still surprise me?" Orpheus dashed over to the homeless man and mouthed a few words. The man picked up his carrier bag and blanket and walked as if hypnotised in the opposite direction.

The statues of Winston Churchill and Nelson Mandela stood vigil, and for a moment, I thought I saw them move.

My heartbeat was erratic, and I shielded my eyes and looked up at Big Ben. There, Tielbu perched, blue on blue against the London sky. It was an incongruous sight. From this distance, he looked like a gargoyle balanced on top of the world's most famous clock. The city had already sustained so much damage. My dragon couldn't cause more.

"We have to get him down," I said.

Robert ran over and joined our motley crew. Dark circles ringed his eyes. He gave Marina a kiss. "Thank God you're here. The Met just called in Special Forces to investigate that bloody thing. The Palace of Westminster is a UNESCO World Heritage Site. You've got mere minutes before the area is flooded. Good thing the Westminster bobby was sleeping on the job, or else that dragon would be wrapped like a joint of seared beef already."

I winced. "Here's what I want you to do. Orpheus is on mind control. Lavinia's are rats for Echo to deal with."

"What do you expect me to do? Lock them in the sewers or make them my breakfast?" said Echo.

"It's your call, but they need silencing. I can't have them reporting every move to the coven."

"I thought you were a healer," said Echo. "A lover not a fighter. A good girl, not a bad one. A soufflé, not a rotten egg."

"Name-call all you want, Echo, but there are times a woman just has to do what it takes."

He growled. "Very well, Alisha. The hunt begins."

Orpheus nodded. "I will meet the dragon?"

"I promise."

"Then make yourselves scarce. I have work to do."

"Marina, Robert, you clean up the chatter online as best you can."

She kissed my cheek. "Be careful, Alisha."

I looked at Ezra. "I need to get up there."

Grey eyes on mine. "Step into my arms, hellfire."

I secured my rucksack. Then I leaned against his chest, tuning into the thud of his heartbeat, and let myself be swept upwards and away.

MY DRAGON PERCHED on the clock tower of the Palace of Westminster. He balanced on the uppermost spire of the clock popularly known as Big Ben, although most Londoners would have told you that it was the bell in the clock tower rather than the clock itself that was named as such. That bell weighed 13.8 tonnes. Almost as much as two Tyrannosaurus rex, twenty-eight grand pianos or fourteen Asian wild water buffalos. Which was why it hadn't collapsed under the weight of Tielbu.

Thank everything that was holy and good.

Because on top of everything else, I couldn't be responsible for the destruction of part of a building that had survived World War II mostly intact and only toppled when it came into contact with me.

When I next saw Gaia, we were going to have serious words.

There wasn't enough space for the dragon and us to balance on the spire, so Ezra deposited us on the level below.

"You're going to have to do this last bit alone," said Ezra.

My throat was a desert. "I know."

His voice was urgent. "I'll be listening. Call if you need me, and I can be there in a flash. Your best bet is to use the air current and your abilities to hover next to him until you can decide if he is friend or foe."

"He won't hurt me."

A sigh. "You can't be sure of that."

"I have to be, or else the courage I have left would be in shreds. Take me up again, Ezra, and leave me there. I won't fall."

His eyes said no, but he opened his arms again.

The bottom dropped out of my stomach as he left me scrambling for footing in the empty air, a hair's breadth from the dragon. It wasn't my brain but my instincts that kicked into gear as wind tunnelled from my palms, making me feel like Iron Man. Only, Iron Man wore armour, and I was skin and bones and cells and blood, and the tower was a hundred metres tall. I didn't know how long I could keep up this hovering move. It was harder than anything I'd done before, with the exception of animating the dragon.

A moment of lapsed concentration and I would go splat.

The dragon's eyes were already on me, molten fury in those amber pools. As if he had no friend in the world. As if only lashing out would make it better. Even now, his beauty stunned me. Ivory horns, both elegant and fierce. Black talons held fast to the golden spire of the clock tower. Turquoise scales that shimmered in the early morning mist, where the clouds seemed within touching distance. I was the size of his forelimb, and he could crack me open like an egg. He hissed.

I flinched. I was invading his space. This wasn't even just about the city. It was about what would happen to him. His next choices would determine everything. Maybe he didn't want to be part of this world I'd dragged him into. Or maybe he fancied a bucket of Kentucky Fried Chicken. Either way, I was about to find out.

"Tielbu," I said, floundering in the air, unable to keep a stable level. "It's me. Alisha."

He blew rings of smoke out of his nostrils.

"I know you can understand me. I'm sorry for frightening you before."

A sound rumbled from his throat, or perhaps it was the sound of my own blood rushing to my head.

My position was getting more and more haphazard. With every word, I feared a failure in focus that would send me plummeting to the ground. "You can't stay here. It's too dangerous. It's dangerous for the people of the city, and it's dangerous for you. If they find you here, they will come with their helicopters and nets, and it will be out of my hands. You have to trust me."

I wanted to touch him, but I couldn't. My hands were my propellers. It was going to be all or nothing. Either I gathered the shreds of my courage and clambered onto his back, or I stayed in limbo in the air.

Beads of sweat broke out on my upper lip.

He opened his mouth, and what came out wasn't the

mewling of a newborn. His voice was gravelly, slow and precise. "You gave me life, druid, but you assumed I was a simpleton. It has taken me mere hours to find my voice. Dragons are ancient creatures. There are worlds hidden inside us. And I find I don't like this world at all."

My movements jerked, and my jaw dropped in surprise. My instinct was to flee and call Marina for help, but this was my mess. Had he learned language so fast because his character had been rooted in Dad's stories? Or because of my affinity with teaching language? Or had this been growth all of his own? Like the time he had fallen through the sky, ambled through the streets or surveyed the city from above had given him words and wisdom. Like he was a sponge that had soaked up our language or that it had always been inside him, and I'd been too stupid or distracted to see it.

I locked my eyes on his, willing him to see my pure intentions. "We were taking you somewhere safe."

The vibrations of his voice resonated in my body. "How can I enjoy safety when you are in danger? You gave me no purpose. We are tethered to each other until you free me. So my purpose here can only be to protect you. Why do you think I am up here surveying the city from this vantage point? I will find this god you will die fighting."

My own words to Ezra came flooding back to me. *I'd rather die fighting than stand by while innocents are in danger. I'll take on the god.*

If I'd kept my mouth shut, we would still be threading our way across the city.

The dragon was taking control of our fate because I hadn't determined his with a purpose. But it was too late to assign him a purpose, as my grandmother had done when I'd forgotten it at the moment of his birth. What I couldn't work out was whether Tielbu and I were equals or whether he needed an alpha. Could dragons be led like a dog, wolf or donkey? I would have given anything to have Marina on a hotline, but all I had was my wits and instincts.

"Tielbu," I said. "You and I are going on a trip. In a moment, you're going to scoop me out of the air, and we're going to fly southwest to Richmond Park. My friends will wipe away the memory of any sightings of us, and we will use that window of opportunity to make sure the god does not pose a risk to any person or creature living in this city. Are you with me?"

He sighed and then stretched his wings, revealing the bony structure underneath, and swooped towards me.

I clung on, exhausted from my efforts to stay afloat, although it could only have been mere minutes. My stomach lurched. This wasn't a falling like into Shanghai Moon.

It was flying. His wings beat the air, and it was glorious.

And as he sped towards the south bank of the Thames, he roared. I had no time to think of Ezra or Orpheus, Marina or Echo. It was just me and my dragon and our common purpose to thwart Pan, just as I had thwarted Ra.

27

I preferred flying to teleporting. Flying in a plane was nothing like riding a dragon. It might have been the wind druid in me. The way I had always loved the wind in my hair and face when using the tube. How mountains and bridges were some of my most favourite places in the country—Snowdon, Ben Nevis, Tower Bridge and Pulteney Bridge—for the clarity of mind it brought me to be buffeted by wind there. I opened my eyes as we soared across the city, knowing I was the first.

Knowing that at forty years old, I was doing something children dreamed of. That I had dreamed of as a child.

Except it wasn't all bliss. This wasn't a joy ride. It was flying into the jaws of danger, and I didn't have the faintest clue how to solve a problem like Pan. When we faced Ra, I wasn't alone. Our plan had been concocted by many brains working together, by those who had experience of the Otherworld. We had rehearsed in Baba Yaga's and worked as a team.

I didn't know if my dragon and I could win this alone.

I didn't know the dragon, not really.

I only had meagre intel from Gaia, Robert and Echo on the

sort of god Pan was, plus my own vague recollections from myths and legends.

And yet, my confidence had grown since the night in the Celestial Library, when I had managed feats I had never thought I, of all people, could bring about. I had spent so long doubting myself as my marriage crumbled and in the wake of Mum's death. But I had managed to change. I had leapt over barriers placed in front of me and grown. I mean, I had killed a ravenous, lawless vamp with as much effort as blowing out a candle. I felt bad about it, but it was pretty damn cool.

The senate had all advised me to focus on my upcoming magical trial. Even Ezra had wanted me to play it safe.

But I hadn't abandoned my principles to hone my skills in a padded room. Instead, I had walked through the world, ready to make mistakes. Ready to fight for what I believed in. To take on the bullies other people wouldn't.

I was proud of myself.

We landed in Richmond Park, amongst a thousand hectares of green space. Woodland, gardens and residences, which Pan had now claimed for his own. Herds of deer scattered like flies on Tielbu's approach, and I held my head up high, reminding myself of what I had achieved and determining to fake it until I made it, even if my courage and confidence failed. After all, wasn't that what men had done for centuries? I was capable of taking on Pan by the very virtue of being the only one willing to do it.

I slid off Tielbu's back and slipped on my baldric. Transcender's obsidian blade gleamed within its sheath.

I might have been in joggers, a T-shirt and trainers that stunk of Echo's urine and needed a wash, but when I put my sword on, I was a dragon-riding warrior woman.

The seed of an idea took root in my head. I turned to Tielbu. "We don't want to pick a fight with a god unless we can help it. We win this fight not by testing our might against an immortal but by persuading him not to use the herds to cause tremors. By taking away the Prime Sorcerer's reason to target the elves."

A rumbling growl came from the dragon. "I will heed your words, druid. Unless the god seeks to harm you."

I turned in alarm at vibrations under my feet. The herd of deer, which had fled on our arrival, parted like the Red Sea for Moses. Six hundred animals doing the bidding of the half man, half goat that came towards us in his stately Englishman's attire. Tweed, cord, a top hat to hide the horns that lurked underneath. In his hands, he held a flute.

"I am Pan, god of the wild, shepherds and flocks, companion of nymphs and lover of musical instruments. Formerly a porn site owner. In recent centuries, for my sins, also a royal gamekeeper and a board member at Battersea Dogs Home." His pale green eyes took in the dragon, and a smile lifted his lips. "That beast does not belong amongst my herds, druid. You would do well to move him before I do him harm."

I stilled my racing heart and clenched my damp palms. "And yet, you are harming innocents in this city."

Pan looked me up and down, lust filling his eyes. "Would you rather I had a different pastime? You might not look like a nymph, but perhaps you can blow some things as well as I can blow the flute."

Legend said he was lecherous and debauched. That he had taken the honour of defenceless maidens.

But I wasn't a maiden. Neither was I defenceless.

I stood in the shelter of Tielbu's body and took out my sword. Its double-edged blade made it hard to miss, and Tielbu's tombstone teeth and knife-edge talons stood ready to defend me.

Pan might be an immortal god, but he wasn't laying a hand on me.

I wrinkled my nose. "Your pick-up lines need work."

I would have said his missing thumb would have been a

disadvantage between the sheets, but judging by his demeanour, it was his own pleasure that mattered most. What a tool.

"You're no fun. Taken a leaf out of the book of modern-day nymphs, have you?" He sniffed. "I prefer my maidens young and fertile. I want to ravish them around a fire while men beat drums and blow horns nearby. Ideally, I would have my wicked way in a threesome while the maidens are high on field mushrooms, performing sensual dances, giggling to themselves. Waifs with voices as sonorous as my flute."

"Well, I've got love handles, a barren womb, and I can't sing for shit."

He frowned. "How sad."

I snorted. "How lucky."

Tielbu's breath ruffled the top of my hair. He was becoming impatient.

Pan's pale green eyes narrowed. "You are here to stop me, but I am having fun. Too often, the people of this city have eaten up the green spaces. They have sullied fields with plastic waste and trampled wildflower meadows. They have forgotten how to marvel at the flocks and herds. They cast out the dogs they bring into their homes as pets. They fornicate as routine rather than for pleasure. And they have forgotten to pray to the gods. Their bleak, prayerless hearts weakened me." He smiled, and the dry skin of his cheeks cracked like the desiccation of a clay pot. "But I am stronger now. They fear the tremors. All I need to do is to move my herds. I cause panic, and panic leads to strength. At least for the one who causes it. Death. Destruction. Prayer. Ra was right. It's a good formula."

Tielbu roared, and the sound made the deer timid but not the god. He stood firm.

I saw it now. I saw how the stories had pegged him right. How he was both playful and terrifying. How he liked the order of the herds but the wilds of the landscape. How his animal nature intertwined with his divine one.

"I will stop you," I said.

Pan laughed with the abandon of a merry drunk. "How pitiful to see a mortal have no sense of their mortality."

I had to give him a show of strength.

I lifted my hands, and my body tensed as I drew from the vastness of nature to send a tornado towards him. When I looked up, I found that his lips rested on his flute, and he had darted to another spot and then another, so my tornado could never reach him, although I myself was utterly exhausted.

Even his hat stayed on his head. He was completely unharmed.

Pan grinned. "Not so easy trapping a trickster god, is it? Especially one so in tune with the land."

I felt the coming heat before I saw it. A warming of my dragon's chest at my back before a column of fire erupted from his mouth, narrowly missing me where I stood between his legs. "No, Tielbu."

The god lifted the flute to his lips, and the flames danced around him. They were even unable to harm a hair on his head or scorch what must have been cloven feet underneath his oddly shaped shoes. He extinguished them with a glint in his eyes, and the sound was so sweet that I was tempted to sit down and listen.

Like this was a game, not life and death.

He stopped playing and licked his lips. "You see, druid? I am not easy to subdue. Even by a dragon-rider."

Tielbu's gravelly voice boomed in my ear. "We must leave."

"No. We must stay." I lifted my sword, willing myself to hear the voices of my ancestors as Gaia had once promised.

My hands grew clammy. I heard nothing. I was fast running out of options, but I didn't want to use the sword. I wasn't stupid enough to think it would kill an immortal, but I did want the voices to return to give a clue about how to beat him.

"That is Death's sword," said Pan.

I shook my head. "Perhaps once. Then it was Gaia's. Now it is mine."

His mouth twisted. "You know her."

"I do. She told me you're not all bad, although sometimes you do bad things."

He gave a sad smile. "And what do you think, druid? Do you think I'm all bad?"

"It's not for me to say. I'm not a judge. I, too, have hurt people. We're all just trying to do our best."

Pan smirked. "It's good you don't judge me. Because a judge also wields an axe. And you have no authority over me or power to assert it. That sword might as well be a baguette in your hand. I'm enjoying myself for the first time in centuries. I'm not going to stop."

Fake it until you make it, I told myself. This was like chess. I didn't need to be physically stronger. I just needed to move the queen into the check position, and then the checkmate would follow.

I gave him a slow smile. "Do you know what my favourite feeling is?"

"An orgasm?" said Pan, looking me up and down.

"When an arrogant man has to eat his hat."

He was built to prance and saunter with his chest stuck out. A strutting peacock as much as a god. "I bought this hat for Queen Victoria's coronation, druid. I am certainly not eating it."

I didn't press the point. Instead, I steeled my nerves and replaced Transcender in my baldric. Gaia had told me not every battle was solved by escalating into war.

In that instant, my friends materialised next to me—Ezra, Marina, Orpheus and Echo—in a horseshoe shape that had probably been Marina's idea.

"What are you playing at, hellfire?" said Ezra, his eyes on the god. "And how on earth did you get the god to run from you?"

"Hello, dragon. You are safe from me. My nose tells me your meat is too tough," said Echo.

Orpheus turned his unblinking gaze on Tielbu. "The honour is mine, dragon. Alisha, this is your fight. Vampires and gods don't mix. I will bear witness to the fact that it is the god and his herds that caused the tremors, not the elves."

My mind whirred as Pan came towards us in his funny, forward-leaning gait. He sneered. "You have brought friends, druid. They will not improve your odds."

Echo roared. "I will chase you off and hunt a deer on my way. Just say the word."

"Will you all just shut up and let me deal with this?" I unzipped the rucksack with my items from the Celestial Library.

Pan's expression froze. "What's in there, druid?"

"Gaia sensed its power and almost figured it out. Can't you?" I pulled out the bag of Odysseus's winds and the remnant of Noah's Ark.

The god's eyes drifted from the wood to my face and back again. Then, he lifted his flute to his lips. A sleepy melody akin to a lullaby filled the air, and Pan vanished.

My stomach dropped. That had been our chance to save the city and put an end to the ridiculous war against the elves, but I had blown it.

"He is gone." Tielbu gave a fearsome roar that scattered the herd.

An idea formed in my mind. I placed the artefacts back in the MC Hammer rucksack for safekeeping. "He's the royal gamekeeper. And there's no way he is abandoning his herd with multiple predators threatening them. A dragon, a leopard, a vampire and a werewolf."

"Hey," said Marina. "What about me? I can threaten the deer."

"Can you, though?" I said. "Pan's still here somewhere. I know it in my bones. Tielbu, this is our chance. Don't harm the deer but fence in the herd with your fire."

Tielbu rose into the sky. His neck arched up and down until he reached a height from which he unleashed hot, orange flames of spite. I wished Dad had been there to see it. And that it was less life and death. That my friends could ooh and aah like it was a particularly dazzling display at fireworks night rather than a gamble of wits.

But I had to focus.

The herd panicked. They darted this way and that, but Tielbu's ring of fire left them with no route of escape.

I steeled my own soft heart against their shrieks. My hands tingled in readiness.

"Stop," said Marina. "You're frightening them."

"Seared meat isn't as tasty as fresh cuts," said Echo.

Pan's voice thundered across the park. "Leave the herds alone, druid. Leave the herds alone, and we will talk."

"You heard the god," said Marina. "Stop it."

"Kill them all," said Orpheus. "And we will have a feast for the ages."

"I trust you," said Ezra. "But that dragon is a virgin. He can't go rogue here."

"I won't let them die," I hissed. "Keep up the bluff. Let me concentrate. I will coax the flames into submission myself. But I'm banking on the god's love for them to bring him to me."

"I'm warning you, druid," said Pan's voice.

Beads of perspiration gathered on my brow from the heat of Tielbu's flames, but I didn't call him off. I couldn't.

Pan had to reveal himself.

Just when I thought those poor deer wouldn't survive the shock, Pan re-materialised a few metres from where he had disappeared. His expression writhed in horror as he determined what to do. Crashing buildings and urgent sirens excited him, but it was another matter for his panicking herds of red and fallow deer in all their elegance and gentle beauty.

He came towards us with the puffed-up chest of vengeance, his flute ready to be used as a weapon. His eyes sparked malice.

My friends stood their ground. A buffer around me that I didn't need, but appreciated.

I let the flames burn until we were inches apart, and I could smell the smoke on his skin, the sweat from his pores. He made me retch, but I had my answer.

Pan's divinity still warred with his beast. He'd not baulked at the bag of Odysseus's winds. It hadn't scared him. So to use them against him would have been the wrong ploy. Instead, Pan had been scared of the holy cedar wood from Noah's Ark. He had proven to me he still loved the father of the gods. Like Gaia, the remnant had awed him. Maybe it had shamed him for his choices too.

He spat on the floor in disgust. "Call the dragon off."

My heart thudded, but I kept my voice cool. "Oh, you need my help?"

I beckoned Tielbu.

The dragon responded immediately. The ground thudded as he came to rest between me and the god.

I raised my hands and coaxed the flames away from the deer before quelling them with an effort that made me quiver and grunt, leaving a scorched ring in the grass. "It is done, Pan."

His voice whipped through the morning air. "You put my herds at risk. Now you will pay."

Ezra and Echo came to either side of me, their hackles raised.

I smiled to set them at ease and to show Pan who had the upper hand. "My dad once said that a man can lose his way if he drifts from his faith. In this bag, I have a reminder of faith. It can be yours for a short while if you wish."

"Open the bag, druid," said Pan.

I brought it out with care.

"Alisha—" said Ezra.

"I know what I'm doing."

Pan's eyes widened. "A piece of cypress wood."

I nodded. "From the bow of Noah's Ark. Found amidst the plains of Mount Ararat. It carried mating animals to repopulate the earth."

"I know what Noah's Ark is, druid. I knew the prophet. I lived through those times." He edged closer, trembling. "Let me hold it."

"First, a promise from you. No more mischief that harms innocents."

He smirked. "I can't promise that."

I couldn't trust him. Of course, I couldn't. A trickster god would always, always betray me in the end.

But this wasn't about me. It was about his longing for a godly item. A millennia-old god would remember all his victims or even all his wins.

He probably didn't even feel anymore.

But touching this disintegrating piece of wood would remind him of his godliness. Wasn't inspiration the basis of all change? I had to believe that holding this piece of lost treasure, knowing its place in God's plan, would remind him of his own godliness. That feeling would be something that was all the more precious for its rarity. It would be something he wouldn't forget.

And that was why I had him where I wanted him.

Checkmate.

I cradled the wood between my hands.

Pan looked at it like an addict at a crack pipe.

The dragon huffed behind us, and Ezra bristled. They trusted Pan as little as I did.

"It can be yours, Pan. I will give it to you," I said. "But if you feel an ounce of connection to this earth or to a greater power when you hold this, you must promise not to cause any more tremors. Or my dragon and I will come back." I swallowed hard, hoping my bluff worked. I couldn't, and I wouldn't hurt an animal. "And we will hurt your herds. We will burn everything to the ground."

His thin lips twisted. Then he sighed. "It is as you wish. Hand me the wood, druid."

A shiver ran up my spine.

I gave it to him, and when it left my hands, I was bereft.

His eyes gleamed, and he snatched it from me. For a moment, I thought I'd made a terrible mistake, but Pan sank into the grass. He put down his flute. A gentleness came over him as he studied its silver-grey colour, every grain, nail mark and dent on it. He held it to his chest.

"I'd forgotten what it felt like to hold something so holy." A tear threaded down his face. "It still echoes with the mark of the heavens. For that, I thank you, druid. I will keep to our bargain."

"Make sure you do." I looked at my friends and motioned to Tielbu. "Our work is done here. Anyone fancy a ride?"

Marina clapped in glee.

As we walked away, leaving the goat god in the grasses of Richmond Park, Ezra grabbed my hand and squeezed.

Echo purred. "You have a hunter's instincts, Alisha. I am proud of you, but I will make my own way to the woods the wolf has found. It is not normal for a leopard to be up amongst the clouds."

Orpheus frowned. "I must beg your pardon for being wrong about the dark elves, Alisha. I have much to discuss with the senate. But a dragon ride is a new experience, so I will join you."

"Tielbu," I said. "Will you do us the honour?"

The dragon inclined his head and sank onto the meadow

for us to clamber onto the sheltered skin on his back. Marina crawled up first, eager as a child on Christmas morning. Next came Ezra, then Orpheus, refusing any help.

"Druid," called Pan.

I swivelled. "Yes?"

"Your womb is barren." Green eyes smouldered under his mop of curly brown hair. "It is within my gift to bestow fertility on domesticated animals."

I shook my head. "No, thank you. It is dangerous to be beholden to a god, especially one such as you."

A goat-like bleat of laughter erupted from him. "I heard your kin is not so discerning."

I frowned, unsure of what he meant.

Pan tipped his top hat to me. "What a strange human you are. You are not like other ones."

I shrugged. "All humans are not alike. And middle-aged women are a world apart. But we are all better off when we look out for each other."

I climbed onto the dragon and nestled close to Ezra. The wind rushed against us as Tielbu took flight, and I thought how far I had come and how the Wildwoods trial would be a piece of cake if I could convince a trickster god to lay down for me.

28

———

Ezra's woodland lay situated between the A127 and the M25. Its position near noisy roads and landscape—comprised of a group of fields around a steep hill and tens of thousands of native trees—made it a perfect hideout. Yet it belonged to the city of London, with panoramic views from the hilltop of the River Thames to the North Downs and west across Docklands and Canary Wharf. It was a place of rest and respite and perfect for hiding Tielbu. Lavinia's rats preferred the sewers and rubbish bins of built-up areas for their natural habitat, and we would see the coven umbrellas approaching a mile off from the woods.

Little did I know, Tielbu wasn't the only secret Ezra had been keeping.

With Marina preoccupied with tending to Tielbu's needs and hooking him up with roadkill, Orpheus, Ezra and I walked into a wooded area when a rustling met our ears. Orpheus reacted first, his speed giving him a natural advantage. He pulled back branches of thick foliage to reveal the slim bodies in torn clothes and dirty, smiling faces.

I blinked hard, clutching Ezra. "Are those—?"

A small, muscular body barrelled towards me and hugged my legs.

Flinar smiled and looked up at me. The cut above his eyebrow had healed, and his milky eyes held joy. "Alisha the druid. I have been waiting for you."

His Roman tunic and knickerbockers had been replaced by an oversized Wham T-shirt and denim cut-offs.

I grinned and couldn't resist giving his billowing ears a tug. "You look well."

Flinar swatted me away good-naturedly. "The werewolf found me after I left Shanghai Moon. I had no place to go. Now, the Defence Minister and her rats can't find us. We sleep under the stars, and I have friends."

"I'm happy for you."

He jumped from one knobbly leg to another in excitement. "I have been eager to see you. You have been fighting for us. The wolf has told us everything. You gave us hope." He brightened. "But now that you are here, I can tend to your every need. What would you like me to do? We have cheese that is turning green, curdled milk and some pickled roots. Perhaps you would like a plate?"

My stomach heaved. "Actually, just a glass of water, a blanket and a place to lie down. I could sleep for ten years."

Orpheus rolled his eyes. "You have a day until the trial, druid."

"If Alisha wants to sleep for ten years, then that is what Alisha will do," said Flinar.

The vampire sighed, a storm cloud on a sunny day. "There are many reasons to dislike elves. Do not add to them."

Flinar frowned. "I have not forgotten that Alisha saved me. I will save her. Even if today that means creating a nest of leaves for her to rest in."

He scurried off. I burst out laughing, and joy danced in my heart.

Ezra leaned down to murmur in my ear. "I take it you approve?"

Butterflies darted in my stomach. "Of course, I approve."

He gave me a wolfish smile. "You didn't think I could stand by while my aunt mobilised against the elves, did you? Especially once we realised they were innocent?"

Orpheus rolled his eyes. "You two are gluttons for punishment. The coven is best kept onside."

Ezra protecting the vulnerable meant the world to me. It made him more of a man than the gung-ho senate.

I reached up to grab his face and planted a kiss smack on his lips. The scent of him—spice and smoke and musty man—intoxicated me. "Ezra, you're brilliant. I love you." I coloured and backtracked. "I don't mean 'I love you,' of course. I mean, I appreciate what you did here. How you put yourself out."

He grinned. "It's okay, hellfire. I don't think you want to marry me. It's nice to be appreciated."

I blushed. "How many are hidden here?"

"Eighty-odd, give or take. Not the ones who can afford to pay for protection in the city or whose money means they are exempt from the worst inclinations of the senate. I brought only the defenceless ones here. The ones too weak or guileless to ride out the storm of the senate's anger. I can only hope they can go back to their lives once this is all over."

I sighed. "It's definitely not all over. Lavinia wants me to bring Tielbu to her by 4 p.m. today."

Ezra frowned. "If you thwart her, your chances of passing the trial plummet. Remember, it's your actions in the maze of London's Underground tomorrow. It's about winning a majority vote of the senate that already has misgivings about you."

"If I hand Tielbu over, her power grows, and any gains we made against Pan tonight will be for nought. If I fail the trial, I won't be around to stop her from controlling him. But that's not going to happen because I'm going to pass the trial, and she can keep her grubby mitts off him."

"And what if my dear aunt decides to kidnap you to prevent you from showing up to the trial?" said Ezra.

I chewed my lip. "I might be wrong, but even though Lavinia is underhanded and difficult, I don't think she'd stoop that low. She has some kind of moral code."

"I hope you're right." His voice dipped into a growl. "But she'll have to come through me, a bunch of elves and a dragon if she wants to stop you from attending. And she'd risk the wrath of the rest of the senate if it came out."

His protectiveness of me sent shivers up my spine.

And then I realised. It was always the same with bullies. Lavinia probably wasn't used to people standing up to her.

Well, that was about to change. I pulled out my phone and began texting.

"What are you doing?" said Ezra.

Orpheus's eyes gleamed. "She's about to tell your aunt where to go. I'd tone down that language if I were you. Velvet gloves are preferable in internal wars."

I pursed my lips. "Okay, Orpheus, but just a smidgen. I've just about had enough of bowing down to people who don't deserve it. In fact, I've never been that good at deferential behaviour."

I typed. *Thanks for the offer of coffee and cake. Maybe another time. The dragon is staying right where he is. I'd think twice about launching an offensive to take him. I'm no longer the woman you tricked into drinking a green smoothie truth serum. I'm far better as an ally than an enemy, A.* I pressed send.

Ezra groaned. "Well, that's going to set the cat amongst the pigeons."

Orpheus nodded. "Your aunt is not a woman to be trifled with. Plenty have tried and lived to regret it."

"She can't fight a battle on two fronts." My phone pinged.

Lavinia's name flashed up.

How interesting you pick a fight on the eve of your Wildwoods trial. Rayna planned it so carefully, but two heads are better than one. I'm sure you'll appreciate my last-minute tweaks, L.

Ezra grimaced. "That sounds like a threat."

I set my shoulders back, pleased to find that exchanging blows with Lavinia didn't floor me like it once would have. My belief in myself had grown, and it felt good. "I wouldn't expect anything less."

Orpheus raised an eyebrow. "The druid is like a star athlete blowing their advantage by running onto the field, having poked themselves in their own eye. As her mentor, you failed to teach her the art of subtlety."

I shrugged. "Hide in the shadows all you want, Orpheus. I am ready to shine."

"Let's hope you all are, hellfire," said Ezra. "Marina and your brother have to face the same thing."

"To be honest, that's not my main worry right now. How can we be sure that the senate won't plough on with their path of malice against the elves?"

"You talk as if the senate speaks as one," said Orpheus. "Not all of us would have made the stark choice to target the elves had we known the allegations were false. The Prime Sorcerer, too, would be appalled that he himself has not acted justly."

I shook my head. "You were at the coven dinner, Orpheus. Phinnaeous Shine took the tremors as an opportunity to crush the elves without a thought for justice."

Orpheus glowered. "That man has done more for the Otherworld than you can possibly know. He is innately good and just."

I massaged my temples, tired of explaining the obvious. "Even good men can be unjust. If I gave you a penny for every time a person thought they were in the right but were mistaken, you'd be a rich man."

"I am already filthy rich, druid." Orpheus's coal-black

eyes narrowed. "I will see to it that the Prime Sorcerer hears of the elves' innocence and that they may return to their homes." He paused. "Your trial is mere hours away. Be on alert. It would be a shame for an initiate of your calibre to throw it all away. As much as I desire you to pass, you and your fellow initiates must weather it alone."

My voice cooled. "It turns out we can handle quite a bit on our own. Maybe the keys to the Otherworld should be ours."

He stared me out. "Be careful what you wish for, Alisha. The burden of power is always heavy."

I sighed. "If you two gentlemen don't mind, it's been a long day. I'm in severe need of my beauty sleep, or else I'll never get back the glowing skin of my twenties."

I woke up as evening had fallen to Echo licking my face with a tongue that felt like sandpaper.

"Wake up, Alisha," the leopard said. "Your brother is here. We have much to discuss. Sky News is reporting that the scorched ring in Richmond Park is the work of a group of feral child flautists, who left an incriminating flute nearby."

I groaned, checked that my MC Hammer rucksack was safe beside me and wiped away spittle from the corner of my mouth. Thankfully, the bag was so uncool that no one had bothered to steal it. Maybe that was what clever Calypso had intended. "Let them dream up all the stories they wish. It's better than reporting what really happened. Seriously though, I'm aching all over, and my forty winks on this compact ground didn't help my back issue. What I wouldn't give for the firm touch of my osteopath and blow dry right now."

"There'll be time for that later," said Echo. "I miss evenings on the rooftop of our flat filled with cubed salmon steak and pussy harems. The world does not leave enough time for frivolity, but the Siberian minx around the corner will be mine soon. I will regain her with tales of our exploits, and she will be mine."

I sat up and pulled my dishevelled hair into a neat bun. "I missed you. How did you find us?"

He purred. "I know how to read a map, as you well know, but in this case, it was Ezra who came to find me. He thought you might appreciate a familiar tongue to wake up to. And it was his idea to bring Sahil and your father here too. A last supper, if you like, before your Wildwoods trial. Come. The fire is burning. Our friends and family await."

Echo led me to a grove where elves broke bread. Their children, in the absence of toys, foraged for golden leaves, smooth rocks and berries to trade. They kept a wary distance from the dragon but giggled nervously when he blew rings of smoke into the air or turned his amber eyes on them. Marina sat at Tielbu's side, but when we approached, she ran to welcome me.

She hugged me, and the words tumbled out of her mouth. "You slept for an age. The men brought the firewood, and Tielbu lit it. He really is very clever. He seared some steak for some of the elves, too, although it was too crispy to eat. Joshi refused to sit down until he saw you sleeping soundly, and Ezra has been checking up on you too. But Flinar turned them all away until Echo scared the living daylights out of him and insisted on waking you." She leaned into me with an air of conspiracy. "Your brother is behaving very strangely. Orpheus was right about his jealousy of you. He almost turned green when he saw the dragon. I'm not sure what's going on underneath the surface, but I'd say he's not the most reliable of our trio going into tomorrow's trial."

"The story of my life." We approached the fire, where forked flames of orange and red hissed and crackled.

Dad rose to greet me. "Let me kiss my daughter, Marina. I can't get a word in edgeways with you two." He grabbed my face between his calloused palms, and the paint smudges on his fingers told me he'd been working at his art again. "Let me look at you. One day, I hope you will let a day pass without this old man having to worry about you."

I squeezed him tight. "How are you feeling, Dad?"

"Oh, much better for seeing you."

"You've been painting."

His brown eyes filled with warmth. "I have. I got home after our dragon dance, and I was inspired. I made a little chapbook of watercolours for you. It's nothing special. But with the trial coming and you being an animator, I thought you should have something in your back pocket. What's an animator without paintings to create from?"

I accepted a small notebook from him with eight drawings and flicked through the drawings: a gecko, a stork, a wasp, a giraffe, a penguin, a rooster, a panda and a crane. "It's beautiful, Dad. Thank you."

All my favourites smiled up at me. Dad, Ezra, Marina, Echo, Tielbu. Okay, Sahil wasn't a favourite, and he was sitting in a weird, pigeon-toed position. But it was about time I checked in on him.

I sat down next to him. "How are you doing?"

"I'm okay. It's been quite a week. My business is suffering from a lack of attention. I have squatters to deal with." He shuddered. "Plus, an invasion of pigeons in one of my North London buildings that the tenants are insisting I call in the exterminators for. And my secretary has left me because I inadvertently turned into a pigeon and then back again and was left standing butt naked with my clothes at my feet. After she screamed, she snapped a pic. It was cold in there. And now she's suing me for sexual harassment in the workplace. I couldn't exactly tell her the truth."

Next to me, Marina turned blue with corked laughter.

"How awful." I patted Sahil's leg.

"Well, it's all right for you. You've taken to this all like a duck to water. I feel like every atom of me has changed. You see the state of what my bowels produce. It's very disconcerting to see the colour change in the toilet bowl. From brown to white." He shook his head. "It's not even like I can see the doctor about it."

I hesitated. "Listen, there was something I meant to ask you. It was something Orpheus said at the coven dinner. He said you'd done something. That you'd made a poor decision that bodes ill for the future."

Sahil grunted. I felt for him. His pigeon nature made him weird, and for a man who had always prided himself on being cool, it was a cruel blow. "Nothing's wrong. My sister is an animator, and I am a werepigeon. What could be wrong? Are you going to listen to that stiff more than your brother?"

I winced. "All right, all right. I was only asking. You know how much is riding on tomorrow, don't you? If we fail, we won't even remember the Otherworld exists. It's so important we work as a team."

"Why are you directing this at me rather than Marina? It's as if you think I'm the weak link."

I frowned. "You're being sensitive."

He snapped. "No, I'm not. I know who you think the weak link is. Every single person around this fire thinks I'm just a laughingstock. Well, what if I did something about it?"

"What did you do, Sahil?" The low warning note in Dad's voice took me back to when we were children.

"Even my own father expects the worst of me."

"Do you see? The Otherworld always tears families apart," said Dad.

I shook my head. "Maybe it's just families that do that to themselves. I want to trust you, Sahil. Do you have our backs tomorrow? I don't want the memories of all we have learned these past few months to warp into something humdrum. For all the truths to be hidden. For Mum's death to be just a car crash. For Dad to be a painter who settles for postcard prints rather than the creator of real-life dragons. For me to be a teacher, not a druid. For Echo to be my missing Bengal cat. For Ezra to have just been a stranger on the street and Tielbu to have been a story. For you…"

A vein throbbed in his jaw. "I was happy being a property magnate until I found out there was more."

"Then we'll do this together. We'll pass the Wildwoods trial as a trio. All of us or none of us."

He sighed. "Yes. Okay. What else do you want me to say?"

Ezra's grey eyes found mine. "That's settled then. Come on, you three. We have some drills to do. A last push at preparation and then an early night. Alone."

"That's a shame." I winked. "Let's get to it then."

29

We stood outside Morden tube station, at the most southerly end of the Northern Line, underneath a crescent moon and cloudy sky. The underground had long closed, and the streets were deserted, with the exception of empty night buses rattling past and a takeaway owner pulling down the shutters on his chicken shop.

The three of us undergoing the trial had dressed in black, like robbers in the night, and shook with nerves. That was where our similarities ended. Marina's pockets bulged, clattering with acorns, crystals, horseshoes and rabbit feet. An unholy assortment of good luck symbols that would make no difference at all to how we fared tonight. Sahil had inexplicably decided to paint his face with stripes like he was on some army drill or a paint-balling jaunt with the lads. I had freed Transcender from my knicker drawer. The inch-thick shoulder straps of the baldric Fei Yen had made nestled against me like a second skin. The sword sat in a short scabbard on my back.

A shiver ran through me. I felt powerful.

But scared. Like knees-knocking-together scared.

I wouldn't give voice to what could happen if I failed. It

was too painful. I had to hope I could see this through because if I lost the Otherworld, I would also lose Echo, Ezra, Tielbu and Flinar. I would think the foxes were two crazy Chinese ladies who ran an occult shop and forget they were *hu hsien*. I would return to being plain old me and forget how strong and brave I had been. I would never feel the wind from my palms or create new life from a page. It would have been for nothing.

"I have no idea what to expect," I said, although my heart ached with unsaid goodbyes.

Echo rubbed up against my legs. "It's the tube, Alisha. A labyrinth. What else could be in there except monsters?"

"Remember," said Ezra, "you have all the tools you need in your arsenal. You just need to keep your heads clear. Come morning, with any luck, you'll be fully-fledged members of the Otherworld, and you'll never have to think about this again until your own children have to go through it."

Dad wailed. "I'm so scared for you. My own trial was a disaster."

"Forget Morden." Marina glanced around uneasily. "More like Mordor."

"I've always hated the tube." Sahil looked like he wanted to run as fast as he could in the other direction.

I didn't blame him.

Echo's emerald eyes flashed. "Not helpful, Joshi. It is times like this I miss Rosalie. Her steadfast nature puts your lily-livered moaning to shame. Alisha, Marina, pigeon—"

Sahil butted in. "I'm a werepigeon, actually. Not a bog-standard pigeon."

"A pigeon is a pigeon. In any case, fight like a leopard. Be courageous. Be bold. Mark your territory to find your way out."

Sahil brightened. "I can help with that."

Echo purred. "Indeed you can, pigeon. We may laugh at your walk and feathery hair, but every pigeon plays his part on this green earth. Mostly, by leaving it splattered with waste."

"Druid. Empath. Pigeon." Rayna Willowsun said, her long, grey hair flowed behind her, intertwined with vines. Her wrinkle-free skin glowed in the moonlight, and the potions on her belt clanked, but she had wisely removed the dagger she usually carried. Old ladies with daggers might have drawn attention after all. Not that I could speak when Transcender sat snugly against my back.

"Werepigeon," said Sahil.

Rayna frowned. "I trust you have prepared well for this day and focussed your full attention on it?"

I plastered on a smile, although my ribcage tightened with anxiety. "Of course, headmistress. It has been the top of our priorities."

"You have no need to lie to me, Alisha. As Minister for Education and Headmistress of Wildwoods School of the Wondrous, I am well used to my students getting by on a wing and a prayer. Talent is no excuse for a lack of preparation. We will see how you all overcome the obstacles in your path tonight," said Rayna. "Lavinia and I have outdone ourselves imaginatively."

My palms were sweaty. I just wanted it to be over. "How do we know that the trial has ended?"

"It's simple, really. You just have to find your way out of the labyrinth. You may not go backwards, only forwards. You may only use force proportionate to the danger you face, and you must abide by the rules of the Magical Constitution. Ignore the orbs. They will be in flight behind you as witness to your choices." She clapped in excitement as if exams weren't anxiety-inducing at any time of life. "The hour is nigh. Mr Neuhoff will teleport you inside, and then we must leave you. He, too, has been preoccupied of late. This is as much a test of his performance as a mentor as it is of yours."

Ezra clenched his jaw. "Who could forget that?"

"I stand ready to come to your aid if you suffer any injuries," said Rayna. "It has been a long time since the senate and school community have taken such an interest in the outcome of a trial. There are bets afoot, and the Defence Minister herself has arranged a viewing party at Baba Yaga's Gym."

No doubt Lavinia wanted us to fall flat and for our shame to be witnessed by as many people as possible.

"One more thing, druid. Some amongst us feel we are indebted to you for preventing harm to innocents in this city. But you have shown a disdain for the rules and traditions of the Otherworld. You have cast away your training wheels and taken it upon yourself to make decisions that your betters avoid. You would have been wiser not to make enemies so quickly. From one druid to another, it is in our nature to be peaceable. Yet you are a whirlwind."

My gaze darted to the dark confines of the underground. "Plants are peaceable. The wind is not."

She gave me a slow smile. "Well, good luck to the three of you. Joshi, leopard, you may view the proceedings with me."

Ezra stepped forward, and his voice trembled. "Ready?"

Both of us knew how much we had to lose.

I gave him a shaky smile. Then I took a deep breath and joined hands with my brother and best friend. "As we'll ever be."

The damp, moist air filled our lungs. The lights had been switched off, but the orbs flickered above us, giving the station the air of an abandoned lunatic asylum. For all Lavinia's love of bubble gum pink, I had to give it to her—she had a flair for horror as well as Barbie chic.

I stood between Sahil and Marina, panting hard, not from exhaustion but from terror. Viewing rooms at Wildwoods and Baba Yaga's and who knew where broadcast our every word. Rayna had admitted there were bets on how we would fare. I wouldn't have been surprised if there was popcorn, too, as if we were actors on a stage, not real-life people trying to survive an ordeal.

Marina turned around and grimaced at the orbs that shadowed our every move. "This is horrendous. It's hard enough not knowing what's in that tunnel without every word and decision being watched."

"Just block it out." I gritted my teeth. I wanted to smack them out of the sky too.

A dark tunnel loomed in front of us. The Northern Line didn't run after 1 a.m., but that didn't make this a hospitable environment. Rats lurked down here, and creepy crawlies, and that were just humdrum creatures. There were other peculiar things that went bump in the night. Who knew what traps Lavinia had laid in store for us?

"Can pigeons see in the dark?" I said.

"Nope," said Marina.

Sahil frowned. "You could let the pigeon speak for himself."

"Sorry," said Marina. "Once a vet, always an answerer of animal Trivial Pursuit."

I pointed to the tunnel. "Shall we?"

"Must we?" said Marina. "I really miss Robert right now."

"You don't need a strapping man to make you feel safe, Marina. You have me." I tugged them with me.

At the platform edge, I jumped down onto the tracks. I was hedging my bets about them not being live. The senate might not like me, but I was pretty sure they'd choose humiliating us over killing us. It would kill the mood of the viewing parties for the night to end in our gruesome deaths.

Marina jumped down next. "So, all we have to do is find a way out. How hard can that be?"

Goosebumps trailed up my arms as the wind whistled down the tunnel. I pulled out my sword.

Sahil huffed as he joined us on the track. "What are you going to do? Quarter the rats?"

I grimaced. "Only if I have to. Shh. Do you hear that?" I looked down in horror as roots emerged from the ground, grasping at our feet. "Run!"

We ran, as only scared forty-year-olds do, with an ungainly, toppling forward motion.

Marina might have been a dancer, but she was no runner. She held her breasts as she ran, her legs akimbo. "I forgot to wear a sports bra."

"Let your boobs bounce, dammit," I panted. "Just move faster."

Sahil's longer legs took him further than us. "Look, a manhole."

He clambered up a ladder, but the roots crept up the wall, developing stems and leaves that covered the manhole in thick foliage in a matter of seconds. He gasped and leapt away as it sucked his arm into the mass.

"That's Rayna's doing." I climbed up and slashed at the vines with Transcender. Voices of the spirits overwhelmed me as I freed Sahil.

I fell to my knees.

"Get up." Sahil grabbed my hand.

We ran farther down the dark tunnels on Marina's tail. The vines reached the manholes before we did.

Panic set in. I didn't know if the rumbling of the ground was our feet or phantom trains or a creature from the unknown. My head filled with scenes from horror movies: Pennywise, the clown, hidden around a corner. Chucky, the doll, waiting in a dormant, abandoned tube carriage. Candyman and his bees behind me, always behind me, waiting for me to slip up. Waiting to devour me.

I had been so arrogant and stupid to think I'd been ready for this. That I could take on a witch of Lavinia's talent, a druid of Rayna's wisdom.

The truth was, I lagged far behind my grandmother. I couldn't even hope to come close. My ego had inflated when we had beaten Ra. It had inflated when I had left Pan unscathed and when I had animated Tielbu.

But any successes so far had been pure luck. They hadn't stemmed from talent. They had come about from stumbling in the dark.

Ezra hadn't trained me because of his faith in my abilities. He'd been strong-armed into it by Rayna. Dad had been right to wrap us in cotton wool. To tell us to stay safe. Even Fei Yen and Faeza had warned us not to trust the senate.

We could have lived as magical outsiders.

Instead, we had stepped into Wildwoods and made a pledge with the devil. All or nothing. Belonging or oblivion.

Why had I thought it would be any different for us?

I ran down those dingy tunnels with no escape and only the pounding of my weak, human heart. We were no longer running in tight formation. Sahil was ahead, Marina in the middle, and I lagged behind. The vines no longer grasped our feet, but they loomed overhead. A reminder that there would be no escape.

I pulled up short to catch my breath, leaning on Transcender. "Anyone else picturing horror movies?"

"Why would we need to picture horror movies when we can picture Jack the Ripper, the Moors Murderers or Fred and Rose West?" said Marina.

Sahil froze. "Will you two shut up?"

A putrid smell filled my nostrils. I gagged.

A man strode from one side of the tunnel to the other, disappeared through the wall and reappeared on the other side, only to repeat his motion, shaking his head and muttering all the while. He wore a threadbare tunic and stockings of coarse, undyed wool as if he'd stepped out of medieval England.

"I knew it," said Marina. "I knew ghosts were real."

"I'm not ready to meet Mum down here," said Sahil. "I can't tell her I'm a werepigeon."

"I hate to break it to you, Sahil, but I expect she already knows." I sighed and sheathed my sword. "I bet they put this in to tickle Orpheus's fancy. He loves a bit of history. No point bothering him. Let's wait until he disappears through one wall and run past. He won't harm us."

"Like hell, he won't," said Sahil. "The man's had to wear stockings for centuries. He must be livid."

"I like Alisha's plan," said Marina.

Sahil shrugged. "Don't say I didn't warn you."

We waited, and the man passed through again. He had hair like Friar Tuck and eyes that were only hollows, with claw marks underneath as if someone had taken them or he had himself torn them out.

I shuddered. "Now."

We stepped forward, but the ghost man came wheeling at us, bigger and wilder than he'd been in his calmer muttering state as if we'd angered him. Although in spirit form, he shoved us back with a monumental force that sent us sprawling.

I raised my hands and tried to return the favour, gathering a wind so wild that my hands stung.

The man sighed and continued his muttering and roaming like he'd not felt a thing, and yet when I stepped forward, he threw me again, the energy surge sending me farther than Marina and Sahil in punishment.

I stood in my signature kickboxing stance, legs braced, fists ready, in case he came at me again, but he continued his route, unseeing, deliberate, like he could continue for another century or seven.

"We can't keep this up, or we'll end up at the beginning," said Sahil.

Marina glanced around furtively. "Every second we stay in here is making me more anxious."

The orbs made it worse.

"Me too. We can't go backwards, Rayna said, but forwards

isn't an option. Unless he lets us pass. So there has to be a way. It's not wind. It's not shapeshifting because he'll do the same. So it has to be empathy, Marina."

She bit her lip. "We need to get him to move on. But how?"

"Sahil, can you get close enough to hear his muttering?" I said.

He indicated the orbs. "You want me to shapeshift in front of all the people watching?"

"Please. What other choice do we have? We said we'd have each other's backs, didn't we?"

He held my gaze, and a second later, my brother's brown eyes shrank and repositioned themselves on the sides of his head. It was gross. They morphed into small, fiery, beady stones with none of Sahil's own handsomeness. Then he dropped to the size of a Wellington boot as we watched, his clothes falling away to reveal his weird, muscly, grey werepigeon chest with his pink, clawed toes, green-tinged head and orange beak. He grunted and took flight, trailing the hollow man, with his personal orb bobbing behind him.

"He's no robin redbreast, is he?" said Marina.

"Bless his heart. I really wish the universe had made him an eagle, at least. He would have dealt with that better."

Sahil fluttered back to us, landing heavily on the floor. "I know why he's here."

"Why?" I wrinkled my nose, desperate for some clean air.

"Because, my dear sister, that putrid smell isn't just the Northern Line. It's the smell of a mass grave underneath our very feet. Three thousand bodies were laid to rest here during the Black Death, and that man's wife and child are amongst them."

Marina's cornflower blue eyes welled up. "I know just what to do."

I grabbed her hand. "Be careful."

She walked with trepidation to the spot where the hollow

man had repeatedly passed through and knelt there amongst the rail line with its gravel, soil, scuttling mice and the mass grave below. Then she dug in her pockets for the lucky crystals she had collected over the years from Shanghai Moon and other shops in Brighton, Norfolk and Stonehenge and all those places where free spirits dwelt. She piled her green jade, citrine, smoky quartz, malachite and rose quartz in a little pile, like an altar.

Then she stood up.

The hollow man made his rotation through the tunnel walls, but this time, he hovered over her.

Marina raised trembling hands to touch him but pulled them back like she'd been burned. Her grief-stricken face turned to look at me, and my heart hurt for her. "He's livid with rage. I can't help him."

I wanted to shield her from him, but this was her task. I was as certain of that as the sky was blue. "You can do it. Remember what you did for Elvira. And for Faeza. Remember how you calmed Sahil in the Wildwoods arena? Remember what you do for the creatures in your care every single day. This is no different. Counter his emotions with your positive ones, just like Ezra said."

She shook with fear and rolled up her sleeves like she meant business. Then she reached up with her glorious, tattooed arms and sank her hands gently into the hollow man. This time, she didn't pull away.

I held my breath, straining to listen.

Marina spoke of daisies and sunrises and the wings of hummingbirds, of technology and vaccines and children who lived to a hundred years old. The hollow man hovered over her and, this time, waited for her to finish. He crouched at the altar of crystals Marina had made.

Then the mass of his bulking shape broke into a thousand segments and rained down on the altar as if his very spirit had blessed it.

And he was no more.

She grinned. "I did it."

Relief washed over me as we joined her. "What did you say to him?"

Maria looked down at the crystals. "That the spirits of his loved ones live on in the beauty of the world and that medicine and technology mean that children born today stand a greater chance of living long lives. He seemed to like that."

"A good thing you didn't tell him about how Lavinia's rats bring death. I'm not sure he would have moved on so quickly," cooed my werepigeon brother.

By now, my trainers were wet with the damp ground. "We can pass now. Come on, before something else stands in our way."

Sahil flew over to his pile of discarded clothes. "Can someone carry these?"

I shook my head. "Best to keep our hands free, just in case."

He swooped past and fired a watery shit on my shoulder.

"Mature. Real mature, Sahil."

"You wanted me to have your back, didn't you?"

Marina sighed and gave her altar of crystals one last look, and we took off at a jog, with Sahil flying close behind. There was a deathly silence to the tunnels that drove fear into my heart. I preferred the bustling of the city to the sound of our feet against the ground, the heaving of our breath.

About two miles in, we came to a junction where the single tunnel split into two.

Sahil flapped his wings. "We should take the right one."

"The left one looks like a better bet," said Marina. "See the flickers of light?"

"Left it is," I said. We ran, and the air became cooler, as if the atmosphere had changed like there had been an airlock. The hair on my nape stood on end.

"This doesn't feel right," said Marina.

A shiver ran up my spine. "No, it doesn't."

A hiss met my ears.

I drew out Transcender, and this time when the sword whispered to me, I deciphered its call.

Basilisk. Basilisk. Basilisk.

30

"Basilisk," I said.

Marina stopped dead in her tracks. "What do you mean?"

I frowned. "The sword said basilisk."

Sahil came to rest on my clean shoulder, his claws digging into me, his toothy beak millimetres from my face. His breath smelt like the mints he liked to chew. "Don't be stupid. They're not real."

"Neither are dragons," I said. "But they exist."

"Whatever you do, if you hear the sound, don't look at it," said Marina. "A basilisk causes death from a single glance. I read up on them after Ezra told us they were real. They are born from an egg laid by an old cock just before his death. A basilisk is born exactly at midnight on a clear night with a full moon."

I gulped as the hissing grew closer. "Thank goodness for your encyclopaedic, knowledge-searching mind because we sure as hell can't Google anything down here. We have two choices. We can run, or we can kill it."

"The other tunnel. Run," said Sahil.

"No! We'll fail the trial. Rayna said we can't go backwards, remember? Only forwards."

He flew ahead. "Well, run forwards then, Einstein."

The hissing grew louder and more pronounced, above and around us.

"Shit." I pulled Marina back to back with me. "Sahil, land on my shoulder. I can channel my powers to shield us. A column to keep us safe as we edge out of here. Keep your eyes shut."

"To hell with this," said Sahil. "I have my own shield."

"You what?" I opened my eyes, although I myself had warned against it.

My werepigeon brother flew before us. And it was true. He had a shield. A fluorescent yellow shield that presented as a cube around him. He tilted his feathery head at me pigeon-style as if riling me to challenge him.

I frowned, ignoring the hissing that drilled into my brain. "I don't understand."

Marina prodded me. "Alisha, now's not the time."

"Since when can you do that, Sahil?"

"You think you're the only one with friends? The only one with bargaining ability?" my brother cooed. "What is money when you've seen power like this? Why should I give it up? Passing this trial is as much my birthright as yours, Alisha." The fluorescent light from his shield revealed an air vent at the top of the tunnel. "I hope you make it out of here, but I'm not sticking around this hellhole to help. See you on the other side."

He looked at it, and the next thing I knew, my werepigeon brother shifted into something small and bulbous, with many more legs than a pigeon. His shield contracted with him, and he scuttled away through the grate.

His orb disappeared with him.

I clutched Marina. He really had left us in the damp tunnel with the basilisk hissing in surround sound.

"Aren't we supposed to stick together?" said Marina.

"It wasn't one of the rules, but I can't believe the wanker left us here and saved his own skin." I sighed. "There's no way we fit through that grate, Marina. Did he just change into a frikkin' bulbous spider to get through it?"

She shuddered. "And I thought a werepigeon was scraping the bottom of the barrel. I'm *never* sleeping with him now. Even if my boobs reach my toes, and he's the only one left on Earth offering some nookie."

The hissing reached a fever pitch, making me break out in a sweat.

Sahil was gone.

So much for teamwork. So much for us all being in it together.

I wasn't sure if I hated him or if I was just disappointed. But for now, we had to focus on making it out ourselves, and we still had no idea if this was one basilisk or many. Or how big and bad our foe was. For all I knew, it could have been a hologram conjured by Lavinia—including sound effects. There was no way Helio would have let one of his beasties loose in London's Underground.

"Er, Alisha?" said Marina. "Something just slithered over my foot."

I jerked her three feet away, flat against a wall. A creature wriggled past, and I thought I might pass out. Two orbs were left floating overhead. I held Transcender aloft in the light of one of the orbs, and my blood chilled.

Reflected there in the obsidian blade was a serpent with a crown-shaped crest. The serpent slid forward. It must have been at least thirty feet long with a girth wide enough to fit Marina and me side by side. And we weren't skinny chicks. We were curvy ladies with a lifetime of chocolate consumption on our hips.

King of the serpents, indeed.

Its venomous tongue flickered, and its eyes loomed larger

than any snake I'd ever seen. Eyes that could kill us with one stare.

It looked like he belonged in the Congo or the Amazon, not at sorry old Morden tube station, which, let's face it, didn't even feel like central London—just some sort of junction between the big smoke and suburbia.

"He's behind us," I whispered. "Don't look at it. At least not directly."

"Is it bad?"

I shuddered.

"Oh shit," said Marina. "Why are we playing musical statues? Shouldn't we run? Bloody thing is probably sentient as well. It will probably quote *Paradise Lost* at us as it devours us."

I winced. "It's really long. Who knows if it can do that winding, suffocating trick I've seen on the Discovery Channel. We'd have to get past with our eyes shut."

She sighed. "Well, mate. It's been a thrill and a pleasure knowing you."

The hissing perforated my mind, making it difficult to think. "We can't give up."

A head emerged out of the wall next to us.

"Alisha doesn't have to give up," said a small voice.

I jumped three feet. "Flinar?"

"You gave me hope. I am going to save you."

I could only see half of his face. His milky eyes glowed. Two cold, four-fingered hands reached out and pulled us into a black hole before sealing it shut, leaving the two orbs and the basilisk in the tube tunnel.

The clamp around my chest eased. We seemed to be on a ledge with a vast expanse of blackness underneath us.

"But Flinar, I thought you could only hide small objects?" I said.

He broke into a smile. "I have been practising, Alisha. Our

people were hunted, and the woods were quiet enough to practice. It is good to be useful."

Marina breathed a sigh of relief. "This is nice. Not cosy but much better than being in a confined space with a serpent king."

Flinar shook his head mournfully. "We can't stay here long. I told the leopard that Alisha needed more sleep. That she should stay safe in the nest I made her. But this will give you a few moments to decide how to defeat the basilisk. But where is the werepigeon? I hope he is not languishing in the serpent's belly."

"Don't ask," I said.

"I am sorry. We will arrange him a funeral befitting a warrior."

"Let's focus on defeating the basilisk. Thank you for this moment of peace, Flinar." I sighed. "What would my grandmother do? Or Echo or Ezra?"

Flinar leapt up and down on the ledge, the only one of us brave enough to do it. "You made a god believe in god, Alisha. Why can't you believe in yourself?"

Marina nodded. "He's right. All your successes, and you still don't get how badass you are. You've had so much on your plate, Alisha—the divorce, your mum's death, coming to terms with all this. Take a breath. We can still win this. But... call it my vet's disposition, but however horrific the basilisk is, I don't want to kill it. You know how animals are. It might be a sweetheart in a serpent's body. Maybe we can sing it kumbaya and lull it to sleep. An a cappella version with harmonies might do the trick."

I rolled my eyes. "That thing is not a sweetheart. But you're right. I don't think killing it will win us any favour. It's probably one of Helio's pets."

"It's pretty much impossible to kill anyway," said Marina. "You can try stabbing it with your sword, I suppose, but that's going to be hard if you're fencing blind. And according to legend, the only way to kill a basilisk is by the crowing of a rooster."

My heartbeat sped up. I hoisted up my arse on the wafer-thin ledge and reached carefully into my back pocket, where I'd stashed the chapbook Dad had made me.

I squinted at it.

There he was: a fat bird standing proud on the page, crumpled by my butt. Bold red and brown, he had a striking plumage on his tail and neck, a tell-tale crest on his head and red flaps of skin hanging on either side of his yellow beak.

I shoved the chapbook under Marina's nose. "Is this a rooster?"

Her blue eyes widened, and she punched the air. "Hell, yes! We are back in business!"

A weight lifted off my chest. I knew exactly what I was going to do. "Flinar. It's time to go back. It might be dangerous. Can you take us?"

Marina frowned. "Maybe you should animate that thing here. You know, in case it takes a while."

I gave a slow smile. "No, I'll animate him in there. Wildwoods wants a performance, and that's exactly what we're going to give them. Are you ready? Just follow my lead."

Flinar stood up. "Take my hands, friends. We will go to the basilisk. But if it's okay with you, I prefer to live."

He spun his back hole magic, and the ledge disappeared from under us.

The three of us stepped out of the wall. The serpent lurked for its prey in the dark. Patient. Vicious. Ready.

I didn't know if time had continued at the same pace or if hours had passed. Ezra had said the trial would take as long as was required to determine the outcome. I had to believe we hadn't already failed. That we had bent the rules enough to give ourselves a chance but not enough to turn the senate against us. Because I realised my advantages in the

Otherworld had come from being an outsider. And I was about to do it again.

The orbs bobbed up and down, eager to find their targets again.

Flinar cowered behind Marina.

I flattened myself against the wall, working quickly. My fingers called out the rooster from the page. Warmth and cells and feathers and rubber-like wattles that weren't my favourite texture. But also shrewdness, daring and gregariousness.

This time, I didn't forget.

"Your purpose is to keep the basilisk at bay for as long as I require it. Don't look him in the eye, and don't crow unless I ask you to." I pulled the rooster out of the page. He was a warm bundle in my hands that I showed the orb, like Rafiki showing Simba to the kingdom. "Nice to meet you, Mr Rooster. Let's call you Roger, shall we?"

Roger clucked and wriggled out of my hands.

The basilisk hissed. It knew what was coming.

Roger was determined. He barrelled around, more sheepdog than rooster. The basilisk might have been long, but it was slow, and Roger's tiny wings propelled him up and over its body.

"Druid," said the basilisk. His voice sounded like the lowest notes of a cello, and it suited this dark, dank place. "You are playing a dangerous game. My venom will immobilise you before the rooster crows."

Marina shuddered. "If it makes no difference to you, can you drag us to the Jubilee Line before you strike? I prefer that one."

I held my finger to my lips to quiet her. Marina had suggested the basilisk might be sentient. I'd been counting on it. "The rooster has no other purpose but to crow for me, basilisk. You will let us pass, or you won't make it to dawn."

"Are you so sure of your talent? The witch told me you are

not cut from the same mould as Rajika Verma," said the basilisk.

I closed my eyes and called my dragon. "The witch is right. I might walk in my grandmother's footsteps, but my mould is my own. You see, she played by the rules, and it got her killed. I don't play by the rules." I turned to the orbs. "I think we've done enough to prove ourselves tonight, but I'll give you one last spectacle."

I could feel Tielbu nearing. My hands tingled as I called forth a cushioning wind to surround Marina, Flinar and me. It didn't matter that I couldn't hold it for long. That I was exhausted and needed my adrenalin to subside because Tielbu wouldn't let me down. The threads of the universe held us together, like mother and child.

He broke through the city street to the walls of the chamber where we stood. My beautiful dragon, with his translucent wings and horned head, roared with passion. My wind protected us from the falling rubble that trapped the basilisk, and the three of us leapt onto Tielbu's back before I held out my hands to the rooster, calling him to me.

"Don't look at him, Tielbu. Seal the tunnel with your fire but leave him alive," I said. "The senate put him there. They can remove him."

Tielbu's roar deafened me, and his fiery breath raged down onto the tunnel, shattering the orbs at last, leaving a pool of molten concrete no person or creature could escape from.

"Thank you," I said as his strong wings took us over London's rooftops.

Marina clung on for dear life, with Flinar clamped between her legs like a misshapen yoga block.

I whooped, enjoying the thrill of the ride, although Roger most certainly wasn't, given how furiously he was pecking my arm.

"Do you think it will be enough to pass?" called Marina over the whooshing of the air.

"Not with all the chaos we left behind. But I don't care anymore. I was fed up with playing by their rules. Weren't you?"

31

As per tradition, the Prime Sorcerer summoned both mentor and initiates to the vaulted cabin at Wildwoods as a new dawn rose. Ezra, Sahil, Marina and I waited in stilted silence outside the great tombstone door to be invited in. It was funny to end my Otherworld life in the vaulted cabin, where I had first understood how much this world had to offer and been introduced to the senate that first magical night when Ezra had led me into Wildwoods.

My heart ached with the loss I was about to face, but I was proud of myself. I couldn't have tried any harder to succeed in this new life. All I could do was be true to myself. I only wished I hadn't shamed Ezra.

He stood, handsome and stoic, at my side. "Maybe Orpheus would have been the better mentor after all."

I swallowed hard. Even now, he was trying to make it easy for me. I didn't want to ask whether he'd still search me out once my memory of the Otherworld had been wiped. How could he be himself around me if he couldn't even share his history and talents with me? If he had to lie about what he did every day? I knew then that he'd walk away. He would have to. But I didn't have to lay any blame at his door. The decisions had been mine alone.

"It wasn't your fault," I said. "And for the record, even with a fail tonight, you were the best mentor I could have hoped for. I didn't want a big dick swinging his opinions around. I wanted a supportive mentor who trusted me to take the lead."

Sahil gave a sly smile. "Well, this big dick is about to walk this trail. I showed my wares, got out of there, and didn't make a mess. Not one splatter of pigeon poo either."

I rolled my eyes. "You arsehole. It was supposed to be about teamwork. Wait until Dad hears you abandoned me there."

"It's not my fault that arachnids can see nearly 360 degrees around them and can't shut their eyes. Forget immobilisation. That triffid or whatever it was would have killed me if I had stayed." He paused. "I didn't want to leave you behind, though, Marina. I was worried about you."

Marina glared at him. "Talk to the hand, werepigeon spider hybrid. How do we even know you're Alisha's brother?"

He frowned. "Because you've known me practically all my life."

She was in full flow now, and watching her go was a thing of beauty—my best friend, scrapping like a cage fighter until the very end. "Yeah, well, maybe you're wearing face skin too. Like in that Nicholas Cage/John Travolta film. Either way, you're a slippery eel."

I studied the emotions flitting across Sahil's face. We'd all struggled to help him reveal his peculiar talents. It had been like coaxing a lotus to grow in the desert. Bloody impossible. But what he was good at was making deals. It was why he had such killer instincts as a property magnate. What was more, he was avoiding our eyes like he'd done as a kid and didn't want to be found out.

I turned on him, still sore that he'd just upped and left us. "How did you get that magic anyway?"

Ezra sighed, his voice rasped like he'd spent every minute of the trial smoking his cigarette roll-ups. By the looks of it, his nerves were as frazzled as ours. "Stop fighting, children. Now's not the time. Just remember the rules. Don't speak unless you are spoken to. Your chance to convince the senate has passed. This deliberation is not another chance for you to make an impact. It is a chance for you to listen."

The door creaked open to reveal the soaring ceilings and stained-glass windows of the inner sanctum. The thousand burning pillar candles burned again, and the meeting was already in full progress around the split stone table. Nine faces turned to face us, their expressions inscrutable, although by now, they were familiar to me. Hadn't we all just dined together at the coven flat? Yet, without batting an eyelid, they would go from breaking bread with me to walking past me on the street like strangers.

My stomach was rock hard with bundled nerves.

The Prime Sorcerer stood. His midnight skin glowed in the candlelight, and his straggly beard was streaked with silver, just as the cloud of hair around his head. A pen and lined paper hovered in the air beside him, recording his every word. "Another day, another group of initiates. Welcome to tonight's warriors. You may sit."

Four high-backed chairs faced the stone table. Sahil and I chose the outer seats, with Ezra and Marina in the middle. So much for sibling love.

"I would like it noted for the record that both the Minister for Education and the Minister for Defence did an excellent job planning this trial. The combination of grasping vines, Black Death spectre and basilisk, is one that was well appreciated by the spectators at our various viewing parties."

Lavinia, resplendent in a full-sleeved, glittering pink

gown and a bouffant helmet of hair, inclined her head in acknowledgement and silently applauded Rayna next to her.

Phinnaeous Shine continued, his eyes glinting with glee. "Now, it is time to put the spectacle aside. I do love this part of the evening. It's almost reminiscent of the white smoke that emerges from the chimney of the Vatican's Sistine Chapel when the cardinals decide the next pope."

Orpheus rolled his eyes, but he didn't look at me.

I had no idea if we could count on his support. But it was clear how many would stand against us from their dispassionate faces. This was simply business for them—another vote.

Whereas for us, it would determine the rest of our lives. Perhaps I'd never discover again who I really was. Like dementia, a cruel uncoupling of who I truly was and how my life unfolded.

"First, we will decide in the case of Sahil Verma and Marina Ambrose," said the Prime Sorcerer. "These two initiates fought with honour during the trial. They displayed their skills openly and with vigour and showed the courage and discerning natures required of peculiars. While Sahil Verma should be censured for escaping the tunnels without his sister and friend, his prowess as a shapeshifter cannot be denied. Marina Ambrose was able to bring peace to a ghost that had disrupted many a commuter train. They both pass the trial. The senate's vote is unanimous. Can I hear an aye?"

"Aye," said the senate.

"It is done," said the Prime Sorcerer. "You may leave the hearing."

Sahil grinned broadly and gave me a wave before prancing out of the hall.

Like I said. Arsehole.

Marina looked at me in awe. "Alisha, I want the same for you. I'll wait in the park with all my fingers and toes crossed."

"It's okay. I'm happy for you. Go." I willed my heartbeat to stop thundering. "I'll be fine."

She kissed my cheek and Ezra's. "Take care of her."

I watched her as she bounded out of the room, lighter than someone who had offloaded a giant poo.

Then I turned back to the senate.

Shadows cast by the candlelight cloaked the Prime Sorcerer's expression. "Granddaughter of Rajika Verma, you involved yourselves in matters that did not concern you."

"I did."

"Why?"

"Because innocent lives were at stake, and facts matter."

He shrugged. "You are young for your forty years. When you grow up, you will realise that sometimes the end is more important than the means. There are always winners and losers. It is our job as the senate to choose only those to enter our fold who will help us win."

"That sounds a teeny bit unhinged to me."

Orpheus shook his head in a pantomime fashion.

Ezra gave me a sharp elbow in the ribs.

"I see. It seems it is hard to teach old women manners," said the Prime Sorcerer. "There remains only one question to answer before we vote. Will you surrender the dragon to us?"

I frowned. "Does the answer to this have an impact on my vote?"

Phinnaeous nodded. "It may well do. Think of it as a way of showing us how hospitable you are to the desires of ministers."

Lavinia's eyes gleamed.

I sighed. They wouldn't let Tielbu be free. I knew it as surely as I knew the lines on my palm. "Then the answer is no."

His brow furrowed. "Then we vote."

They voted, one by one—my fate in the Otherworld in their hands.

The formidable shapeshifting wizard Prime Sorcerer, Phinnaeous Shine, as wealthy as the Queen and with connections deep into humdrum government, cast the first vote. He, whose plans for the elves I had derailed, whose motivations were entirely unknowable. "The druid raised a dragon, but her ego knows no bounds. She is incapable of collaborating with the senate and follows only her own mind. That bodes ill for the future. For that reason, I vote no."

Brooding vampire Orpheus, Minister for History and the Today, with his Roman nose and heavy brows, who could read my hopes and fears, even now, from across the room. Whose vampire I had haplessly killed without really meaning to. His hooded eyes turned on me. "She wasn't distracted by the fiction of an unjust war. I appreciate her uncovering who really caused the tremors. She has achieved things other peculiars could only dream of. Tonight, you sealed the tube line like a tomb, but still, she got out. I vote yes."

Ezra's witch aunt Lavinia, the Minister for Defence, with her love of bubble gum pink interiors, deadly weapons and rat spies, who I'd made to look stupid with my meddling. Her eyes twinkled with mischief. "It may come as a surprise to you, given the druid is sleeping with my nephew, that I am voting the way I am."

I scowled and opened my mouth, but Ezra squeezed my thigh. The wily witch meant to sway Gunnolf's vote against me, no doubt, by saying Ezra and I had slept together. Hadn't Ezra said he preferred werewolves to be with their own kind? And to add insult to injury, it was partly Lavinia's fault that Ezra and I had been so embroiled in work rather than play.

Lavinia adopted a sombre tone. "I have tried to welcome this druid into the Otherworld. I have helped her save humdrum lives, although it led to the loss of one of my own, led her in an aerobics class, although she quite frankly has no rhythm, and invited her to dine with the coven. But she is a disappointment. What good is a peculiar of her quite remarkable talent if they refuse to be a team player? The druid could have shared her elvish intel with me. Worse still"—she clutched her chest as if it personally pained her—"she escaped our orbs tonight and cheated. I vote no."

I rolled my eyes. No word about knocking me out with a truth serum, then.

Her rats had plenty of intel. She hadn't needed mine.

The druid headmistress of Wildwoods School of the Wondrous and Minister for Magical Education, gifted healer and mentor, whose gleaming hip dagger never left her side, played with the vine trailing her shoulder. "Alisha helped during the crisis at Wildwoods. The students look up to her. She didn't strictly play by the rules by involving the elf and the dragon, but she is inventive and brave. There is no doubt that she is too wild, but we can tame her still. She is a valuable member of this community. I vote yes."

I sighed with relief. The vote was even stevens with five more votes to come.

The fairy Bestiary Minister Helio, whose beasts included the octopus Kraglek and surely the basilisk we probably maimed that night in our escape, propped his elbows onto the stone table in a pensive mood. "I am torn. The basilisk lives, although she animated a rooster who could have killed him. She commands a dragon. But she refuses to share him with us. How I would have loved to study him. To command him myself. I vote no."

Shit. It wasn't looking good.

The leprechaun Minister for Finance, Cillian O'Meara, whose job was to move money for magical needs from rainbow to rainbow, to deal in good luck and to keep the armoury stocked, was up next. Wouldn't he, too, lust after my dragon and be on Lavinia's side? Shrewd eyes darted to my face as I held my breath. "She takes on foes that would make others tremble. I'm a money man, but we need fighters with balls of steel amidst us. Luck is on her side. I vote yes."

It was down to the wire. Two more votes to go.

Ezra tensed next to me.

Gunnolf, Ezra's brawny, denim-loving werewolf alpha, the Minister for Justice who was a stickler for the rules and who, even now, curled his lip at me. Presumably, because he knew of the sparks flying between Ezra and me. "She is disobedient and insolent. She doesn't know her place and has no respect for the Magical Constitution that governs us. She is a distraction for our best seeker, and her choices tonight show she is willing to break the natural order to further her own goals. With absolute certainty that we would regret admitting the druid into our fold, I vote no."

Margola Silver, the selkie Minister for Information, with her flame-coloured hair, cat-like glasses and perfectly pointy bosoms, dabbled in divination. Ezra had told me her allegiances shifted depending on the story of the day. Her voice tinkled like a bell, high and thin. "There are dark times coming. We need all the help we can get. Besides, you saw her tonight. She's more skilled than even her grandmother. And the magical community loves her. Heroic stories sell. I vote yes."

Erelim the angel, Minister for Diplomacy, with his dirty wings, stringy blond hair, washboard stomach and a bottom that could crack a nut. As a conflict mediator, wouldn't he be on my side, given that I had helped solve the problem of Pan and the elves? "She damaged humdrum property. That causes difficulties for me. What is more, she conducted diplomacy with the elves without consulting me. I vote no."

The candelabras flickered.

The floating pen stopped writing.

Lavinia broke out into a wide smile.

My ribcage contracted, and the senate blurred. I felt like I'd been punched in the stomach. It was over. I was about to lose part of me. I didn't even know what life would look like on the other side. Whether this would somehow drive a wedge between Marina and me, whether I would see Echo or my creatures again. What would happen to Tielbu?

Ezra took my palm in his hand. "Take a deep breath, hellfire."

The blood rushed to my ears. "You can't teleport us out of here. You'd lose everything."

"Like hell, I can't. They're not taking away your identity. Damn the consequences."

"The yew tree rune won't tolerate you teleporting."

He rolled the binary code charm on his necklace between his thumb and forefinger. "I have a little trick to bypass that."

Orpheus stood up, a tall shadow looming over the stone table, as if he knew what we were thinking.

The arched door to the vaulted cabin opened, and in strode Calypso, with her blade runners and dreadlocks and a kickass pocketed trouser suit, like she meant business. She smiled at me, and it was like the warmth of the sun on an icy winter's day.

My consciousness came back into the room, tethered by a thread of hope.

Phinnaeous Shine stood up, grimacing. He waved his hand, and the floating pen began once again to scribble on its page. "This is very unorthodox to leave the Celestial Library at such a dark hour."

"The threat has passed, has it not? In large part thanks to the druid."

"The vote is over," said Phinnaeous to murmurs of assent from the rest of the senate.

The Custodian set her shoulders back and spoke in clear, soaring tones. "The vote is not over until the initiate leaves this room as a fully-fledged peculiar or a humdrum revert. You know this as well as I do, Prime Sorcerer."

He inclined his head. "Still bookish, I see, Calypso? Very

well. In that case, let it be said, it is not your place to meddle here."

Calypso's amicable tone cooled to ice pole levels. "My place is anywhere I choose it to be. I'm an equal. As much a member of this senate as you, Phinnaeous."

His eyes flashed with anger. He wasn't used to being challenged. "Yes, in theory. But why would you choose to intervene in this particular matter, Calypso, when you are usually far happier with your nose buried in books amongst the stars?"

"My role in the Otherworld is all about learning. The Celestial Library is perhaps the greatest source of learning in the known universe. And what is this sitting if not about learning?"

"You don't know what you are doing. Our laws cite—"

"I know what our laws cite. And I know why it is worth raising my head above the parapet to invoke this one. How often do we have initiates where the vote is so close? Alisha Verma is not just anyone. She is the granddaughter of the most celebrated Custodian in the Otherworld. She performed feats tonight that are exceptional for an initiate. She did something not one of you has done in years. She faced a god without fear and with candour. And she gained access to the library. It deemed her worthy. My vote is yes, making it a tie." She drew a deep breath. "Our laws state that in the case of a vote tie following the trial of a new peculiar, the balance must be tipped towards acceptance based on the principle that everyone deserves a chance." The Custodian turned to smile at me. "Alisha Verma passes her trial."

Sparks of happiness dispersed my mountainous anxiety. I jumped up from my chair and pranced around like a kid at a school disco.

Damn Lavinia and her assessment of my sense of rhythm. Dancing was joy.

Ezra picked me up and spun me around as the senate stared. "It's over."

"You are one of us now, Alisha," said Rayna.

The Prime Sorcerer's face shuttered. "Let's hope we don't live to regret it."

32

———

For once, my bedroom didn't smell of Echo marking his territory. Pink rose petals trailed across my bedroom floor and onto my bed. My silken bedsheets wafted of summer rain fabric conditioner. A breeze drifted in from the open window. A bottle of Prosecco and two glasses waited on my side table. Ezra lay on my bed—not naked and wrapped in a bow—but in bare feet and jeans, with his hands behind his head. Like he'd stepped out of a Levi's advert.

Yum, yum, said my brain.

"Hey, you," said my mouth. "What are you doing here?"

His soft lips curved into a smile. "I thought we could celebrate together."

I kicked off my shoes. "What, the rooftop karaoke with a drunk detective, two foxes, my empath bestie and a crooning leopard hogging the microphone isn't your idea of a celebration?"

He winced. "Those tracks from the *Glee* soundtrack that he keeps choosing are really starting to grate. Maybe we should sneak him into a real gig. Something with a mosh pit at the Hammersmith Apollo. What do you say?"

I neared the bed, my senses tingling in the low lamplight. "I'd say you're out of your mind."

His grey eyes held mine. "Out of my mind for you."

He caught my hand and pulled me on top of him.

My chest crushed his. I wasn't a double D cup for nothing. "Would you really have whisked me out of there in front of the senate just so I could keep this side of my identity? They would have thrown the book at you."

Ezra pushed my loose hair back over my shoulder and played with the front fastening of my bodycon dress. "I was following my instincts. It's hard to think straight around you. And besides, Gunnolf wouldn't have thrown me to the wolves. And if he had, he would have given me a cushy suite."

I caught his finger and nibbled it. "You have that much faith in his love for you?"

"He brought me up after my parents died, didn't he?" He rolled me over onto the velvet layer of rose petals, and I had never been as turned on.

"We really pulled it off," I said.

He caught my lip between his teeth and murmured against me. "We did."

Ezra kissed me, and I breathed in the mossy, earthy scent of him. The pressure of his lips was firm against mine as if he'd grown impatient of waiting, as if he couldn't get enough of me. Everything else—all our efforts and striving and exhaustion—receded into the background as it became only him and me on a bed of rose petals.

I could have spent a lifetime within that moment, feeling wanted and loved and the centre of his universe.

He propped himself onto his elbow as his hand toyed with the zipper of my dress and looked deep into my eyes. My nails dug into his back, and my vision blurred with passion. I didn't need the alcohol on the bedside table. Being in Ezra's arms was heady enough.

Ezra unzipped my dress, trailing featherlight fingers down my exposed ribcage.

I hadn't felt like this in so long. To hell with my divorce. I was ready to claim my flirty forties. I pushed impatiently against him, kissing his jawline, hooking one leg around his legs to bring us closer, his hard chest against my soft one.

He dipped his head to my lacy bra and kissed me on each breast through the material.

I wanted this so much.

A head of silver curly hair popped up next to the bed like a nightmare clown.

I almost lost control of my bladder there and then. The words burst out of me like machine gun fire. "Oh, my god. Lavinia?"

Ezra stiffened like a corpse before swinging around with a growl.

I shoved him off me and scrambled to pull down my dress, feeling like a teenager caught by their parents.

She shimmied over to sit between us in her yoga leggings and sports bra, swinging her umbrella, ruining the romance in a lightning blink. "Hello, darlings."

A vein throbbed in Ezra's clenched jaw. "Auntie, what the hell are you doing here?"

She pouted. "Can't an aunt come to see her beloved nephew?"

"Cut the crap, Lavinia." He quivered with anger. Or sexual frustration.

She shrugged. "Very well. I came to warn you about her. She might have passed the trial, but you might want to think twice about how easily she is driving a wedge between us."

Ezra sighed. "Leave Alisha out of this. When will you and Gunnolf realise I'm not yours to influence? I have independent thought. I know you, auntie. You came specifically to ruin our celebration out of pique. Like a dog urinating on a picnic because they aren't allowed to eat from it."

Lavinia clutched her hand to her chest. "How you wound me. Never mind. I do love you, you know." She scowled at me. "Alisha, on the other hand, I'm not so fond of. He'll find out soon enough that you're not worthy of him. Oh, and I'll find the dragon. It's only a matter of time before he's under my control." She stood up and dusted herself off. Then she glanced around my room, pinched his cheek and winked. "It's not going to be so easy to get it up now, is it, Ezra dear?"

Her laughter hung in the room as she slipped out the window in a fine display of the granny acrobatics that had impressed me the first time I had met her.

Ezra stood up, sighing heavily. "God, she can be awful."

"Families, eh?"

He took my hand and pulled me into his arms, then turned me around, pulling my back against his bare torso. His hair brushed against me as his lips found my neck.

I nestled into him, butterflies darting in my stomach.

A dreadlocked head loomed through the window as a woman—who lived amongst the stars and books with a horse named Nightfall—leapfrogged into the room.

"You've got to be kidding me. What is this, a train station?" said Ezra.

Calypso pointed to the wall. "Sorry about that. Nothing a lick of paint won't fix."

Gratitude bubbled up in me. "Calypso."

I'd not seen her since the senate vote when she'd intervened on my behalf. I disentangled myself from Ezra and ran to hug her.

Ezra groaned and grabbed his shirt.

She patted my shoulder awkwardly. "Apologies for the intrusion. I figured it couldn't get much worse after the witch parachuted in here with that brass-handled deathly umbrella of hers."

The sounds of a raucous rendition of "Don't Stop Believing" drifted down from the rooftop.

Ezra sighed. "The mighty leopard has really failed at his protection duties tonight."

"I suspect Lavinia Drach has been waiting outside your window to pounce during the least opportune moment," said Calypso. "That woman always was too spiteful for her own good. She really should take more sugar in her tea. It might make her less bitter."

"You were brilliant the other night, Calypso," I said. "Thank you. Why didn't you say you were a senate member?"

She patted my shoulder awkwardly. "There are lots of things you don't know. And I rarely leave the library to take up my seat there. There are far more efficient ways to change the world. In any case, congratulations, Alisha. You deserve to be one of us."

My heart sang. "That means a lot."

"Actually, I didn't come to say that. I came to collect what you borrowed from the library. At least, what you still have in your possession."

I nodded and delved into the bottom of my wardrobe to retrieve the bag of Odysseus's wind and *The Rose of Jericho* book Mum had loaned.

She winced as I tripped. "Careful, careful. I'll take the bag."

My legs were still jelly after those stolen minutes with Ezra. Imagine what he could do with an hour.

Calypso looked inside the bag. A stormy wind erupted from its folds, lifting her off her feet and swelling her hair like she'd stood in front of a megawatt fan, sending the rose petals swirling through the air. She shut the bag with deft fingers and nodded.

"All present and accounted for. But you should keep the

book. You and your friends might yet need it. That reminds me." Her hand delved deep into her pocket to retrieve a velvet pouch no bigger than her palm. "Now you've passed the trial, it's time to give you this. Your mother only gave it to me for safekeeping."

I accepted the pouch and tipped the contents onto my hand. A necklace fell out: an oval amber stone on a choker-type gold chain. Chokers had fallen out of fashion in the early nineties, but my eyes filled with tears all the same.

"It's beautiful," I said. "I wonder why Mum wanted me to have it."

She frowned. "For you and the empath to finish the work she started, of course. Why else do you think she needed the book on the Rose of Jericho?" She glanced at her wristwatch. "I must go. I have a Battersea Dogs Home board member to see about another borrowed item."

"I'm not sure whether you'll get a hospitable welcome. Do you need my help?"

Calypso shook her head. "My dear Alisha, I can handle myself. I have the power of the Celestial Library behind me. Besides, the god has had a reminder of the heavens. In my experience, that softens the heart." She headed for the window. "This isn't goodbye, though. More like an *au revoir*. We still have our swap day to look forward to. And you can always come and find me, can't you?"

"Do I have to pass the test again?"

Her eyes lit up with mirth. "Of course. But everything's easier the second time."

***

Lavinia was right about one thing. All the interruptions ruined the frisson of desire between Ezra and me. Not entirely, of course. All it took was a lingering, heat-filled glance from him to make my heart leap again. They said twenty-year-olds had all the fun, but seriously, my lady parts smouldered in his presence.

That fire didn't need to blaze today. I could wait a bit longer. It would make the experience all the sweeter.

If all else failed, at least I could purge the image of Lavinia out of my head beforehand.

So, a whispered word from me, and we teleported across London. A velvet black sky dotted with stars blanketed the woods as we arrived. The wind rustled through the firs and oaks and sycamore trees, making me feel right at home. Quiet reigned, disturbed only by the gentle lull of the distant motorway.

I stepped out of the circle of Ezra's arms.

Ezra was still a little peeved at his thwarted efforts earlier. "Are we here to say goodnight to the dragon?"

"Something like that."

"Going to read him a bedtime story?"

I grinned. "Stop sulking."

He shrugged. "It feels weird here without the little guys, that's all."

The elves were home at last after Erelim had led diplomatic talks between injured parties. Rumours had spread across the Otherworld that the elves had received a tongue-lashing from the senate. That played well to those who wanted the persecution to continue. But Flinar didn't mind. He was just happy to return to his hovel and had invited me over for elvish flatbread when the dust had settled.

"You were so brave to help them. Now there's one last soul to take care of." I cupped my hands around my mouth and called out, although the magical trial proved that the dragon didn't need to hear my voice to respond. "Tielbu."

Our thoughts were connected. Maybe it was my fear that called to him, or maybe because I was his mother in a strange sense. I could work all that out later.

He came, his wings beating in time to my heart. The ground shook as he landed in the clearing, dwarfing us. "Druid."

"I'm here too," said Ezra.

Tielbu snorted like he didn't care a jot. His ivory horns glowed in the moonlight. He turned his gentle amber eyes on me, and it was as though he could see to my very core. "I knew you would come, but I can't do as you wish."

My chest tightened. "I listened when you perched on top of Big Ben, just as I listened when Dad told me stories about you. About your courage and heroism. How you always saved people in need. And then I realised you were happiest in those stories when you were soaring free."

His slow, precise voice sent a shiver down my spine. "Those stories are like a dream to me. Vague memories. They tell me who I am. But I can't tell whether the voice I hear is yours, your father's or my own."

I nodded. "It doesn't matter which parts of you are us. It just matters that you are a force for good."

"Perhaps. But I still have no place in the world. These woods are little more than a jail now the elves have gone."

I gave a small smile. "That's why we must take you somewhere safe. You don't belong to me. Just as you don't belong to the senate. You are free, Tielbu."

His roar made my bones rattle. "What about my purpose?"

"If I need you, you will come if you are able." I walked towards him so I could feel his hot breath rippling through my hair one last time. "But I'll let you in on a little secret. I think I am different to my grandmother. I think I don't have to assign a purpose at the moment of animation. I think you can find your own purpose, and purposes change."

"There's a settlement of peculiars in Eastern Europe," said Ezra. "On the surface, it's like any old ski resort. With brochures about the snowy landscape, spas, picturesque chalets and restaurants serving fondue. But when you get there, it's something else altogether—a haven for peculiars. I went there a long time ago with my parents. I go there sometimes to be close to them. I think the dragon could be safe there too. There are deep forests and caves where he wouldn't be seen and witches from other covens who could help with a glamour."

I nodded. "Then that's where I'll ask the goddess to take him."

"That sounds like quite the plan, druid. It's nothing less than I have come to expect from you and your merry group of friends," said a familiar voice.

I swung round to see Gaia in the shadows, dressed in a simple green chiffon sari with a blue border and her hair in a neat chignon at her neck.

Tielbu gave a roar of deep pleasure. It rumbled through me, making me feel alive.

"I've just come from a lovely dinner with Pan. What a wonderful artefact you brought him, Alisha," said Gaia.

"Hello, goddess," I said. "I was hoping to see you tonight. I thought maybe you could help Tielbu to a safe haven far from here in exchange for leaving it up to me to deal with Pan."

Gaia beamed. "Of course, Alisha. I am happy to help a druid and her dragon." She planted a kiss on my forehead. "Bravo. You did very well against that mischievous beast of a god. I'll have you know my absence during your shenanigans with him was entirely intentional. You didn't need a new mother. You needed to find out what you could do on your own. I gave you just enough counsel to show you that a war can be won with gentler means. Besides, a god is more beloved when they make themselves scarce. Nothing worse than a meddler. We are much better when we pull the strings from behind the curtains."

"I don't much like riddles, goddess."

"More fool you. They are very good at keeping the brain synapses firing. Forget all this New Age nonsense about multi-vitamins. Dig up some greens from the earth and add a few mind games. I credit Sudoku and *The Times* crossword for lubricating the wheels of my old head. They haven't let me down yet." She dug around in her sari blouse and pulled out an old Nokia with a cracked screen. The screen cast her wrinkled cherubic face in a glow as she peered at it, sticking out the tip of her tongue in concentration. "Such a sturdy little thing. Let me just find the browser. Google Earth is a godsend, even for me. It jogs my memory about all the changes on the planet." She offered it to Ezra. "Just type in where this ski resort is, werewolf, and we'll be on our way."

Ezra did as he was told and handed it back to her.

Gaia's sari fluttered in the wind behind her as she approached Tielbu, who lay down at her feet, much like the effect Gaia had on Echo. She murmured a few inaudible words to him before climbing onto his back with a hop, a skip and a jump that belied the centuries of her age.

We gawped at the sight of the goddess sitting atop a dragon in her green chiffon sari.

"Well, this is going to cause a bit of bother with the flight plans from City Airport," said Gaia. "What fun.

"He will be safe?" My voice quivered, and Ezra's fingers found mine.

"You have my word, Alisha." Gaia paused. "Although the night is still young, and more mischief awaits, and I haven't yet had my nightly cup of masala chai. Do you remember the place I mentioned?"

I nodded. "A café opposite Tooting Broadway tube station, squeezed between a fast food restaurant and a betting shop."

She clapped her hands in glee. "That's the one. Perhaps you lovebirds would like to join me there in an hour? Your treat."

I burst out laughing. "How about it, Ezra?"

He grinned. "It would be wise to say yes. And I quite like masala chai."

"A man of hidden depth," said Gaia. "Say your goodbyes, dragon."

I swallowed the lump in my throat and walked closer to the dragon. "Go now, Tielbu. Go now under the cover of darkness, and don't let the senate catch you. We will come to visit."

The dragon's amber eyes didn't move from my face, as if he wanted to remember every detail. Then he dipped his great head to draw level with my face. He could have torn the flesh off my face with his tombstone teeth. But he didn't.

It hurt to let him go, but he wasn't mine to keep.

"Goodbye, druid," the dragon said.

I breathed in the charred scent of him. "Goodbye, Tielbu."

Tielbu lumbered across the lawn and launched himself skywards, reptilian scales glimmering in the moonlight, and we watched as he disappeared from sight with the goddess on his back.

I thought of all we had accomplished, all the stories I had to tell and the secrets I had to keep. For the first time in years, I was excited about what came next and damn sure I could handle any curveballs life threw at me.

ACKNOWLEDGMENTS

To my husband Jan, who played Monopoly with the children and took them to the park during the brief windows of clear skies during this washout British summer. *Midlife Tremors* literally would not have been completed without you holding the fort while I locked myself in our garden office for weeks. Take my heart and hold it in your hands like a bird because there is no one I trust more.

Thanks again to the Fab13, who founded this genre and who allowed me to host a takeover in their gorgeous Facebook group for fans of Paranormal Women's Fiction. I'm so grateful for your support of new authors. Books about wise women over forty kicking arse have been so fun to read and write this past year, and I have you to thank for that.

My deep thanks, as always, to my book team. To my editors Jeni and Toni, your skills take my stories to the next level and, in doing so, give me more confidence. To my cover artist Maria, your patience and skill astound me. Debbie and Sherry, my beta readers, I am grateful for your book instincts, kindness and support. I'm lucky to have you in my corner.

To my children, seeing the world through your eyes makes me a better writer. Never lose those sparks of pure joy. Sorry-not-sorry for how often I've told you to keep the noise down.

Thank you, readers, for following Alisha's story. My feisty, caring, control-pants-wearing, dragon-raising druid has so much more to come.

FREE SHORT STORY

If you enjoyed this book, please leave a review online to help other readers find this story.

The Druid Heir novels are written in Alisha's perspective, a 40-year-old teacher living in London. The short stories explore the world from an alternate character's viewpoint.

You can get the Druid Heir short stories for free by signing up for my fantasy newsletter at www.nillunasser.com.

MIDLIFE NEWS: DRUID HEIR BOOK 3

One minute, I'm just your average forty-year-old Londoner, past my sell-by date and going nowhere. The next, I've animated a dragon, kicked a few godly backsides and become an overnight sensation. My head is spinning. What I need is peace and quiet to catch my breath and enjoy the first flushes of my relationship with half-werewolf half-wizard Ezra. What I get is a taste of being a celebrity. And I don't like it one bit.

As if midlife couldn't get more challenging, dark omens appear quicker than I sprout grey hair. First, Ezra is called in to investigate dead wolves found on pack land. Then the last raven leaves the Tower of London, provoking fears that Crown and country will fall. But the senate couldn't care less, and their breezy indifference means my middle finger gets a workout.

As enemies close in, the goddess Gaia is too busy in pursuit of the perfect cup of chai to be of any use. I can't deny that I'm a druid with a flair for magic, a nose for trouble and a drawerful of big knickers unlikely to impress a new lover. Can I put my own needs aside and prove once and for all that I'm a match for anyone in my path?

If you're a fan of Paranormal Women's Fiction and magic-wielding heroines over forty, get your hands on Druid Heir Book 3 today.

ALSO BY N. Z. NASSER

DRUID HEIR

Midlife Dawn, Book 1

Midlife Tremors, Book 2

Midlife News, Book 3

Midlife Drift, Book 4

Midlife Portals, Book 5

Midlife Eclipse, Book 6

Midlife Battle, Book 7

Druid Heir Collections

MAJESTIC MIDLIFE WITCH

To Save a Sister, Book 1

To Curse a Rival, Book 2

To Trick a Raja, Book 3

To Hunt a Foe, Book 4

NEWSLETTER EXCLUSIVES

The Magical Grandmother, Druid Heir Short Story 0.5

A First Date in Paris, Druid Heir Short Story 1.5

Midlife Battle, Druid Heir 7 Bonus Epilogue

To Become a Witch, Majestic Midlife Short Story 0.5

Biryani Junction, a Majestic Midlife Witch Cookbook

ABOUT THE AUTHOR

N. Z. Nasser is a writer of paranormal women's fiction. Her stories are about women who change the world, filled with magic and rooted in friendship.

A lover of barefoot walks along the beach, she is glad to have left behind her career in the civil service and to never wear heels again. Whether she is writing in her garden office or wrangling laundry, she is happiest with a cup of tea at her side.

She lives in London with her husband, three children, two cats and a fox-mad dog.

For new release alerts, you can follow her at Bookbub or Goodreads. For a more personal touch, join her Facebook reader group Nasser's Book Nymphs, say hi on social media, or visit her online store at www.nillunasser.com.

facebook.com/nillunasser

instagram.com/nillunasser